PRAISE FOR LILLIAN M. ROBERTS

Riding for a Fall

"Hang on tight and prepare yourself for a flat-out gallop of a book with enough twists and turns to give whiplash."

—JODY JAFFE
Author of *In Colt Blood*

"Good humor and delightful empathy with animals."

—*Publishers Weekly*

The Hand That Feeds You

"Grabs you in its jaws and doesn't let go . . . This [is] a truly unique mystery series worth following!"

—TESS GERRITSEN
Author of *Harvest*

"Read this book. . . . You'll love it."

—ALAN RUSSELL
Author of *Multiple Wounds*

By Lillian M. Roberts
Published by Fawcett Books:

RIDING FOR A FALL
THE HAND THAT FEEDS YOU
ALMOST HUMAN

ALMOST HUMAN

Lillian M. Roberts

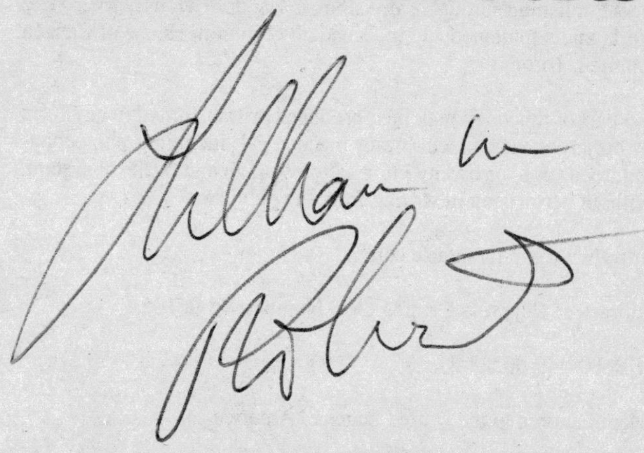

FAWCETT GOLD MEDAL BOOKS • NEW YORK

A Fawcett Gold Medal Book
Published by The Ballantine Publishing Group

http://www.randomhouse.com

Library of Congress Catalog Card Number: 98-96105

ISBN 0-449-00228-4

Manufactured in the United States of America

First Ballantine Books Edition: October 1998

10 9 8 7 6 5 4 3 2 1

This book is dedicated to Kitty Flanders.

And to all the veterinary support staff who do it because they love it, and not because it pays so well.

Acknowledgments

As always, this book would not have been possible without the help of others. Dan Westfall, trainer of Cheeta and other primates, inspired my fascination with chimpanzees and has patiently answered innumerable questions over the years. Michelle Leland, DVM of the primate research center, answered my queries by phone, fax, and e-mail.

Ronald B. O'Gorman, MD, PhD, thoracic surgeon, gave generously of his time and expertise.

Officers Greg Jackson and Dave Costello, and Lieutenant Joe Rodriguez of the Palm Springs Police Department allowed me to ride along and answered innumerable questions. As always, I am grateful to them and their whole department.

David Garcia, Pharm. D., provided crucial instruction in the working of a certain narcotic-delivery device, as well as a description of the duties of home-care nurses with whom he works.

Fellow author and psychotherapist Alex Matthews lent insight into the workings of a character's mind.

All errors of omission or commission are mine alone.

My agent, BJ Robbins, as always listened patiently and cheered or commiserated, depending on circumstances.

My staff at Country Club Animal Clinic keep things

running smoothly, allowing me to use my time away from work to concentrate on writing.

And above all, I am ever grateful to the extraordinary clientele of Country Club Animal Clinic for their constant enthusiasm and encouragement.

Chapter One

"I want to die, and I want you to make it happen."

The woman's eyes, even on the videotape, held mine without wavering. I'd watched it three times, yet could not look away. Gilda Hopkins meant every word.

"I've thought this out." A sardonic twist of her mouth was my first glimpse of the willful woman who had walked, straight-backed, out of my office four years earlier. Who'd left without the little dog she'd loved for nearly fourteen years. Whose last words at the time were, "That's all there is to it?"

"I've thought of little else. It's all I have left," she continued on the tape. This, too, was reminiscent of the Gilda Hopkins I'd known. *She's the only thing I have left.* A strange statement from a mother and grandmother, but she tended toward melodrama.

My focus had been my patient, Maui. The old sheltie was my introduction to "real" medicine—such a contrast to the routine vaccinations and boring skin cases Philip had trusted me with till then. Mrs. Hopkins's trust in me, and the fact that Maui responded so well initially, had opened my eyes to the wonder my profession could hold. More than that, I began to realize the range my profession offered to its practitioners. Philip—the man who founded Dr. Doolittle's Pet Care Center—would have euthanized Maui the first day. Since graduation, he had been my only mentor. If Maui hadn't entered my life, I might have followed my employer's lead, learned not to try too hard. *Wasn't worth it,* he said. *You'll burn yourself out. It's only a job, it's only a dog. Don't take yourself too seriously.*

I bought Maui almost six good months. I glimpsed what was possible. He and his owner gave me my career.

So much had changed for all of us since then. Philip had sold me half the practice, then died. Maui's cancer finally had made his life unbearable, and we'd done the right thing. Mrs. Hopkins eventually got a new dog, a delightful little cavalier King Charles spaniel named Frankie.

And now Gilda Hopkins was dying. Truth be told, I'd thought she must have died months ago. I'd known she was ill, visited a few times early on. But the sessions were awkward and dragged. Despite what we'd been through together four years earlier, I didn't like the woman much. She was domineering, snobbish, didn't converse easily. The hovering, saccharine presence of her daughter Alexandra further discouraged comfort. I'd made excuses, stopped going at all once she left the hospital. Forgotten. Until today, when the video arrived by Federal Express, nothing had happened to remind me of her.

Now the tape captured every nuance as Mrs. Hopkins struggled to maintain her rigid composure. It was subtle; I had to look beyond the oxygen line and the feeding tube and the constant pain that twisted her features into a caricature of their former strength. But she knew exactly what she was asking. I had no doubt she knew that.

And how impossible it would be to say yes.

"I would have liked to do this for myself," she went on. Her voice quivered slightly, whether from fatigue or the strain of her plea I could not tell. "As you see, that has become impossible." Her words mocked my thoughts. *Impossible for me—not for you, Andi!*

She cast her eyes briefly at the useless hands folded across the white blanket that covered most of her. I wondered fleetingly who had placed them there, for she was clearly incapable of doing so herself. I pictured Mrs. Hopkins—I had never learned to call her "Gilda"—choreographing the scene, going for effect. The twisted hands visible, her fragile shoulders beneath the hospital gown; the dark wig that only emphasized her ghastliness. Mrs. Hopkins would not want to be seen coiffed in less-than-perfect fashion, and the drugs had taken her real hair. She even wore rouge over the vaguely cyanotic pallor of her cheeks.

"And while it was still possible," she said, "I was too much a coward. Or perhaps did not believe how unbearable life would later become. Has now become."

She stopped for air, coughing but trying not to. I took in the pleasant floral wallpaper that backdropped enough medical equipment to furnish a third-world hospital. Did she know how much I owed her? Did I owe her anything at all?

Another memory tugged, this one deeper, more uncomfortable. My own mother's death, when I was twenty-one, before vet school. Primary lung cancer had been the cause, my mother too young, made old by cigarettes and illness. Begging with her eyes, dying by inches. She was only fifty.

But that was years ago. I could not have been expected to do anything about it. Could I? I pushed the image away, forced myself to study the video, noticed again the feeding tube that transported nourishment to Mrs. Hopkins's body.

The tube. Innocuous, expected even, given her condition. But why was it in place? If Gilda Hopkins wanted to die as badly as she insisted, why had she permitted the tube's placement? Perhaps she was not physically capable of preventing it, certainly not of removing it without help. But this was a strong—emotionally strong—woman who surely could have found a way to avoid such prolongation of her life.

It wasn't the only question I had for her, but at the moment it was the most troublesome.

The video ran into snow. Answers would have to wait until I could see her in person.

I picked up the phone.

Why me? I wondered as I scanned the medical summary included with the tape. After all this time, why did she dump this on me?

She'd trusted me to operate on her precious pet to remove the diseased and bleeding spleen, and through the subsequent chemotherapy that added six months to his life. She did not want to hear about "gentle death" when life was still practical. But when the seizures began, and the paralysis, Mrs. Hopkins knew when to quit.

The owner's progression had not been so different from her little dog's: adenocarcinoma of the breast, radical mastectomy too late to prevent its spread; more surgery. Metastases to the lung and various bones. Pathological fractures of the right ulna, right tibia, and the fifth cervical vertebra. Swelling into the spinal canal that squeezed the life from motor neurons without interrupting the pain—severe, unrelenting pain. They finally abandoned the chemo when she aspirated and developed chronic bronchopneumonia. Now the cancer sprang up randomly, with a demonic glee, in the various parts of her body. According to the summary, her doctors had been giving her two weeks to live for three months. Yet the capricious disease refused to take her life.

I was grateful I would never have to allow this to happen to one of my patients. And I bitterly resented the woman's request.

"So, are you gonna do it?" Trinka asked later. Her eyes glittered with a certain mischievous twinkle they sometimes get, when she doesn't approve of something I'm doing but still wants to know how it turns out. Trinka had been my partner, half-owner of Dr. Doolittle's Pet Care Center in Palm Springs, California, for about ten months. Veterinary medicine is the only thing we have in common.

"I don't know yet," I said irritably. I'd just finished a particularly tough surgery, a closed pyometra in a bulldog. Pyometra—"pyo," for short—is a condition where the uterus fills with pus, becoming, in essence, a giant abscess. "Closed" refers to the cervix. When it's open the pus can drain, which makes it a lot less urgent. The only good treatment for a closed pyo is total hysterectomy, the sooner the better, or the dog will die. Not maybe, not probably, but one hundred percent of the time.

Except this dog's owner didn't believe it. She'd read that hormonal therapy had been tried, and wanted it for her dog. I tried to explain that this was only feasible with an open cervix, but the distinction was lost on her. Trinka did not help when she tracked down a reference and showed it to me in the client's presence. Daisy Bell's owner wanted to breed her again. She would not approve surgery without first attempting drug treatment. This set us back until the uterus ruptured, causing a near-fatal and totally avoidable peritonitis.

Bulldogs are terrible anesthesia candidates anyway, they're so heavy and don't breathe well under the best of circumstances. Daisy Bell arrested twice—once when first anesthetized and a second time while waking up.

She'd resuscitated fine, but I was angry at the owner and resentful of Trinka for the role she'd played in the delay.

"Andi, you can't just leave her hanging!" Meaning Mrs. Hopkins.

I spun around, snatching the surgical mask from my face and tossing it and the matching hat into the trash. "You think it's so urgent, go do it yourself!" I snapped.

I immediately regretted the outburst, but didn't say so. Trinka glared at me, neither of us willing to apologize.

I stomped into the office and dialed Mrs. Hopkins's number again. The first time I had called, her daughter had answered and the ensuing conversation had left me feeling like I'd just stepped out of a *Twilight Zone* episode. "Oh, Dr. Pauling! Thank you so much for calling. I know Mother will be so sorry she missed your call! I'll be sure and tell her when she wakes up."

As if I were a long-lost friend of the family. As if I hadn't been asked to put her mother to death. And no one had held the video camera while Mrs. Hopkins made her request, and no one had put the tape in the mail.

This time Mrs. Hopkins was awake. She would see me immediately. I took directions and left without telling Trinka where I was going.

But first I called Daisy Bell's owner and told her about the operation. Then I told her the cost. It didn't make up for the frustration she'd caused, but it sure did help.

It was hot in the desert. August hot. A hundred twelve, according to the thermometer stuck to the outside of the window in the office. And it was only noon.

It was also muggy. Not what I expected when I moved to the desert. Palm Springs and the surrounding cities comprise an alluvial plain known as the Coachella Valley. Mountains sweeping upward on all sides—it makes for a dramatic view. But something in late summer—

high pressure or low pressure or some coastal weather system, I can't remember—traps evaporating moisture from thousands of swimming pools and the constant watering of a hundred-some-odd golf courses. A few people actually stayed and played all summer. The rest fled north and would begin trickling back in November or so.

"We really need covered parking," I muttered to myself as I started the Miata and turned the air on high, standing outside the open door while the inside temperature dropped into the life-sustaining range. My scrub top clung to my skin when I finally got behind the wheel. Then I drove to Gilda Hopkins's house. It wasn't far but I drove slowly. The AC was actually making some progress by the time I parked.

Alexandra Dixon smiled when she answered the door of the sweeping stucco house. "Dr. Pauling! Thank you for coming. May I call you Andi? I feel as though I know you! Mother hardly talks about anything else."

I had met Alexandra at her mother's bedside a year or so ago. She never seemed to connect with the events around her.

I stood blinking on the doorstep. Cool air invited me, but the woman had not. Against the backdrop of a sweeping staircase, she stood in a three-story entry hall with a potted palm extending nearly to the ceiling. The grandeur was astonishing, but a faint odor of corruption wafted out with the air-conditioning.

Alexandra wore a classic black-and-white suit—skirt, pantyhose, and all, with black heels. Her hair was styled and lacquered in place. Diamond studs adorned each earlobe. Red lipstick. Very formal attire in a town where even the best restaurants admitted people wearing golf shorts.

"Are you on your way out? Is this a bad time?" I asked, almost hopefully.

"Oh, no, of course not! I wouldn't miss this for the world! Silly me. Come right in. Mother's waiting for you. Come in, come in, right this way."

I followed her and she strode into a big, gloomy living room. Baskets of potpourri failed to mask the virulent stink of impending death that permeated the house. Vertical blinds were drawn over the windows. A dusty baby grand piano occupied a quarter of the room. A giant television received pride of place across from overstuffed furniture that looked ready to grab unsuspecting occupants and never let them go.

"Have a seat! I'll get tea." She swept out of the room, appearing moments later with a tray of cookies and iced tea. It had clearly been readied before my arrival.

"I hope you don't mind sweetened. I simply can't abide any other kind."

"Um, no, thanks. Really, I can't stay long."

She placed her tray on the coffee table. The cookies were arranged artfully on a china plate. The tea swirled gently in a crystal decanter. "Oh, nonsense. There's always time for a glass of tea!"

"I left work. I really can't stay away. I was hoping I could spend a few minutes with your mother?"

Her face crumpled like tinfoil. Then she said, "You don't like tea? I can make coffee! Sit down, please sit down!"

Jeez, what have I walked into? Then I realized she must have been cooped up in this house with her dying mother for months. A little pleasant tea-sipping probably seemed like a vacation. I felt terrible saying, "I'm really sorry, but I just don't have time. Maybe later?"

For a suspended moment I thought she was going to insist. Her lower lip actually trembled. Finally her smile found its place and she said, "Of course, what *was* I thinking? Come this way, this way right back over here. Just up these stairs."

I touched the banister and my hand came away dusty. But the elegant curve of the wood had not been diminished by time or neglect. The stench grew stronger with each step. We turned left and moved toward an open door at the end of the hallway.

"She insisted on keeping her own room, you know. It's been a terrible strain, I'm sure you can imagine, but I wouldn't have it any other way. No sir, my mother is going to die peacefully in her very . . . own . . . *bed*!" With that she stepped to one side of the doorway and held an arm toward the interior as if presenting Her Royal Majesty.

From here the odor was a strong wind, impeding my progress into the room. I've smelled worse, I told myself. But never from a living human being.

The wasted figure half-upright in the hospital-style bed could not be the woman I once knew. For a dizzying moment I felt sure I'd wandered into the wrong house. But she saw me. Her eyes moved from me to her daughter to me, then to another woman who was fussing with her IV.

"Andi?" The voice a croak. She licked her lips, tried again. "You came. Good. You've met Alexandra."

"Yes."

"This is my nurse, Eva Short."

I offered my hand. The nurse, hearing her name, turned and smiled at me. A professional smile that fit her oval face. She then finished attaching something to the IV, picked up a plastic cassette a little narrower than a CD case, and tossed it into a red-lined biohazard waste can under the bedside table.

"There you go," she said to her patient. She touched her hair with her free hand and straightened up, revealing her full height, six feet or close to it. "I'm gone. See you tomorrow?"

"I'll be here," Mrs. Hopkins said bitterly.

The ironically named Eva Short slipped past me. Her footsteps echoed in her wake.

"And you know Frankie." The little dog lay at his mistress's feet. He had waited his turn and now began wiggling in anticipation of being petted. I didn't let him down.

Alexandra came in, leaned over her mother and fluffed the pillow. "Honestly, Mother, I don't know why we put up with that nurse. She doesn't take proper care of you, half the time she leaves you stinking, she—"

"Stop it!"

Alexandra gasped. The command, though barely above a whisper, rang through the room.

"I always stink! Don't pretend for Andi, she's smelled worse." She turned her eyes to me, her head moving only an inch. "She can't clean me properly because my bones break if she moves me. Once a week two of them come in and change the sheets and wash me. The rest of the time it's diapers and catheters and do the best we can."

"Oh, pooh! They should clean you every day. It's not like we can't afford it!"

"No, I can't stand it! Now get out of here, Alexandra! I want to talk to Andi alone. Go on! Go!"

Alexandra's fury was obvious, but only for an instant. Then she smiled sweetly and said, "Oh, that's all right." And winked conspiratorially at me. The sound of her retreating heels stopped just outside the door.

I was alone with the woman who'd asked me to put her to death. I didn't know what to say. "How have you been?" felt singularly inappropriate. Somehow "It's good to see you" didn't work either. Likewise "Is there anything I can do?" since she'd already made her request impossibly clear.

"Hello," I finally said. I was still having trouble meeting her eyes. Kept glancing behind her at the array of machinery. IV pumps, an oxygen concentrator, a portable suction unit. Those were just the ones I recognized.

"You're uncomfortable." She spoke quietly, somewhat slowly, but very clearly. "Come, sit next to me. Let me explain what I'm asking."

I came and sat, increasingly nervous. This feeling was only partly a result of what had drawn me here. Frankie dropped into my lap and I stroked his soft back, grateful for something normal to do. Oddly enough, I'm ill at ease around sick people. I can sit with a dying dog, rub the cheek of a cat as it breathes its last. But show me a human invalid and I get all fidgety.

She started to speak, but instead her mouth wrenched open and she gasped, her features paralyzed in what could only be pain. I half stood, helpless to give any relief, embarrassed to witness such a personal moment in the life of so private a woman.

Then the paroxysm passed, and she lay with her eyes closed for a long minute, struggling to catch her breath. I sat back, breathing quietly in sympathy.

Finally she looked up, took another deep breath and said, "You see what it's like."

I nodded. I didn't see at all.

"By the time I found the lump, it was in my lymph nodes. Then they took part of a lung. Now it's in both of them." Deep, shuddering breath, tinged with the odor of decay. "The drugs helped for a while. So they told me. But my spine is falling apart." More breathing. "It hurts," she finished simply.

"How long—" I stopped.

The twitch that passed for a smile. "That's the worst of

it. No one knows. I could go anytime. Or I could linger for years."

Not years. Surely not that long. I tried again to think of something to say. Failed.

"You're young. Healthy," she said. "You think me selfish."

"No, of course not." The words jerked from my mouth before I had time to think. *You bet I do. I was barely part of your life. Why are you dragging me into your death?* Followed by that unnerving silence, while the tiny *ticks* and *whirs* and *hums* of the machinery continued uninterrupted.

"You, of all people, know how it's done. You could end this farce and not botch it up."

I didn't answer because she was right. I was already thinking about what drugs might be used. But that wasn't the same as actually using them.

"If money would persuade you, I would offer you everything," she said quietly.

I shook my head in horror. Opened my mouth and couldn't speak.

Again that twitch-smile. "Then again, if I thought that, I would have chosen someone else."

I shifted in my chair. My sense of unreality deepened. The room was too much like a hospital. Too much like that other hospital, so many years ago. The white linens, the stench of death. I wished I were almost anywhere besides sitting at the bedside of this crippled, pathetic woman whom I'd once admired. Wished she *had* chosen someone else.

Frankie whimpered and I realized I was pulling his ears fiercely. I apologized and gave him a few gentler strokes before placing him back on Gilda's bed.

"I could go anytime," she repeated wistfully, watching me with her calm, tortured eyes. Telling me that no one would suspect. If she died in her bed, her doctors would sigh with relief, write "Complications from carcinoma" on the certificate under "Cause of Death," walk away and look no further.

"Why did you let them put in a feeding tube?"

Her mouth twitched. A frown this time. "I can't swallow well anymore. Alexandra insisted."

"Your daughter? But what about you?" I didn't believe she would bend to anyone's will on such a thing.

"They threatened me with surgery. A big, ugly tube sticking out of my side." She must have meant a gastrostomy tube, through the skin directly into her stomach. She blinked, slowly, as if it were difficult. "This, at least, I don't have to look at." It was true; the thin nasogastric tube was taped to her nose and snaked between her eyes to the bag of opaque liquid via yet another pump. "And," she admitted, "I fear starvation almost as much as I hate . . . all this." She moved her eyes from side to side, indicating the trappings of the room. Most of the medical equipment was, I now realized, behind her and out of sight. All quiet, discreet, but nonetheless constant in its function.

"What you did for Maui . . . we don't inflict this sort of thing on our pets. Animals. Don't you think I deserve the same *quality of care*?"

"I . . . Mrs. Hopkins, what you're asking—"

"Gilda. Please, Andi, don't you think you can call me Gilda?"

No. I couldn't. I remembered her too well. She'd begin with something innocuous: *Please, call me Gilda.* Then she'd have me bringing her a glass of water, or combing her hair, and before I knew it I'd get used to following her instructions.

Gilda Hopkins was highly skilled at getting what she wanted.

Chapter Two

There must be questions I should ask. I cleared my throat. "What about your doctors?" I mumbled.

She looked disappointed. "You never called me Gilda. Why is that?"

I regarded her carefully. What harm could such a small thing do, really? It seemed important to her. I sucked in my breath and let it out as if embarking on a long and treacherous journey. "Gilda, then. Have you broached this subject with your doctor?"

She let her head fall back, closed her eyes, breathed so deeply I thought she'd fallen asleep. "Which doctor? The oncologist stopped coming months ago. I outlive his predictions. I'm an anomaly to him, little more. My geriatrician, good Dr. Frank . . . Alan. Known him for years. Stares in horror when I ask for a little extra morphine. It's possible Alexandra has . . . made it difficult for him." She stopped, coughed, spent most of a minute catching her breath.

"Would you mind if I spoke to him about your condition?"

"I asked him to talk to you. Don't know if he'll do it. Before I lost my body, my treatment involved a cardiologist, three internists, a nutritionist, respiratory therapists, four or five nurses. . . . Why do the nurses leave, do you suppose? I have been examined by a dizzying array of specialists, mostly men, few of whom bothered to learn my name."

Damn her, I thought. The name thing again. Then, *poor Gilda.*

"I'm sorry," I said, thinking that "before I lost my body" was an interesting way of saying "when I could move."

"Sorrow does not help. I am at the end of my life. Do not be sorry. I am not. If only this . . . *damned* heart would realize the game is up and cease its interminable beating." She enunciated slowly and with great dignity. "I did not realize how bad things could get. You've no idea how I wish I'd . . . taken things into my own hands long ago."

I sat silently, gazing at the monitor behind her that proved yes, her heart was still thumping along quite well.

"She thinks I don't know how she makes me suffer." I barely caught the words. Mrs. Hopk—*Gilda's* eyes were closed.

"What? Who makes you suffer?"

She focused on me, as if surprised to find me there.

"You came." Her voice strong.

"Of course I—"

"See that," she said abruptly, her voice fading noticeably.

I looked where her eyes pointed, at the same device Eva Short had been fussing with when I arrived. It was a flat cassette, about four by seven inches. A digital readout on the front indicated a flow rate of only 20 milligrams per hour. The cassette was supposed to separate into two halves, but I couldn't immediately see how.

"You need a key," Gilda said.

"This holds your morphine?"

"Yes. She just changed it."

Examining it, I found where the key would go. It required something shaped like a hollow-tipped Allen wrench, but I thought a narrow hemostat would work to twist the lock and open the device. Apparently, once used, the whole cassette would be disposed of. In veterinary medicine we would have reused them until they fell apart, if we used them at all. I wondered how tight the record keeping was. Were they opened, measured, accounted for? Or simply returned to the pharmacy and thrown away? I'd seen Eva Short toss the old one in the biohazard bin. It would be a simple matter to retrieve it.

Gilda's motivation in showing me this device was clear. It was the simple way to give her what she wanted. I wouldn't even have to use my own drugs. There was more than enough morphine in this room to give the old woman the gentle death she craved. All I had to do was open the cassette, remove the contents into a syringe, and inject it directly into her IV line. Perhaps add water to the bag, to replace the missing volume in case anyone checked. Gilda would slip away peacefully and no one would suspect.

Her eyes opened briefly and held mine, and I had the feeling hers could suck through mine all my conflicted feelings—my dismay at her condition, my agreement that she should be allowed to end her own misery, and my abject horror at her request. *I want to die, and I want you to make it happen,* she'd said. As if it were a simple thing.

But I was thinking about it. Wasn't that the first step toward doing something? Yet I could not shut the idea out of my brain. I felt bewitched.

Then she closed her eyes and became merely an old woman again. An image of my mother superimposed itself on Gilda's face. I caught my breath. My vision swam.

She had it all planned out, needed only to manipulate me into doing her bidding. I opened my mouth to speak, knew that angry words would help nothing, closed it again.

Gilda had drifted off to sleep anyway, or had tired of me and pretended to sleep so I would leave. I was glad for the excuse. But as I turned away she said, eyes still closed, "Before you go, crank me flat." A command this time.

It took me a few seconds to understand that she was asking me to lower the upper part of her hospital bed so that she was lying flat. I searched for the controls, found them at the end of a cord on the table by the morphine pump.

"Don't!" This sharp directive issued from the doorway.

I spun, surprised, as the bed began its quiet descent.

Alexandra stomped over and snatched the control from my hand. "She's not supposed to be flat out. You want to kill her?" She'd probably eavesdropped on the entire conversation.

I blinked in confusion.

Gilda mumbled, "Of course she doesn't." She lay now with her head elevated only slightly, and looked quite comfortable. "If only it were so easy."

Alexandra was glaring at me. "She could aspirate and die. I thought you were a doctor."

I glanced from her to her mother, momentarily cognizant of all the things human caretakers could control in their patients—such as body position—that I could barely influence in my own. But I had the ultimate control with mine—the power and authority to say "Enough!" and to end pointless suffering.

"Wait!" Gilda ordered. "Frankie . . . needs a good checkup. Take him to your office, clean his teeth and whatever he needs. Then bring him back later."

Hearing his name, Frankie looked up at his mistress, wagging his tailless back end happily.

It's starting, I thought. Asking simple favors, reasonable impositions at first. Working her way up to the Big One.

But I could hardly refuse. In fact, taking care of Frankie would help assuage my guilt when I declined to put his owner to sleep. And if that wasn't a bizarre thought, I couldn't imagine what would be.

Alexandra followed me out of the room. "Well?"

I slowed and she caught up at the head of the stairs. I turned, one foot on the first step. Frankie settled in my arms, a memory of having been carried a lot.

"Your mother is suffering so much. I just can't imagine what it must be like."

"Oh, I know you'll set her straight. You think she needs different medicine? Some kind of Prozac, maybe, something to cheer her up. Right?"

She waited for my answer. This went beyond denial, and it occurred to me that this was one screwed-up family. At the same time my mind repeated the refrain, *She's not my mother, she's not my responsibility!* I just shrugged.

"Well," Alexandra said when I failed to respond, "do come back. I've got to run now!" But she didn't move.

I didn't say anything. All I wanted was to get away from this grand, shabby house and the horror in that room.

"What are you going to do?" Alexandra demanded.

I couldn't tell what answer she wanted. "I'm going to take Frankie back to the office, examine him, take some blood, clean his teeth and ears, and have him groomed."

She laughed nervously. "I guess we've kind of neglected him a little."

"I'll see you this evening, okay?" I shifted Frankie's weight and turned to go.

"I . . ." She swallowed, glanced over her shoulder, lowered her voice as if her mother could hear. "I don't want her to die, okay? I know she will anyway, and I know I can't stop it. But you have no right . . ." She trailed off, swiped at her dampened eyes with the back of a hand, watching me to see what effect her words would have.

Suddenly the front door burst open to the sound of laughing young voices. A young woman, maybe eighteen, stepped through with her back to us, followed by a young man in baggy clothes and dreadlocks. They were joined at the lips. Their bodies gradually separated as they drew the kiss out until both leaned at precarious angles. Their grinning mouths parted at the last possible instant.

The girl, giggling, said, “See ya.”

The boy’s smile vanished as he glanced at Alexandra and me, then back at the girl. He hesitated.

“She’s sleeping,” Alexandra said without raising her voice.

The boy mumbled, “Later,” backed out, and pulled the door shut behind him.

The young woman came toward us. She was exquisite. Fragile features, perfect tanned skin against sun-bleached hair, taut flesh displayed by a white halter and cutoffs. As she passed she looked at me with frank curiosity, a hand darting out to pet Frankie’s head, but she didn’t speak. She glanced toward Gilda’s room then disappeared into another, down the hall to the right.

Alexandra frowned after her. “My daughter,” she explained unnecessarily. “Rainie. Short for Lorraine.” The resemblance was there, but Alexandra’s beauty was harsh and shallow and designed to keep people at a distance.

When the girl had put a door between herself and us I asked Alexandra, “Why do you want to keep your mother alive? Surely her doctors could increase her morphine, ease her pain. It’s what she wants, and her life is nothing but agony at this point.” I knew I’d prefer death for myself given the same circumstances. Thought I would, I corrected myself. Who could really know?

"After all she put me through, you'd think I'd get a little more appreciation for taking care of her. No one knows how hard this has been on me."

I did not want to hear this. I did not need to know what sins Gilda Hopkins had perpetrated on her offspring.

"I had a terrible childhood. I don't have to stay here, you know. I don't have to take care of her."

This conversation wasn't tracking. Steeling myself, I said, "I'll see you tonight."

Alexandra stared hard at the floor, nodded abruptly, rubbing her upper arms. The movement had a restless quality, as if she didn't know what to do with her hands.

"She's my mother. Of course I want her to live as long as possible."

I had no answer to that. "I'm sorry," I mumbled, and started down the stairs.

Outside, the boy waited beside a motorcycle that had seen better days. Unlike his personal appearance, which seemed carefully cultivated to induce dismay, the bike looked like cheap transportation and nothing more. That he waited patiently in the full, relentless sun made me think either he was on drugs or I had casually underestimated him when I mentally dismissed him on first sight as a spoiled rich kid dressing the part of the punk.

"Can I talk to you a sec?" he asked.

I paused on my way to the Miata. He might look weird, but he didn't look threatening. Frankie wriggled and strained to greet him.

"You're the vet, aren't you?"

"I am a veterinarian, yes." I shifted Frankie as if to prove it.

"The one Rainie's gramma called in? Rainie told me. She wants to help so bad, even held the camcorder for the tape. She told me you're gonna put an end to"—he cocked his head toward the house— "all this bullshit."

"I don't know what I'm going to do." *And I certainly wouldn't tell you if I did.*

His declaration hadn't generated the response he wanted. "It's ridiculous, all that money to keep her alive when she's gonna die anyway. Man, when my grampa died, he didn't have any of that shit."

I wasn't sure what he wanted from me. "Well, I'm sure Gilda would choose to go quietly. I need to get back to work." I moved past him and opened the door of the Miata. As I started the motor I glanced up. He stood unmoving, staring after me.

Daisy Bell was fully awake, but groggy from post-op pain meds as well as from the infection, the surgery, and its aftermath. She gazed blearily at me, barely able to hold her head up. Her gums were still pale, her hydration status not great—septic animals tend to leak fluids into odd body compartments, and kidney function is compromised, so they remain clinically dehydrated. But too much fluid too fast could overload an already stressed heart, so the infusion rate had to be watched closely. With Daisy Bell's short, twisted bulldog legs she could cut off the IV flow simply by bending her elbow. I wished for one of the infusion pumps I'd seen at Gilda's, a simple way of insuring that fluids kept running at the rate I selected.

IV pumps were on the cumbersome list Trinka carried in her brain, of equipment we "definitely had to have as soon as possible." They were available used, at a realistic price. But there were so many other things on the list, and so little extra cash, that we had yet to purchase one. In the past year our client base had grown dramatically. But so had our overhead. We'd hired two new employees, doubling our staff. Trinka had insisted on upgrading the archaic computer system. I found this ironic, since my previous partner had barely tolerated the one I had before he died.

But Trinka introduced me to the Veterinary Information Network, or VIN, an on-line continuing education service for veterinarians. It drew me to the Internet as nothing else had managed to do. Now I made a point of checking the boards several times a week. They constantly reminded me of just how much equipment we did not have.

And now it was summer. Everyone who could leave the desert did so, and business dropped off. After we paid the staff and overhead, there wasn't much left to pay ourselves, let alone buy new equipment. So we were "stuck in the Dark Ages," as Trinka said at every opportunity. The lack didn't usually bother me—I'd been at Dr. D's since I graduated five years earlier, and hadn't known anything different. But Trinka used to manage the local emergency clinic, and recalled fondly all the "toys" she'd left behind.

There were maybe half a dozen appointments scheduled for the whole afternoon, simple things all clustered between two and three. When they were done I joined Trinka in the office and picked up a journal from the stack that had accumulated since the previous fall. I'd been making quite a dent in my reading lately, and the stack was less than six inches thick now. I turned to an article about wound healing and began reading. Or pretending to read.

Trinka stopped tapping at the computer and I sensed her watching me, waiting. Roosevelt, her ancient and nearly featherless African gray parrot, stood at the edge of the desk, head cocked to one side as if he, too, wondered how my meeting had gone.

"Well?" Trinka finally asked.

I shrugged, not looking up. I knew I'd tell her about it, but wanted to make her work for it.

"What did you do?"

I turned my attention to her. "Talked."

"Andi! Come on!"

Roosevelt said, "Cool!" Then he gave a wheezing chuckle, pushed his beak against the worn desktop, and began stalking toward Trinka, shoving any object that got in his way to the floor. When he reached Trinka's arm, resting on the desk, he climbed it to her shoulder where he prepared to nap.

"Trinka, I honestly don't know what to do. She's so pathetic, and still controlling people around her. I don't like her, but I wish I could help her, I really do." Thinking ironically that I'd said enough already to incriminate myself should the old woman die under suspicious circumstances. But who could I talk to if not Trinka?

She narrowed her eyes, studying my face. "Oh, my God! You're gonna do it!"

Where did she get that? "Trinka—"

"Have you told her?"

"I haven't decid—"

"What are you gonna use? Morphine? From here? How are you gonna record it? I mean, you can't just write down 'used to euthanize former client.' We've got almost a whole bottle of Demerol up there. I guess you could just tell the DEA you broke the bottle."

My partner is a little strange. Half-Gypsy, half-Jewish, she wore her hair (that month) in a severe French braid down the center of her scalp, the sides very short and slicked back so from a distance it looked something like a Mohawk. Fortunately she's gotten away from the bizarre colors she used to dye it, and it's back to its natural black. Her outlook on life is unlike anyone else's I've met.

"I don't know what I'm going to do," I said. "Okay?"

But she was too far into the idea to give up that easily. "Could you kill someone with Demerol? I wonder how much it would take? Her tolerance would be increased, right? Since she'd have been on narcotics for months at least. Except her organs would be starting to fail, which might make her tolerance *lower*." She got up and pulled the PDR—*Physicians' Desk Reference*—off the shelf and began thumbing through the index.

"Trinka!"

She flipped pages, found what she was looking for. "Christ, Andi, there are enough drugs in this clinic to kill a lot of people, you ever think about that? If we turned into psycho-killers tomorrow, we could do a lot of damage before we ran out of ammo."

"You're sick, you know that?" I said, laughing. "And you're enjoying this way too much. I do not, repeat, *do not*, plan to euthanize Gilda Hopkins. That I would even consider helping her is only due to the fact that she so obviously means what she says." *And that I keep seeing my mother when I look at her.* "She's quadriplegic and in horrible pain, and totally helpless to do this herself."

Trinka shut the heavy book with a loud *thwap*. Roosevelt jumped but recovered. "NO!" he said. Trinka picked him up.

"All you had to say was one word: quadriplegic." She shuddered. Trinka's free time is invested in things like rock climbing and competitive cycling. "I would definitely want you to do this for me." She set the book on the desk and looked at me, suddenly serious. Her free hand absently scratched the parrot's head. "Would you? If it were me, would you put me to sleep?"

"I—" How had we gotten into this? I stared at Roosevelt, his head down for the massage. I tried to consider Trinka's question seriously. "It would depend on how you felt at the time. I think I'd want to die under those circumstances, too. But I don't know for sure."

"Well, I do. And if you wouldn't do it, I'd find someone who would. I mean it." Like it was a threat.

I don't know what I would have said in response. I was saved from answering because that's when the chimp came in.

Chapter Three

She was screaming: huge, freight-train shrieks that were nothing I'd heard in any zoo. She was staggering and near panic, and very, very pregnant.

Her name was Sally. I knew her, had treated her once before. When she was seven, she'd caught a cold from her owner and it developed into streptococcal pneumonia. That couldn't have been more than four years ago—she seemed young to be having a baby, but I didn't really know. She was the only chimp I'd ever gotten that close to.

"She's in trouble," her owner screamed over the noise. "Hurry!" Holding Sally's hand, he half carried her past Trinka and me as we stood in the doorway to the office.

This was Wayne Williamson, a pediatrician, and half of Sally's "parental unit"—his term. The other half was Bradley Jones, animal trainer extraordinaire and one very peculiar dude. If there was good news to be found here, it was that I only had Wayne to deal with.

"Brad'll be here in a bit."

Oh, well.

"She needs a section," Wayne shouted over the noise of Sally's shrieks.

"She *what*?" I stood momentarily frozen. A cesarean on a chimp? Me? With no preparation?

"Wayne, I can't—"

"You have to. The baby's early and she's placenta previa."

"But how—" Sure, we'd anesthetized her as a baby, in order to place IV lines and get a throat culture, but I'd had a whole day to prepare. I'd consulted a zoo vet, a respiratory therapist, a human anesthesiologist, another vet in LA who worked on primates but had since retired to Florida, and a pediatrician (Wayne, who this time might be no help at all). He could at least have warned me she was pregnant and this might happen. He didn't even call to say he was coming in.

"What's placenta previa?" I trailed after him in my own clinic.

"Trust me, she needs the section. Now!"

Didi and Diane, our two technicians, followed eagerly as Trinka and I joined Wayne in the tiny OR. Wayne helped Sally climb onto the stainless-steel table. The chimp's soft brown eyes were wide with terror, but gentle with trust as well. This was a good thing, because she could easily have ripped apart the room and everyone in it.

Chimpanzees in captivity are normally one-person-oriented. But Sally had been rigorously conditioned to tolerate other people. She'd been socialized from birth, and always wore a harness on her back, with electrodes similar to a shock collar made for dogs. Wayne and Bradley wore remotes like pagers on their belts. I'd never seen either of them have to use one.

"What do I give her?" I asked. If she'd been a dog, the anesthetic dose would have been automatic—enough ketamine to intubate, then gas for maintenance. We'd used ketamine on Sally when she had pneumonia, but I couldn't remember how much. I held the bottle in one hand, a syringe in the other. In dogs it was slow to cross the placenta, but was that true in primates?

Wayne crouched behind the table, holding her hand

and stroking her head, so like a nervous father-to-be it was uncanny. Sally lay tensely on her back, legs bent beside her dark and hairy body, the gray-pink bulge of placenta protruding from her vagina.

I'm used to anxious owners, but my patients normally have four legs, a tail, and a muzzle. Seeing the two of them like this, but without the time to assimilate it, was just plain eerie.

"Just mask her!" he moaned. "Come on. Let's move!"

Diane had the anesthesia machine out and was attempting to hold the cone-shaped mask, designed to go over a dog's muzzle, against Sally's face. Sally pushed it away. Wayne grabbed both her hands, and Sally reached up with a foot. Fortunately, her belly was in the way.

"This won't work," Diane said flatly. And she was right. Sally's noise output had not abated, and was taking on a somewhat threatening note.

"I'll hold her down," Wayne said. But everyone in the room knew that was ludicrous. Sally, head flailing from side to side, freed one hand and grabbed Diane's thumb. Diane screamed and her legs folded. Then Sally took the rubber diaphragm in her teeth and did what no dog had been able to—tore it in half.

"Holy shit!" Diane dropped the mask as the chimp let go of her hand. She clutched her fist against her, scooted into a corner, and began rocking, eyes tightly shut.

"Damn it, Wayne. Are you all right, Diane?"

"I think she broke my thumb." A harsh whisper barely heard, as Sally wound up for another shriek. The noise increased my anxiety and that of everyone in the room. Someone had to slow down and inject some rationality. And some ketamine. Diane was in pain, but could wait. My first priority was to immobilize the chimp before someone else was hurt.

"How much ketamine did we give her last time?" I

demanded in my best I'm-taking-over-now voice. My hands, I noted, barely trembled. Bottle in hand, I calculated the patient's weight—around a hundred pounds, I thought. A dog that size would take five cc's just to immobilize. But I thought the primate dose was less.

"I don't want the baby anesthetized."

"If we get moving it won't have time to cross the placenta." I hoped. I didn't have time to research it. Trinka was bravely attempting to clip the hair from Sally's belly, yanking the electric clippers back as the chimp grabbed at them. Sally reached up tiredly with her feet, but couldn't get around her distended belly. A contraction seized her and she shrieked. Wayne held her hands, glancing nervously at Diane, who still sat clutching her injured thumb.

"It'll be okay," I said, hoping it was the truth. *How much time does this baby have, anyway?* "How much ketamine?"

"Don't put her out, you can't. Use morphine and a local."

"I need her out, Wayne! She could kill someone! Come on, how much?"

"She'd never hurt anyone on purpose!"

"I won't work on her like this! I won't let my staff!"

"Girls!" Trinka's voice cut in. Wayne and I stopped, turned to look at her.

"You gonna stand here and argue or we want to get this kid born?"

For a second even Sally didn't make a sound.

"Try three hundred milligrams," Wayne muttered, looking back at Sally. "That's what a kid her size would need." His eyes were moist. "Hurry!" he said again, but this time it was more plea than command.

I kept the syringe out of Sally's view and handed it to Wayne with a strip of latex tubing. Using the latter as a tourniquet, he injected the ketamine into a vein. It worked in seconds and the ensuing quiet calmed me a little. Trinka rapidly scrubbed her belly. With Wayne's help, Didi slipped an endotracheal tube over her epiglottis and connected her to the gas machine, so that a mixture of oxygen and anesthetic flowed into her lungs with each steady breath. I pulled on cap and mask and went to the sink for a fast hand scrub, while Didi got me a gown and surgical gloves.

"What are you doing?" Wayne screeched at Trinka.

"What?" She stopped midscrub.

"That's not where you want to cut!" Without letting go of Sally's hand, he stepped around and drew an imaginary line with his finger an inch above her skin, describing an arc that made her belly look like a cyclopean smiley face with her navel as the one eye.

"That's where they make the incision in women," I said tensely. "This is an animal. I don't think she cares how she'll look in a bikini." Didi tied the gown behind me. I slipped the gloves on and opened the sterile inner wrapping on the instrument tray.

"But she's not a dog! She's . . . she's almost human!"

I inhaled deeply and let it out. Repeated. "Wayne, none of us really knows what we're doing here, okay? You're asking me to perform major surgery with no time to prepare. The midline is what I'm familiar with."

Trinka went back to her task with barely a pause, probably thinking as I was, *Just shut up, Wayne. Pretend you're a doctor.*

"It will be fine," I said again, with patience I wished I felt. "Our goal is to get the baby out alive and Sally sewn up so she'll heal. Right? And there's less pain if I don't have to cut through muscle." So they say.

Trinka wiped the belly one last time with Betadine. I draped and picked up a scalpel. We left Wayne to monitor anesthesia. The pulse oximeter beeped reassuringly with each heartbeat, and I wished I had some means of monitoring the fetus.

Diane roused herself to muster a stack of towels, suture for the umbilicus, and a suction syringe for the baby's airway. Her thumb stuck out stiffly and her face was pale, but that awful just-injured shock had passed. This was an adventure she wasn't about to miss out on.

Trinka got the crash kit out and drew up emergency drugs. Even Sheila from the front desk stood by, ready to help if needed. C-sections were something we all understood, even if the shape of the patient was a tad unfamiliar. They might bicker at times, but when we needed them, our staff went into team mode.

Sally's skin and *linea alba*—the "white line" that separates the two sets of abdominal muscle—parted smoothly beneath my blade. Her uterus bulged into the incision, a tiny foot kicking slightly. A good sign, I thought, and cut into the membrane.

The amount of fluid was manageable, but I hadn't anticipated the blood. I wiped ineffectively with gauze sponges, finally giving up and reaching in with both hands to lift out the baby and place it into Wayne's towel-draped hands. While he held it I clamped the umbilicus; after that he was on his own. Sally was still bleeding.

I dimly recalled learning the various types of placental attachments back in physiology, memorizing them for test purposes and promptly losing the information. There is a reason primates tend to hemorrhage following delivery, and it has to do with the way the mother's and fetus's blood supplies join together.

"Trinka, give me some epi," I said sharply. "Didi, get an IV in."

"Done," said Diane. "LRS okay?" Lactated Ringer's solution, our fallback for intravenous fluid administration.

"Yeah, full bore." It wasn't like I had a supply of

chimp blood in the fridge to transfuse her with. "Then go get some oxytocin." How much? Damn it. "One cc, IV." Didi ran to the fridge in the other room.

Diane, thumb protruding awkwardly, dropped a sterile syringe in my hand, then gave me a needle and inverted the bottle of epinephrine as I filled my syringe. She was pale but functioning. Trinka was helping Wayne.

I mopped up blood, sprayed with epi, repeated the procedure. Unlike other species, there was no local area I could inject with the drug, which constricts blood vessels thereby limiting hemorrhage. Nor, in other species, had I ever needed to.

As Didi gave the oxytocin—a synthetic hormone—the uterus contracted feebly. Not enough.

Diane gave me more epi. I considered injecting a uterine artery. The problem was, the uterus has a redundant blood supply, and the organ was huge and floppy and surrounded by fat, making it hard to locate and isolate even one artery, let alone four. The ongoing hemorrhage didn't help, nor the alien nature of the anatomy. I resorted to clamping the vessels as I found them, then carefully slipped the needle into the last branch, knowing the needle was too big as I did so, watching with my heart in my throat as the blood welled around the needle and began spilling into the abdomen, spurting over my hands as I reached through the slippery disaster to pinch the artery above the puncture, with my gloved, inadequate fingers.

I opened my mouth, thinking, *Shit, shit, how can I tell him,* and said, "Wayne, I've got to spay her."

No answer.

"Wayne!"

"Huh?" He and Trinka were bent over the tiny infant, from which I'd heard no sound. Not a good sign.

"She's bleeding all over the place. I'm afraid if I don't

spay—do a hysterectomy—she'll die. Please, I need your permission."

For what seemed like ages, the only sound in the room was the bleeping of the pulse oximeter, belying my prognosis by proclaiming the chimp's blood to be perfectly well oxygenated. But we both understood this represented a percentage of available blood, unrelated to the amount pooled in her abdomen, soaking the pile of gauze sponges, clotting on the floor around my feet.

And Bradley Jones chose that moment to arrive.

"Oh, my God, what have you done to her?" And before I could stop him he was in the room, brushing my sterile instruments as he moved past me, leaning over the bleeding uterus.

"Brad, *get back*!" I yelled, hoping the urgency in my voice would do what I'd never managed before, to make an impression on Wayne's partner. "Do. Not. Touch *anything*!"

He seemed belatedly to realize where he was, took in the blood, the noncrying infant chimp, the open nature of Sally's abdomen.

"Oh, you bitch!" I couldn't tell if he meant me, Wayne, or Sally. "This is horrible! How could you just . . . cut her open like that?" Managing to brush against both my gown and the drape covering Sally's belly, he moved away and bent over his new "grandchild."

There wasn't room in the OR for all these people, all this drama. And I had no time to re-gown, let alone open a new pack.

"Wayne?" I said quietly, beseeching him with my eyes not to tell Brad just yet.

Wayne's eyes reflected a desperate indecision, moving from me to his partner, to Sally. He knew, he had to, that there was only one answer.

"Please," I said.

"What?" demanded Brad, finally catching on to the fact that something wasn't right. Something beyond what he could see.

"Go ahead, Doctor," Wayne said clearly. Perhaps it was the title that did it, but Brad went into hysterics.

"Someone had better tell me what's going on here! This decision is half mine. What did you tell her to do?" His voice rose into the soprano range.

"Trinka, get them out of here," I said. I could feel myself about to lose it. She glanced at me and hustled them into Treatment, taking the crash kit with her. Seconds later she ran back in and grabbed the pulse oximeter, leaving me with no objective way of monitoring my patient.

Thus I spayed my first chimp. Nothing to it. The principles of surgery are the same across species lines: Don't cut an artery unless you tie it off first, and double-ligate everything. The uterus never did contract much, and was still a flabby mess when I lifted it out of Sally's body and placed it into a tray—well, a large stainless-steel dog-food bowl—that Diane solemnly held out for the purpose.

I sewed her up as quickly as I could, burying the sutures since I knew Sally would pick them out if she found them. A bandage was pointless for the same reason but I put one on anyway, mostly for Wayne's sake, and Brad's, too. As Didi turned off the gas I wished for the first time that I hadn't had to give ketamine.

While Sally breathed pure oxygen, I went to see if the baby had survived.

Chapter Four

Trinka had her IV'd and intubated and had given Brad the job of ventilating her lungs. This was brilliant on her part—Brad's entire concentration was focused on counting to ten then gently squeezing the ambu bag. Unfortunately, it wasn't doing the trick for Sally's baby—her gums were bluish gray and the oximeter report was dismal.

The creature lay, dark and woolly, on a stack of towels on the treatment table, no bigger than some puppies at this stage. Her weight, obtained from the scale I used for birds, was noted on the chart Trinka had begun for our newest patient: 1220 grams. Barely over two pounds. A newborn chimp should be able to cling to its mother's back while she clamors through trees and lumbers over hills. This one couldn't even breathe for itself.

I just stood in the doorway for a moment, watching. Wayne and Brad with their heads together, focused on the impossibly tiny life. I felt exhausted and inadequate. This creature I'd delivered into the world didn't have a chance.

"Where's the surfactant?" Wayne demanded.

Trinka raised her eyebrows, the abyss that separated human medicine from what we did suddenly yawning wide. Whatever residual energy I'd had evaporated.

"Her lungs aren't developed. She needs surfactant."

Several potential answers crossed my mind: *Do you have a clue what that stuff costs?* foremost among them. But I was too tired to explain, and Trinka just said, "We must be out."

I gathered she'd already told them our nonexistent automatic ventilator was in the shop. Neither of these was even on her list. In fact, our primitive ambu bag only delivered room air instead of oxygen. I could imagine Wayne's reaction to learning there was no IV pump available. Wait until they found out how long it took us to get lab test results.

"You *do* have an incubator?" Wayne asked monotone.

Smiling, finally presented with a request I could readily fulfill, I went to the office where we stored it when not in use. I was rather proud of this little gem, a retired human infant model we'd picked up for a thousand dollars a few months earlier. It had everything we needed: heat, cooling, humidity control—if not very precise—and hookups for oxygen input and body temperature monitoring. I wheeled it into Treatment, glad I could produce something that would impress our client.

Wayne glanced at the Plexiglas-domed cart and did a classic double take, his mouth falling open in horror. *"That?"* he demanded. "That's it?"

Brad glanced from Wayne to the incubator, to my stricken face, trying to follow Wayne's objection. Brad was white-blond, dark tanned, melodramatic in all he did. His lips moved: *seven*, *eight*, *nine*, *ten*. He squeezed the bag, pumping air into the baby's lungs.

"It's great," I said defensively. "Everything works, and this is almost what it was designed for!"

"But it's twenty years out of date!"

My mouth opened but I couldn't speak. After all that had happened that day, somehow this self-important pediatrician insulting our best equipment was just too much. For a horrifying moment I thought I would burst into tears.

Trinka's face had darkened dangerously. "Now you look," she growled. "We've pulled off some damned miracles in this place. We might not have all the electronic bells and whistles, but Andi just got this kid out alive and saved her mom, and I think you should be the tiniest bit appreciative. You march in here with no warning and start throwing out orders and now all you can do is sneer at everything we do. This is what we have. If you aren't happy, you can move her over to CVG." This was delivered with the sarcasm it deserved. Coachella Valley General Hospital wasn't likely to welcome a baby chimpanzee, and Wayne knew it. He had privileges there. Dr. D's was just a humble veterinary clinic, but for now he was stuck with us.

I felt a surge of gratitude toward my partner. She hates working on exotic species, and doesn't care for clients in her workspace. By belittling our equipment, they'd managed to touch every one of her sore points.

"We're just not set up for this," I said. "As soon as possible, we'll send you down to one of the referral centers in Los Angeles." If I could find one that would take her. Few veterinarians were willing to work on primates. And stabilizing this one enough to transfer seemed an impossibly optimistic goal.

Brad had stopped midsqueeze. "What? Take her out of town? Don't you even suggest it! She's staying right here!"

Wayne turned to Brad, studied the baby, whose heart beat irregularly and whose oxygen saturation was just over 60%. The adrenaline rush had passed, and he looked tired. How long had Sally been in labor before he'd brought her in? How long had Wayne been awake?

"I'm going to get some things," he said. "We'll talk when I get back." And he left.

I went to check on our new mom, who was moving a little. Diane pulled the trach tube, and Didi took the anesthesia machine into Treatment so Trinka could use it to give oxygen to the baby.

Diane guarded her thumb, which had swollen to twice its normal size and was darkening around the base. "You'll need to get that looked at," I said.

She glanced down. "I'll x-ray it later."

I sighed. It was a temptation I'd succumbed to before. If I sent her to Urgent Care, the first thing they would do was take radiographs. Theirs would be no better than ours, and if no fracture was apparent they would bandage it and tell her to put ice on it and refrain from using the hand. They would send her home with a prescription for Vicodin and tell her not to work.

I'd x-rayed my foot once after the anesthesia machine fell on it; Trinka had regularly taken pictures of her own ankle after a bad rock-climbing-induced sprain. We both felt that was different; theoretically we knew the risks. But the law specifically forbade me from using my equipment on humans, despite the X-ray machine being built and certified for human use and newer than some currently utilized in medical clinics.

"I don't want to know about it," I said.

I helped Diane move Sally onto a blanket on the floor, where she could wake up safely. The chimp curled into a fetal position.

I got the morphine and the log book from the lockup in our office, checked the PDR, and gave her the low-end human dose. It would mute the pain when the anesthetic wore off, and I didn't see how Wayne could object to that. But her dose finished the bottle, leaving only one full—not enough for prolonged treatment. When I got the chance I'd ask permission to apply a Duragesic patch, which would release a steady infusion of narcotic through her skin.

I had no idea where to put Sally, though. Our cages were all too small and the runs were full of dogs being boarded while their owners vacationed in cooler climes. Maybe I could move a dog into the ward to free up a run for Sally until she was ready to go home. I wondered how long I would have to keep her, and decided she could go home as soon as she was standing and had an appetite. For now I dragged the blanket into Treatment so we could keep an eye on her.

One or two clients had come in while we were in surgery. I sat with Brad, taking turns ventilating the new baby's lungs, and let Trinka see them. A small dog, excited by the smell of chimp, barked incessantly. The boarders chimed in, background music I'd long ago learned to tune out. I was exhausted, despite the fact that nothing I'd done that day had required physical exertion. That was kind of interesting—if I'd discussed the euthanasia of a terminally ill pet with its owner, then performed an emergency cesarean on, say, a cocker spaniel, it would be a normal day. Even considering Daisy Bell's awful laparotomy and stressful anesthetic complications, it would simply have been a day I was glad to see the end of.

"When can we bring our baby home?" Brad asked.

I didn't answer immediately, wondering if his denial was deliberate or if he truly didn't realize that most newborns could breathe without assistance.

I wasn't up to the discussion. I said, "I don't know."

"Thanks to you and Wayne," he went on, bagging the baby without losing his rhythm, "Sally can't have any more children. Have you any idea how much this little one is worth?"

The question was outrageous, especially under the circumstances. I didn't even attempt to answer.

"*And,*" he complained, "I'll *never* get this blood out of these shoes!"

My eyes were drawn involuntarily toward his white loafers. Formerly white. Served him right. I wondered if he'd noticed the large red stain on his white shorts. I refused to point out the obvious blood stains on my own clothes.

I made a show of auscultating the little one's heart and lungs. This was the first time I'd touched her since handing her off to Wayne during the operation. I wondered if he'd done what I was doing: placed the seemingly enormous bell of my stethoscope against the tiny chest of this new, indeed humanlike creature, and heard a disorganized cacophony of whistles and *whooshes*, where a simple two-step rhythm should have been.

"What?" Brad demanded, seeing bad news in my face. Brad had Presence with a capital *P*, and the voice of one used to receiving answers to his questions. "What is it? Tell me."

"Let's wait until Wayne gets back," I said. *When in doubt, evade.* "He has a lot more experience with this sort of thing." Which was true on two levels: He was used to primates and their various idiosyncracies, but he was also a pediatrician, and this patient more closely resembled his than my own.

But this couldn't be normal. One glance at the oximeter, which had improved with oxygen but not by much, told me I'd heard right. Sally's baby girl had a congenital heart defect, one that could require thoracic surgery to correct. With her immature lungs that was a highly iffy proposition, even with the best equipment in the world. And we still had no way of knowing how much damage the prolonged delivery had done to her other organs, especially the brain.

Wayne was gone for most of an hour, but returned with an amazing array of equipment crammed into the back of his minivan. Trinka and Diane helped him bring it in: a portable ventilator with a small tank of oxygen; not one, but two, intravenous pumps; a multifunction device including an electrocardiogram, pulse oximeter, and temperature probe; a portable suction unit; and a pediatric blood-pressure monitor. Trinka was practically drooling by the time we squeezed it into our treatment room.

"We'll have to make do with your incubator," he told me grudgingly. "Larry Jenkins will be out tomorrow to sound her heart."

"Who?" Trinka asked.

"To what?" I said simultaneously.

Wayne paused in his assembly of the instant neonatal ICU long enough to glance at us. "Larry Jenkins. He's a radiologist who owes me a favor. He's bringing an ultrasound unit out so we can see what's happening with her heart. You *did* hear the murmur?"

I nodded, wondering if the tiny ape would make it till the next day. "PDA?" I asked. Patent ductus arteriosus, a shunt that detours blood from the main pulmonary artery into the aorta, bypassing the lungs and preventing the blood from being mixed with oxygen. It's necessary in mammals prior to birth, when oxygen-rich blood comes not from the lungs but from the mother via the umbilical vein. But it should close as a baby takes its first breath.

"At least," Wayne said. He had calmed down quite a bit, and spoke to me as if he were "the Attending" and I was a slow intern. "She could have a VSD."

Oh, damn. Ventricular septal defect, something else I'd memorized for board exams and promptly forgotten. It involved a hole between the chambers that could only be repaired with open-heart surgery. Open-*heart*. Opening the chest cavity was scary enough. Cutting into a beating heart was unimaginable.

Not that I'd be doing either one, I reminded myself. If this kid made it to surgery, it would be somewhere else. A referral center full of exotic equipment and specialists and round-the-clock attendants. That should satisfy Wayne.

Wistfully, I considered the gulf that separated my skills from those of a specialist. A residency, board examinations—the professional equivalent of the Grand Canyon. I was utterly unqualified to treat this baby chimp, and I knew it. It would be unforgivable not to recommend referral.

But *damn*, I wanted to try.

Chapter Five

It was nearly eight when I left the clinic, relieved to escape the heavy atmosphere, at least temporarily. All I wanted from life was to soak in a hot tub full of spice-scented oil, drink a beer while reading Janice Steinberg's new mystery, and fall asleep before the news came on TV.

The temptation was huge, but had to go unfulfilled. I was due back at the clinic at midnight. Wayne, Trinka, and I had agreed to take shifts watching the infant chimp during the night.

And before that, I had to visit Gilda Hopkins. With the unexpected excitement of the afternoon, I had not gotten Frankie's maintenance work done. He'd be fine at the clinic overnight and we'd do him the next day. But that meant an extra trip to that oppressive house.

I'd managed to avoid thinking about her for most of the afternoon, but now her request hit me full force, making my heart heavy and my feet feel like lead.

My four dogs mauled me at the door, and it was impossible not to smile. I'd brought home interesting odors before, but this was like nothing they'd ever smelled. Gambit, my coonhound, was entranced. At least twelve, he was the oldest, but he had an exquisite nose and memories of wild scent. The combined aromas of chimp, placenta, and strange blood had his gray muzzle twitching like a pup's.

I stripped and left my clothes in the hallway. Della, my slightly brain-damaged "Canine of Uncertain Ancestry," immediately rolled on them. Fifty pounds of black-and-white, with speckled legs, a hint of brindle in her uneven coat. Born with a liver shunt that made me think of the little chimp's heart, her symptoms had been awful—seizures, stargazing, and coma, with periods of apparent normalcy if her diet excluded the protein her undeveloped liver could not process. Her operation had been straightforward, though fraught with post-operative complications. Her spirit pulled me in and I kept treating her after her original owner gave up.

The professional challenge was part of it. Normally I'd refer her to the same specialists to whom I wanted to send the baby chimp. But the owner had declined referral and I'd done it myself, after clinic hours, Didi staying late to assist. No one else, just me and one technician. I'd been out of school just over a year. And Della had done fine.

But she was familiar. Canine. The chimp was not. I'd trained on dogs, not on primates. I'd at least scrubbed in on a similar operation in school. Surely Wayne wouldn't expect me to do this procedure. Surely I wouldn't agree to it?

Romeo, mostly Doberman, attempted to shove his long nose between Della and my shirt, finally snatching a sock to investigate at length in his corner. Zeke alternately sniffed my shoes and barked at them, glancing at the others as if confused by their reactions. Part Lab, part chow chow, some shepherd, and a drop of pit bull tossed in, he was found by police as a young adult, worm-infested and starving in an abandoned house. That was two years ago, but I sometimes had the feeling he was still trying to learn how to be a dog.

Even some of the cats had to check this out. Carbon

yawned aloofly from the back of the sofa, and Hara and Kiri were nowhere in evidence. But the Ayatollah wandered over, yowling with artificial Siamese nonchalance, and ginger Clyde, who had no ego at all, ducked happily between the dogs' feet to see what drew them. Gray Evinrude arched herself glancingly against my calf before joining them, purring already, drooling and kneading her paws as she plopped herself in the middle of the pile.

Just another homecoming. I watched them for a long moment then headed for the shower, emerging somewhat refreshed. Then I let the dogs out, collected my clothes and tossed them in the washing machine—except for the socks, which Romeo had gnawed thready holes in—and checked the answering machine. One message. My heart gave a little leap when I heard the voice.

" 'Lo. I'm back. Long day? I could try you at the clinic, but you're probably too busy to chat. Give me a ring when you can."

I couldn't tell where the relationship was going, but I sure enjoyed listening to Clay Tanner talk. Unfortunately, our schedules conflicted. Most of his weekends were occupied with horse shows, and during the week, I was rarely available for more than dinner. I carried the cordless phone into the kitchen to return his call while I fixed myself a salad.

"Tough day?" He sounded tired himself.

I laughed. "I spayed a chimp today."

Silence on the line. Then, "As in, chimpan*zee*?"

"Very much 'as in.' "

"For a sec there I thought I was back home!" He was most likely teasing me. Did people who lived in South Africa feel compelled to keep chimps as pets? Performing animals? But I smiled anyway, and told him about Sally.

Then he told me about his show, which had been in

Salinas. He'd brought home the dressage trophy, and a promising new mare he'd been training had earned herself a blue in the "Open Hunter." I'd picked up bits of horse-show terminology from Clay, but tonight most of what he said washed over me. I was too tired to absorb it, felt removed from everything in his life. But his voice was pleasant background music until my salad waited, dressed and mouthwatering. And I realized I was famished.

"So, what nights are you free?" he asked.

I hesitated. "I don't know. I've got this baby chimp to watch, so it looks like a long week. Maybe a quick dinner Wednesday night?" That was far enough away to sound like a safe bet. Two days.

"Sounds good. I'll talk to you before then."

Practically drooling now, I said, "Great. 'Bye."

"Toodles. Oh, and Andi?"

"Yeah?"

"Good luck with the little one."

"Thanks, Clay. I'll need it. Good night."

I hung up, realizing I'd never once been tempted to tell him about Gilda Hopkins. I wondered idly about the significance of that.

I ate slowly, half hoping it would be too late to visit her. But when I called, Rainie answered. "Yeah, Gramma just woke up from a nap. She's, like, expecting you."

I filled the animals' food dishes and let the dogs back in, then dragged my unwilling body to the car.

The Miata seemed as reluctant as I to be out again, and took longer than it should have to reach the Hopkins house. Someone was opening the door of a pale Honda as I pulled in the drive. I rolled down my window and the figure turned to face me. The nurse, Eva Short. She paused with her car door open, the dome light casting its glow unevenly over her tall frame.

"You work a long shift," I said.

She leaned against the car. "Alexandra's always having emergencies. Most patients I see two, three times a week. I'm lucky if I get by with once a day here." Gilda had wondered out loud why the nurses left. "We're shorthanded. I can use the overtime."

"How is she?"

She shrugged. "The same, every day." Besides being tired, she seemed nervous. I wondered what Gilda had told her about me.

I hesitated. Then asked carefully, "What does her care involve?"

"You mean what do I do in there? Everything she can't do for herself. Clean her, check her catheters, change her urine bag, her diaper, the sheets. Give her bowel treatments if she needs them." Seeing my confusion she said, "Fancy word for an enema." She wasn't looking at me now. "There's a tumor on her sacrum. I can feel when I . . . you've got to be careful with the tube. Lately there's been blood. She doesn't know."

I felt revulsion, imagining the wasted body of this once-powerful woman reduced to such elemental needs. Revulsion, along with niggling memories I'd suppressed in order to make my own mother's death seem, well, nicer. And no desire whatever to enter that awful room again.

The nurse hesitated, one long leg in the car, and said, "I gotta get going." She folded herself into the driver's seat, then let the window down and leaned out. "It's nice that you're coming to visit. No one comes anymore. And that family . . ." She glanced toward the house, shrugged. "It's good you came." And she left.

Now what did she mean by that? Did she know why Gilda had summoned me? Damn, who else knew? Or was I reading too much into a simple statement?

I stayed in my car, listening to the sound of crickets,

smelling freshly mowed, artificially watered grass, and watching the window I knew to be Gilda's. It was at the side of the house toward the back, the closed blind surrounded by light that seemed to sneak out. A lamp was on downstairs, and the porch light shone. But the effect, rather than being cozy or domestic, was almost sinister.

Finally I got out, not really thinking, too tired to wonder what I was going to do.

Alexandra opened the door. This time she wore denim shorts and a polo shirt. She said, "I knew you'd come! I knew it! Rainie didn't think you'd show, but I told her you were as good as your word!"

Rainie didn't think I'd show? Was she kidding? I gave her a wide berth and she closed the door once I was in. With a smile that felt fake I said, "I know the way," and headed resolutely up the stairs.

Gilda was waiting, with an expression that might have contained a hint of triumph. I'd come back, and she assumed that meant she'd gotten her way.

"How are you?" I asked, sitting in the chair by her bed.

"Is that the best you can do?"

I didn't say anything, just watched her. If my gaze made her uncomfortable I couldn't tell.

"Something happened to you today," she said.

That jolted me.

"You're tired. And you didn't bring Frankie back."

Damn, for a moment there I'd thought she was psychic.

I wasn't sure what to tell her. "I'm sorry. Frankie's fine, ate a good dinner. We'll take care of him first thing in the morning. I have a very sick patient that took up the whole afternoon."

A shadow crossed her face, a memory perhaps of Maui. "Dog?"

"No, it's a baby chimpanzee."

She raised her eyebrows in question.

"I don't work on them very often, but this one's mother came in needing an emergency C-section." I paused. When Sally had been sick the first time, I'd tried to refuse. But no one in an hour in any direction wanted to treat primates. They were smart and strong and dirty and dangerous, and few people had any business keeping them. Many, obtained as "cute, irresistible" infants, wound up shackled or caged for life once adolescence hit. And few veterinarians were willing to do the extra research. But I enjoyed working on exotic species, and had finally agreed to see Sally. I still had her baby picture on the wall of my office.

"I had to spay her. The baby might not make it."

Her brows knotted. "Wish I could give her my life. Stubborn damned thing."

I recoiled from that subject. "She has a heart defect and I don't know who can fix it."

That I would even consider taking it on was due in part to this woman's faith in me those years ago. I wondered if she knew it.

A silence ensued, broken only by the sound of Gilda's wheezing breath. "You'll do fine," she said in her quiet, impatient voice.

Her sentences were shorter tonight. "You're tired, too," I said, and stood up to go.

"Andi."

I paused, afraid of what she was going to say.

She coughed softly. "Come see me. Anytime. I'm up at all hours. Don't worry . . . about Alexandra. She's up late, too." Another cough. "You'll do fine."

I thanked her and left, oddly grateful for the vote of confidence.

And for the fact that she hadn't once asked me about my decision.

* * *

It was only eleven-thirty, but I knew if I went home I'd fall asleep. Wayne had taken first watch, and wasn't expecting me yet. I found him sitting on the floor, Sally curled in his lap. He was humming what sounded like a lullaby to her. It took me a long moment to recognize it as the theme song from *Rocky*.

The baby slept on, tiny ventilator whooshing its measured air into her lungs, monitor beeping to its unrelated cadence. After a few minutes I could tune them out, though if anything changed I knew I'd hear it instantly.

Sally turned her wide, expressive brown eyes up to me. So like human eyes, yet so alien. The prominent brow jutted above them, her hairy forehead sloped sharply back. She had hands with opposable thumbs, and feet with opposable toes. Long, coarse hair on her head, and on her neck, and her back, and her legs. She had large, brown ears that protruded from her head at an angle that was slightly wrong.

She was not human, but that was easy to forget when she looked at me. As expected, she had removed the bandage, but seemed to be leaving the suture line alone. Her eyes had a glazed expression that transcended species lines. The narcotic patch, given her post-op anemia, had her mildly stoned.

"How's she doing?" I asked, nodding toward the baby.

"No change," Wayne answered. "Sally's great though. She's not bothering her incision. Yet."

On the treatment table were the cold remains of dinner: pizza, half an apple, and a skeletal grape stem. The banana peels had found their way into the waste can.

I picked up a slice of cold pizza—ham and pineapple, not a favorite of mine, but I was hungry enough not to mind.

"We named her Andi."

I stopped, looked at him sharply, then resumed chewing. The idea wormed itself into my ego. I was pleased.

"It was Brad's idea."

I tried not to let this comment deflate me. Why did he have to take everything away? The slightest grudging compliment had to be qualified. Then again, why did I need his approval?

"That's nice," I said weakly. Really, I was touched. But suspicious. "What about transferring her?"

He shook his head, slowly, full of sorrow.

"Brad hates hospitals, and you know how he projects. He's afraid a big facility will frighten little Andi. And that Sally won't be allowed to visit."

I just stared at him, the pizza forgotten in my hand. I couldn't address anything he'd just said, because Brad wasn't here to answer for himself.

My eyes moved to the infant, a creature no longer than the width of my two hands placed side by side. She barely twitched.

"What about you?" I asked Wayne.

"I agree with you, she needs a bigger facility. More modern." He was just being honest, I told myself. "But this is close to home," he said. "I can be with her, do whatever I need to for her. It isn't perfect, but we'll have to make do."

I could hardly stand to breathe as I asked my next question. "What about her heart?"

"I've given her a drug called Indocin. PDA is common in preemies, and sometimes it will close within a few days. Otherwise, we'll have to go in."

I didn't answer. He hadn't asked me, he'd told me. In the pedantic tone of one lecturing a slow student. I knew I should protest, tell him to find another vet, I was sick of his arrogance. But I didn't say a word. I was afraid he'd change his mind.

As soon as Wayne left to show Sally to her run, the baby's—Andi's—heart rate, evidenced on the ECG monitor, increased sharply. I glanced at it, alarmed. The little chimp was awake, kicking a little, but in no apparent distress.

Wayne returned. Andi's heart rate dropped. I told Wayne what had happened. He seemed perversely pleased.

"It's a sign that she recognizes me."

Together we suctioned her endotracheal tube, a frightening procedure that required disconnecting the ventilator and inserting a tiny suction probe into her throat to remove the accumulated mucus and fluid. I held my breath until she was reconnected, a reminder to myself that Andi would not be breathing during that time.

Then Wayne left for home. I locked the door behind him and stopped in the office for the PDR. I was being manipulated on two sides: On one hand, into something I simply could not do, and on the other, I might wind up stretching myself professionally, meeting a new challenge. It was exciting and terrifying, and infinitely more attractive than hoping Gilda would die before I had to tell her my decision.

I would start by looking up the drug Indocin.

Chapter Six

Indocin, I read, is a trade name for a drug called indomethacin. I was surprised to learn that it belongs in a class of drugs known as nonsteroidal anti-inflammatory drugs, or NSAIDs. Its use in infants apparently took advantage of a side effect, discovered when the drug was given to pregnant lab animals and caused the ductus to close prematurely. The list of other side effects was nauseating, with kidney and liver toxicity and stomach ulcers leading the worrisome pack.

Nothing in life could be easy for baby Andi. I mentally added an H_2 blocker to the list of medications she needed. Then I noted on the chart that Wayne had administered Zantac intravenously at the same time he'd given the Indocin.

Seeing this on the chart irritated me. I knew the medical treatment was right—assumed it was—but finding out about it this way made me angry. This arrogant man was taking over my clinic. Maybe he did know more about treating a chimp than I did. And sure, he had the emotional investment. But how much trouble would it have been for him to discuss these things with me? Seeing the familiar chart written up in this unfamiliar hand separated me from my patient. And made me feel superfluous.

Stop it, Andi! Don't you dare let your ego get in the

way of this baby's survival. You never asked Wayne what he was doing. Maybe he assumed you knew.

And maybe I didn't want him to find out just how foreign all this was to me.

I rolled my chair in from the office and brought half a dozen textbooks, determined to learn all I could about baby Andi's condition. The veterinary literature was limited primarily to puppies when discussing heart defects, and the descriptions of surgical technique seemed impossibly simplified. Indocin wasn't even mentioned, probably because PDA in dogs was rarely caught before weaning, by which time the drug was useless. But the procedure had been extrapolated from human medicine, and these books were the best sources I had.

Wayne had made a pot of coffee. I sat with my cup next to the congealing pizza, a six-pound surgery text in my lap, and watched my namesake struggle for life.

It was not so different from sitting by Gilda's bed.

Two beings, one at the beginning and one at its end. One craving death, the other too feeble even to contribute to its own survival, while we forced life into a body that nature would have destroyed. Or wasn't that the aim of modern medicine?

Either I was getting cynical or I was too damned tired. Daisy Bell, for example, would have died had nature been left alone. She was now doing fine, and might go home tomorrow. Then again, nature would never have created so maladapted a creature as a bulldog, so maybe that wasn't a good example.

Anyway, medicine still had its limits. And veterinary medicine would always be a poor relation, years behind its cousin and willing to accept handed-down knowledge and used equipment, because of the gap in the value of lives in the eyes of society.

I recalled a colleague's frustrated harangue on the VIN:

An MD can spend thousands of dollars on tests to get a "maybe," but a vet had damn sure better know what's wrong, for forty dollars or less.

It is a matter of patient perception as well. Animals seem to accept death as inevitable. They are intuitive, not intellectual; they don't understand the alternatives. One could not explain to Ruffian why she must guard her shattered leg. Nor can I implore a cat whose kidneys are failing to drink more water, take in calories, when her body insists it is time to quit. We have tricks—injectable fluids, drugs, manipulated diets, sedatives, restraining devices, anabolic steroids, even antidepressants. We can sometimes prolong their lives, but we cannot bargain with our patients.

A dog with cancer must expect on some level to die. No one could prove it, but it must be true. I, as a veterinarian, direct my treatment of that cancer toward giving my patient the best quality of life possible. But part of the therapy is convincing the animal it's all right to live.

Gilda Hopkins's body had been blasted with the highest doses of toxic drugs it could survive, still the tumors had thrived. No apparent thought had gone into the woman's ability or desire to tolerate the life inflicted upon that body.

But she'd had a choice. Had she understood that? When she found the first lump, when she signed the form authorizing surgeons to remove her breast and the muscles and lymph nodes beneath it, she had at least some idea of what she was in for. The statistics were there: one in four women dead within five years of diagnosis. This despite everything. Had she delayed? Did her own hesitation give the disease the chance it needed?

And if she had? Did an understandable reluctance to have a breast cut off, somehow mean she deserved what came later? Not in my mind.

Beneath the carefully honed intelligence that purports

to separate us from lesser creatures, there lurks a primitive brain. An instinctual brain. One that knows when to throw in the towel.

Useless speculation, late-night bad philosophy. I sipped my coffee, browsed the textbooks, and tried not to wonder what I would do about Gilda Hopkins's request.

I did not like her, but that was irrelevant.

I owed her, at least I felt I did. But that, also, was not pertinent.

She was a fellow being suffering greatly, and everything in my training and instinct urged me to end that suffering. But that same training, and the laws of our society, dictated that I was not qualified to do anything about it. The law, in a way, seemed to dictate that she suffer as long as possible. Alexandra had made her feelings clear. The threat of a lawsuit hovered over Gilda's bed. As long as Alexandra felt as she did, Gilda's doctors would keep her morphine dose low for fear of being accused of accelerating her death. After all, it was only supposed to last a few weeks. No one had expected this to drag on as long as it had.

I watched the infant chimp sleeping, and wondered if I was doing the same to my own patient.

Baby Andi represented a bridge between two branches of medicine. She breathed with mechanical assistance while a pump delivered carefully titrated electrolyte mixture through a minute catheter in her umbilical vein. Another pump delivered baby formula to her stomach via a tube through her nose. Her tiny body was overwhelmed by equipment: leads and tubes and lines that sprouted from every orifice and limb as she lay without moving, in an incubator that, despite myself, I'd begun to think of as antiquated. The new models had simulated heartbeats and a warmed gel mattress to minimize the shock of leaving the womb. They had open tops and attachable ventilators and monitors and digital controls and alarm bells. And bright lights to minimize jaundice.

Mine had a heater, a fan, and an ice pan. And a lot of holes in its plastic dome for tubes and wires and hands to travel through.

But once upon a time it had nurtured human infants. I was tired enough to imagine the machinery humming more smoothly, the metal-and-Plexiglas sides standing straighter, as if the old incubator felt proud to be entrusted with so important a task.

The difference was hope. Andi had it. Gilda did not.

Trinka is not a morning person. She's always prompt, but even at eight she's not always civil. At four AM she can be downright surly.

"How long are we going to keep this up?" she demanded crossly, sipping orange juice. Trinka insists caffeine is a crutch. I believe crutches have their place.

I didn't say anything.

"Christ, even I can see this one's hopeless."

"Do you want me to leave the books out?" I asked.

"Have you talked to them about what this will cost?"

"Not really. The guy's a physician, Trinka. Our fees can't be much of a shock."

"You know what we're getting into? This kid needs full-time care. How long do you think we can keep this up? I got out of the E-clinic so I wouldn't have to stay up all night anymore. We are not set up to monitor this ape!"

No, but we're doing it anyway. I remained quiet. If I got started, I was afraid I'd lose it with her. I'd volunteered for the worst shift, and was now jittery from coffee and antsy from the cramped environment.

"You just can't say no, can you? Anyone asks you for something, no matter how hard it is on you, you'll do it."

I stared at her. This wasn't about the little chimp.

"This is so not fair to the staff. They're already attached to her," she persisted.

"If she makes it, this will be the best thing that's happened all summer. This is the kind of case they'll tell their friends about."

"But what if she doesn't go home? Have you thought about that?"

What if she doesn't—

"Of course I've thought about it. Her odds are terrible."

The high-pitched beeps accelerated with Andi's heart rate. Almost as if she understood our words.

"Her odds. Say it like you know it. Her *odds* would give Las Vegas wet dreams! This chimp is on a ventilator. She's getting pure oxygen, and her sat's below eighty. She does not—"

The monitor whined. Andi, suddenly awake, had reached up with her tiny hand and pulled the tube from her throat. Trinka and I spent a frantic minute getting it back in, bagged her manually for a few breaths, then reattached her to the ventilator. While the top was open, I changed her diaper and weighed the old one to measure her fluid output.

"Plus, she's her own worst enema."

The pun was so bad I had to smile.

We placed cotton balls in her hands and wrapped them lightly in gauze. It was the best solution we could come up with on short notice.

Trinka turned to me and said, "Andi, I don't want to see you get all involved in this case. We can't afford it."

"He'll pay his damned bill!"

"That's not what I mean! You can't afford the emotional involvement."

"Trinka, it's August. The hottest damned August I can remember. It's not like there's a waiting room full of people every day. We have time to deal with this."

"You're not tracking me. I've been watching, Andi. You care too much, and it weighs you down. You can't say no. You take on everyone's problems, and you can't go on like that. You're burning out. Ever since that thing last spring, you're only half here. Your workups aren't always complete, and you're not following up on cases."

"Damn it, Trinka, do we have to talk about this now?"

"When would you rather I brought it up? At a staff meeting? Over lunch in some restaurant? Will there ever be a good time to talk about this?"

"I'm not burned out."

"Five years. That's when it hits."

"Well, I'm not burned out. I'm not." *Was I?* "I have to go." I grabbed my purse from the office and left.

I should have gone right home to grab the few hours' sleep I could before the next day began. But the first faint glow of dawn from the east—the valley side—convinced my brain it was early rather than late. My nerves twitched from the caffeine and the silent streets beckoned.

Palm Springs is a hybrid city. It calls itself a village, and in summer genuinely feels like a small town. But our residents are sophisticated and often part-time, and the sustaining industry is tourism. At four-fifty on an August morning, the only cars on the street were the odd police cruiser and a few contractors trying to beat the heat of day.

I hated fighting with Trinka. She had salvaged my practice after a disastrous series of events the previous autumn, but there were times I wished I'd never taken on a partner.

I drove, inevitably, to the house where Gilda Hopkins lay fighting for death.

I was *not* burned out. I loved my work. Sure, I'd rather see fewer skin cases, less diarrhea, not so many chronic ear infections. Of course I wished we had better equipment.

Naturally I got tired of the never ending struggle to pay the damned bills.

But that didn't mean I was ready to hang it up.

A light was on in Gilda's room. Another in the living room, and an upstairs window in front glowed faintly, as well.

Stop by anytime, she'd said. But surely not at this hour.

The woman's predicament gnawed at my mind, drawing me to her, repelling me at the same time. I wanted to help her, saw the impulse as the same one that led me to salvage abandoned strays—a need to make things right. I resented the hell out of her for dragging me into her life, but was powerless to turn my back.

What would be the consequences? Would anyone even know? What would Alexandra do if she believed I had caused her mother's death?

As if responding to my thoughts, the front door opened, beckoning like something from a children's spook movie. Alexandra, in a bathrobe and framed by the lamplight, did nothing to dispel that disquieting image. I was caught, now I had no choice but to go in.

"What are you doing here?" she demanded. Her voice cut through the stillness like a foghorn. Next door, a dog barked.

I stepped out of the car and walked silently to the door. When I was close enough to speak normally I said, "Your mother said to come anytime. I just left the clinic and wondered if . . ." I didn't have to explain myself to her. "Is she up?"

"You have any idea what time it is?"

I gave her a look that must have conveyed all the don't-mess-with-me exhaustion I felt, because her eyes dropped quickly. "She's awake. What do I care if you talk to her?"

I hesitated just inside the door, wanting to offer something. I imagined this woman's boredom, cooped up with her dying mother day in and day out. Where was Rainie's father? What had happened to cause this once-attractive person to end up so, well, strange?

"Alexandra, I'm sorry about your mother. I knew Gilda a few years ago, and she was one of the strongest women I've ever met. I admired her greatly, even then." An exaggeration, but surely a harmless one.

Alexandra's scowl deepened. "What would you know? You've always had everything you wanted. No one stopped *you* from going to school. You don't know anything about Gilda."

What was that about? I gazed around the huge house with its unused piano in the living room. Mentally compared it to my fixer-upper, then to the cramped, drafty house in southern Illinois where I grew up. I had everything I wanted? I considered telling her about my own mother's drawn-out death, but glanced at her face and rejected the thought. Instead I shook my head in bafflement.

Perhaps that very strength I remembered was her complaint. What would it be like, growing up in the shadow of such a woman?

"Forget it," she said. "You'll never understand."

I hated to walk away on that bizarre note. Ruefully recalled Trinka's accusation: *You take on everyone's problems.* "Does she get many visitors?" I asked quietly.

"Not anymore. You going up? Or what?" The eyes on me again, narrowed and unapproving.

I went up.

Gilda was listening to the audio version of a bestseller. For a moment I stood unobserved in the doorway, watching her. Her face hung slackly, head sinking into the pillow, weary with suffering. This was a face she hid from me, her pride not allowing her to display self-pity even to the one she hoped to persuade to end the ridiculous struggle. I saw her mouth twist in a grimace of pain. Then she was racked with a coughing spasm, dislodging the oxygen tubing from her nostrils.

I moved to replace the line. She looked up in mild surprise as I entered, her glance flickering toward the clock as if to confirm the hour. Did the days blend into each other, when there was nothing to do but listen to tapes and count the hours until your next enema? *Not many visitors, not anymore.* I imagined the flood of well-wishers thinning to a trickle as Gilda outlived doctors' predictions by a lengthening margin. I realized with shame that I had been one of those visitors.

"Hope you meant it when you said come anytime," I offered lightly, wondering why I was here. Her skin had the dry, fragile look of old dollar bills.

"Come," she said. "Sit." It seemed harder for her to form words now. Maybe she'd persuaded her doctor to increase her dose of morphine. Her mask of stoicism was firmly back in place, with perhaps a hint of anticipation. Suddenly I felt terribly guilty, afraid she'd misinterpreted my reasons for coming.

I hit the pause button on the stereo and sat. "I'm sorry, it's very late. And I still haven't decided." I leaned back, gazing again at all the equipment, not wanting to look at her face.

After a lengthy silence she said, "You're welcome to all of it when I'm gone."

My face must have expressed my shock and horror.

"The machines. You must have a use for them."

"I . . . Is that what you think? That I've been sitting here, coveting your medical equipment?"

She didn't answer, whether from embarrassment or exasperation I couldn't tell.

"Well, I haven't," I said, but it sounded unconvincing.

"It isn't a trade," she mumbled. "I haven't changed my

mind, I want you to assist me. But should you decide not, the damned machines are yours. I'll tell Alexandra. I'll tell the nurse."

I didn't know what to say. It was too bizarre.

"The baby chimp is hanging in there," I blurted.

Her gaze turned hard, indifferent. Surely I hadn't come for sympathy?

"Is there anything you want?" I asked.

We both knew what she wanted from me.

"I mean, I could read to you, or bring a counselor. . . ." I trailed off. Gilda could arrange anything she needed. Except for the one thing she did want. I simply couldn't focus on that. Not now, maybe never. Trinka was both right and wrong. I cared about Gilda's pain. But not enough. If I did, there would not be this terrible dilemma. I would simply do what she asked and forget the consequences.

I blinked, and my mother lay in that bed. Blinked again, Gilda was back.

"Coward," she said, accurately sizing me up. "Turn the stereo on as you leave."

Chapter Seven

The needle zeroes in on an injection port, smoothly penetrating rubber. Plunger depressed, clear solutions mingle invisibly. I slip the syringe into my purse, spin around as a monitor alarm whines. A hand seizes my wrist.

I bolted awake, gasping for air. My own heartbeat would have set off alarms. The sudden movement dislodged Carbon, who must have been playing "Pounce" with my hand.

Automatically stroking the disgruntled cat, I shut off the digital clock that had jerked me from sleep. Six-thirty. Damn, I should have reset it for later. I was still beat, but that was it for sleep this morning. I let the dogs outside, dragged my body into the shower and let its chilly cascade wash away the images.

Gilda Hopkins's image. Superimposed on that of my mother, who died with none of the stoicism of the other woman. In that era, people did not die at home. Ma coughed and retched her way into death under the frowning supervision of a phalanx of nurses and doctors, each of whom expressed patronizing dismay at her request for something to speed up the process. None, of course, acceded. No one helped with anything more than the same inadequate morphine that dripped into the veins of Gilda Hopkins.

Nor had I. How could I? I hadn't known how. I could not have been expected to do anything. It wasn't my responsibility. Wasn't.

What was I going to do now about Gilda? She was hardly my responsibility either, but I could no longer claim ignorance of method. I wanted to help, couldn't help wanting it, and was disturbed to the point of obsession by the request. Wanted, also, to make a statement. *Not fair, not right, what we do to other humans, in the name of humanity.* But, Jack Kevorkian aside, was the act worth its consequences for me?

You take on everyone's problems. But how could I turn away?

It was as much a struggle in my mind as between myself and Gilda.

Gambit waited by the back door till I emerged, padding naked from the bathroom with a towel around my head. He ambled in and flopped onto the cool ceramic tile in the kitchen, ready for a day of sleep. The other dogs took advantage of the early-morning coolness to run off some energy. They all handled my altered schedule without noticeable effect, but the cats were out of sorts, glowering at me and each other from various vantage points above and beneath the furniture.

I did not make coffee. I toasted a bagel and reconstituted some orange juice for breakfast, clearing a space on the dining table among a week's worth of mail. Alternately I stroked Evinrude and then Clyde, as they grudgingly took turns in my lap. Carbon tried three times to sneak up on my bagel, before giving up and slinking off to groom himself. Gambit's eyes followed my movements wistfully—as always, when food was involved. Anything below table-top level was his, and he would slither arthritically after the smallest crumb that fell. He'd been middle aged when he came to me, a working coonhound broken in body but not in spirit. He had adapted readily to indoor life. The rest of the dogs—all of whom had been near death when I took them in—chased each other in the backyard and tussled over one of the toys that littered my sandy lot. The more energy they burned off this morning, the less they'd roughhouse inside later. At least that was the theory.

I went to Starbucks on the way to work and picked up a large latte and a dozen muffins. Trinka had gotten over her grumpiness, was hungry and glad for the food.

I took a muffin into the ward and offered it to Sally through the door of her run. She examined it, pulled it apart, tasted it, and used it to draw an abstract design on the floor. Well, it was a preferred medium over the pile of feces in one corner. But as I watched, she reached over and stuck a hand in that, too. It added color to her finger painting. She was still listless, but doing well considering how much blood she'd lost. Her breasts were swollen with milk, and I wondered if there were some way to harvest it for her baby, instead of the infant formula that dripped through a tube into the little one's stomach.

What did Sally understand? When she gazed into the incubator, did she see her own infant struggling for life in there? Could she know it would be her last? Did she have some dim concept of how near she'd been to death?

If so, she wasn't telling. She was, however, making a bigger mess of her cage than most of the dogs. But I knew better than to try to handle her on my own. As soon as Brad or Wayne showed up I'd get someone in here to clean her run. And it might be time to get her back home.

I went next to check on Daisy Bell. She would gladly have eaten a muffin instead of the high-calorie recovery food, which she had not finished. But she was much brighter than twelve hours previously. Her short, piglike tail wiggled in greeting and she licked my fingers. With an effort I rolled her over far enough to check her incision. It looked great. If her blood count held, I saw no reason not to send her home later that day.

Brad brought a rag doll—an old favorite, judging by its torn and faded condition—which Sally hugged to her chest. Wayne had office hours so would not be in until afternoon. Brad wore a body-hugging, silver-black muscle shirt with white spandex shorts, and that appeared to be all. I easily pictured him prancing before a bank of mirrors, studying the rippling effect of the fabric. I felt slightly embarrassed to be in the same room with him.

"Come on, Sally-potato. How's our little Andi-boober this morning?" He directed the question at Sally but she didn't answer. Finally he turned raised eyebrows to me.

"The same," I said.

"Does she need her didies changed?"

"Diane just did that." Actually, Diane had demonstrated the technique while Sheila looked on. Sheila was getting married in a few months and suddenly found everything to do with babies fascinating. The little chimp put out an amazing volume of pale yellowish feces.

"Then I'll just sing to her." He settled into my office chair, still wedged between the incubator and the treatment table, and Sally snuggled into his lap. He began crooning a lullaby in a surprisingly melodious tenor. It would have put me to sleep in a second.

I went into the office, looked up Alan Frank in the phone book, and dialed. A receptionist informed me that Dr. Frank had rounds this morning, but she'd be sure he got the message to call me.

Roosevelt, in his corner cage, said, "Kee-rist. Baa-aad bird! Cool!" And he whistled like a bomb landing, then stared at me until I gave him a peanut. On a small blackboard next to his cage, I made a tally. It was his second of three peanuts allowed per day. Trinka got to give him two, but he was, after all, her bird.

Our appointment load was light, the usual cluster of first-thingers, all gone by ten o'clock. It was Trinka's day in surgery, but only a cat de-claw and one dog neuter were scheduled.

In the meantime, I saw a dog with profoundly itchy skin. The client was new to Dr. D's.

"I've had him to three vets, and no one can tell what's wrong," the woman muttered.

I studied my patient, a white standard poodle named, with great originality, "Snowball." He had reddened, weepy eyes and inflamed ear canals; red, scaly skin with more black pigment than one should see on a white dog; and no hair on his belly or flanks or upper legs. This could take a while, and I was tired.

"What medication has he been on so far?" I asked.

Mary Wilcox, Snowball's owner, sighed as if I should have known that. "Everyone just gives him a shot. The last one gave me these pills." She began fishing through her purse.

"Have you seen any improvement at all?"

"Hang on." She kept rooting. The purse wasn't that big, how could she lose a prescription vial in there? "Guess I forgot them." This fact did not outwardly distress her. She folded her hands over the bag and looked at her dog.

"Did he get better?" I tried again, more slowly.

She shook her head vigorously. "Not at all. That's why I'm here."

Sheila would already have called the other clinic for his record, but it might be the next day before they faxed it over.

"Does the word 'cortisone' ring any bells?" I was sure

that's what had been given to the dog, in one or more forms.

She perked up. "Yeah, that's what the shot was, I think. But it didn't help. Only, he got real tired and he's hungry all the time and you wouldn't believe how much water he drinks. But he still scratches constantly."

As if to demonstrate, Snowball sat down and began kicking at his ear with his left hind foot.

Mary looked at me: *See?*

I went over the dog carefully, saw no sign of fleas, which are rare in the desert but becoming more common. The skin along his belly was thickened and scaly. Snowball's ears had a faint odor and slight discharge, but clearly the infection was secondary.

I really hate skin cases. But they make up close to half of what I see, and every now and then I can work a miracle. Miracles, of course, are generally the result of diligent diagnostic work and judicious pharmacology, but in the eyes of the person who lives with the animal, I get to be a hero.

"Okay," I said. "So many skin problems respond well to a corticosteroid, that's often what we try first. But since it didn't help in Snowball's case, we'll need to look a little deeper. I'll start by scraping a sample of skin off with a dull scalpel blade, to look for parasites under the microscope. I'll need to pluck a few hairs to culture for fungal infections. An ear culture will help us treat those specifically. And with Diane's help, I'll take a small sample of Snowball's blood, which we'll send off to the lab to make sure—"

I stopped, because Mary was shaking her head.

"You're just like that last vet. He wanted to give him a bunch of tests. When I asked him what was wrong, he just hemmed and hawed and gave me these pills. They didn't do any good. I can't afford all those tests, I just want you to make him stop scratching." She was standing up. She was a blocky woman, in T-shirt and shorts, the uniform of the desert. This bullying technique probably worked sometimes. I was sitting on the floor with Snowball, but was way too tired to feel intimidated.

I didn't ask how much she'd spent hopping from clinic to clinic. I didn't offer to give Snowball yet another steroid injection and another handful of useless tablets to swallow. It was a tempting way to get rid of her for good since she'd be off to do the vet-clinic shuffle somewhere else as soon as she realized my treatment hadn't worked either. But I resisted. My obligation was to Snowball.

"It's up to you. He's your dog, I can't insist on anything. But if it turns out he's got mange or ringworm, you could catch it, too."

I watched the emotions play out on her face: determination to get what she wanted, dread conjured by the word "mange," stubborn refusal to display her ignorance by asking for more information. As if by its own volition, her right hand went to her left arm, and began to scratch.

I jumped in while she wavered. "Look, skin has only a few ways to respond to disease. It can turn red and itch, turn dark, grow lumps, or get thicker. In some cases it blisters, or gets greasy, or very dry. But it's impossible to tell what's causing it without running some diagnostic tests."

She sat down slowly. Snowball stopped scratching long enough to accept a pat from his owner.

"But as I said, the decision is yours," I finished.

"You take Visa?"

Of course we did.

I suspected Snowball suffered from an allergy to the grocery-store-brand dog food Mary had been feeding him, but that's almost impossible to prove. So I set about ruling out worse conditions. The skin scrape was negative for mange mites, the blood work would take a day, the ear culture three, and the ringworm about a week. If these weren't diagnostic we'd talk about a biopsy. In the meantime, I sent Mary home with a bag of special dog food, a bottle of essential fatty acid supplement, ear flush, an antibiotic, and some medicated shampoo and conditioner. These ought to give poor Snowball some relief, and make the owner part of the solution. Her bill came to over three hundred dollars, which she paid without further complaint. Some people are like dogs that way—establish dominance one time, and they'll do whatever you tell them to. I'd call her in a few days to see how Snowball was doing.

Feeling slightly triumphant, I looked in on Brad and baby Andi. Sally was sitting on the floor beneath the treatment table, playing with bandage materials. She'd pulled a drawer out and upended it, and now examined her discovery. She had several rolls of gauze draped over her head, around her arms, legs, and neck. She was chewing on a roll of adhesive tape, and had scattered the cotton cast padding everywhere on the floor.

I didn't know whether to laugh or cry.

"Brad, do you think it's time to put Sally back in her run?" I asked in the calmest voice I could muster.

Brad glanced at me, then at Sally. "Oh, Potato-bo, what naughtiness have you gotten up to, Bo-bo? Did you find a good-good?" He went to her and gently extricated her from the mess, which he tossed on the floor. "Really," he said to me, but without changing the inflection of his voice, "you need to baby-proof these cabinets. No telling what she might have found. We're so lucky her picked the soft bandages to play with, aren't we, Bo-bo?"

Sally inverted her lips in an enormous grin, or, that's what it looked like. She grabbed for a roll of gauze as Brad pulled it away. He took Sally's hand and led her over to the incubator. "Lookie-see. This is your baby, Potato-bo. See the widdle fingers?" He squeezed the fingers on Sally's hand, one by one. "And the teeny, tiny toe-toes?" He pointed, then reached down to touch Sally's toes. The anatomy lesson would have seemed ridiculous, except that Sally appeared to be following closely. The wonder in her huge brown eyes was remarkably human. She made it through eyes and ears before losing interest.

Sheila came on the intercom. "Dr. Pauling, there's a lady on line one, she wants to know how much ether she should give her German shepherd to put it to sleep so she can sew up a cut on its side it got from running too close to a stack of firewood."

The mischievous undertone in Sheila's voice tipped me off.

I said to Brad, "Try to keep Sally out of the cabinets, okay?" and went to the office, still shaking my head. I picked up the phone, hit line one, and said, "We haven't used ether for years. Why don't you just give him a big slug of whiskey? Then when he passes out, you can grab the old needle and thread and stitch away. Better yet, use fishing line. And just ignore any big old chunks of wood you might see in the wound. They help it heal faster. They're organic, you know."

"Damn, I can't fool anyone anymore." But Lara was laughing. My friend isn't normally a jokester, but when she calls the clinic she finds devious ways of getting me to the phone.

"You're slipping, Lara. I told you about that guy last month." That one had been for real.

"So are you free for lunch?"

I thought about it. Wayne would be royally pissed if he came in and I wasn't there. And it was hardly fair to ask Trinka to stay. But I wanted badly to talk to Lara. If anyone could advise me on the Gilda Hopkins situation, she'd be the one. I'd work it out with Trinka.

"There's something I want to run by you," I said. "Lunch sounds like just the thing."

Chapter Eight

El Burrito is a cozy Mexican restaurant in a converted house around the corner from Dr. Doolittle's. It's owned and operated, as they say, by real Mexicans. The menu is printed in English, more or less, and the food is straightforward and uniformly good.

It was possible to speak with at least an illusion of privacy, since ours was the only conversation not taking place in Spanish. That did not preclude eavesdropping in English, of course, but the overall noise level made that unlikely. We ordered—the usual gooey plate of enchiladas for Lara, and a burro pollo, the house specialty, for me. The waitress, one of numerous Garcia daughters, placed tortillas and salsa and large glasses of iced tea in front of us, and hurried off to another table.

I spoke as quietly as I could and still be heard. "I'd like to ask you about something, on a purely theoretical basis."

Her green eyes, clear and skeptical and surrounded by a mass of wavy, deep red hair, zeroed in on me like lasers. "Shit, Andi, what have you gotten into now?"

Sometimes it's not good to have friends who know you too well. "Theoretical, okay?"

Lara sipped her tea and didn't answer.

"Okay, say there's this woman. She's older, not ancient. She's dying of cancer."

Lara's eyes narrowed.

"Just listen, okay? The doctors gave her a few weeks to live, but that was months ago. It started as breast cancer but it's metastasized to her bones, including her spine, and now she's totally helpless. Bone cancer is one of the worst, the pain is unrelenting. So now she's quadriplegic, in constant agony from the parts of her body she can still feel, bedridden because her bones break if she's moved. Diapers, catheters, oxygen lines, feeding tube, the works."

Lara's expression did not reflect the horror I felt just describing Gilda Hopkins's condition. She's a lawyer, and sometimes her ability not to see others' pain scares me. She waited. Our food came, the plates too hot to touch, and neither of us picked up a fork.

"She can talk, and she can cough. That's about it." I took a bite of rice and beans, washed it down with iced tea. Lara waited.

Then, "What does she want from you?" As if she already knew.

I put my fork down. "She wants to die."

She was shaking her head before I had the words out.

"Lara, I knew her before. She was such a strong, vital woman. . . ." I trailed off, wondering why I kept trying to put Gilda on a pedestal. "Okay, she was pushy and overbearing, and manipulative and hard to be around. Still is. But if this is some kind of punishment for that, she's done her time. Can you imagine how awful it is for her to beg for something so basic? All she wants is—"

"Is murder." Lara's flat, uncompromising statement cut into my speech.

I blinked. "But she's almost gone. Her life is horrible. If she could move she'd commit suicide."

"But she can't. The law doesn't see degrees of life. If she's breathing when you go in, and dead when you go out, and you did something to make her dead, that's murder."

Okay, I knew that. Time to regroup. "But what would happen? I mean, really happen. You're part of the system. And the system is run by people, who use discretion sometimes. Would they prosecute?"

"Do you hear what you're saying?"

I shut up for a minute, eating. Thinking. As if, by convincing Lara this was the right thing to do, I could prevent the consequences.

"If you saw her—"

A shake of her head.

"Kevorkian's been acquitted how many times?"

Lara's fork hit the plate. "Jack Kevorkian has made this his life's work, and still he never killed anyone. He hooks up his machine but it's up to the patient to turn it on. There's a big difference between facilitated suicide and active murder."

"I wish you'd stop using that word."

"Murder? That's what it is, Andi. Plain and simple. The law is carefully devoid of compassion."

We ate in silence. Then Lara said, "Please tell me you're listening. Don't do this, Andi."

I didn't answer.

"Please."

I shrugged. Still trying to find a way. "Most likely, her doctor would just sign the death certificate and that would be it."

"Shit."

"If only her daughter wasn't so adamant."

"Great. The prosecution has their star witness in place. This person knows you're thinking about this?"

"She's the, um, primary caretaker. She wants her mother to hold on. In fact, she may be responsible for the fact that Gilda's morphine rate is so low. I think she threatened the doctors with legal action."

I told Lara about the videotaped plea, about the sheltie I'd treated when I was barely out of school, about the faith this woman seemed to have in my infant skills. I did not mention the ever present memory of my own mother, since I've never been able to talk about that. "How often do you get a chance to really make a difference?" I finally asked.

"Andi, you can't go through life righting other people's wrongs. Life is not always nice. This is not your problem."

Lara can be harsh sometimes. But she's unerringly practical, which makes her a good sounding board. I did hear what she was saying. Gilda's agony could not go on much longer, no matter how it had persisted thus far. But if I did what she asked, the act could ruin my life. It wasn't worth it.

If I could just keep that in mind when I went to see her that night.

Wayne arrived about the time I returned from lunch, with Larry Jenkins, the radiologist, in tow. The two of them set up their ultrasound equipment while I saw a cocker spaniel with recurrent ear infections. Again.

Baby Andi's cardiac sonogram proved that she did not have a ventricular septal defect, a hole in the wall between chambers. So open-heart surgery would not be necessary. Thank God. It wasn't even possible.

The left side of her heart was already thickening, a result of having to work harder. The right side was dilating from the overload. This confirmed the PDA, of which there had never been any real doubt. It still showed no sign of closing on its own, despite the Indocin Wayne had prescribed.

That did not entirely explain Andi's condition, either. Wayne muttered angrily about the lack of diagnostic equipment. "I can't believe there's not even a primitive CT scanner available. You can pick them up for nothing on the used market."

"Nothing" was in the range of fifty thousand dollars. It cost around three hundred dollars just to turn the thing on. I did not ask Wayne how many dog or cat owners he thought would pay for that. I didn't inquire where he thought I should keep such a space hog. Nor who would maintain the machine, or read the films once I got them. Instead I said, "I once took a dog into Coachella Valley General after hours for an MRI."

Jenkins nodded. "We could do it."

Wayne looked at me, then Jenkins, and blinked as if the idea hadn't occurred to him. Then he shook his head. "I can't see moving her that far right now."

I was disappointed, and annoyed at Wayne for once again shooting down a good idea, apparently because it was not his own.

"If the PDA doesn't close by Thursday, we'll have to go in," he said.

That got my attention. Today was Tuesday. Andi's lungs were underdeveloped, and in time, if she lived long enough, this would probably correct itself. But the prospect of anesthetizing her loomed like a walk through a viper pit.

"Just reach in there and clamp it off," Jenkins said. "Nothing to it."

He was skinny, with wiry brown hair, and made unfunny jokes while his magical machine displayed an image of baby Andi's beating heart.

No one laughed. Wayne held Brad's hand, and Brad stood there with quiet tears dripping onto his iridescent clothing until I handed him a box of Kleenex. The diagnosis was good news for Andi, but the absence of other defects meant we were committed. It cast a greater responsibility on her caretakers, specifically myself and Wayne. I saw in Wayne's face the battle between doctor and parent, the effort it cost him not to break down.

"Hey, come on, guys," Jenkins said cheerfully. "It's just an animal." Not seeing that baby Andi was the closest Brad and Wayne would ever come to having a child.

Radiology was a good choice of specialties for Jenkins. It kept him away from patients.

When I could get Wayne alone I asked him if he knew Alan Frank. Gilda's doctor had not returned my call.

"Ye-es," he said slowly, "but I don't see what good a geriatrician would do us."

"No, I want to talk to him about something else. Do you know him well enough to introduce me?"

"I suppose so. His office is in the same building as mine. I have to go back in an hour." He seemed reluctant but I pretended not to notice.

"Great. I'll follow you over." I left the room, not giving him a chance to ask any more questions.

The time passed uneventfully. I saw two clients: a vaccination and another skin case. Trinka had said she didn't mind if I left early to see Gilda's doctor. I just had to make it back in time for the first shift on baby watch.

Wayne's office was on the second floor of a professional building across the street from CVG. Alan Frank's office was at the opposite end of the same floor. He walked down with me and we entered a typically sterile reception room. Two older patients waited, a man and a woman, and I could not tell if they were together. The usual glassed-in counter sat at one end of the room, and a generically pleasant medical assistant slid the partition open. Her eyes slid from me to Wayne, as if she couldn't figure out what either of us was doing in a geriatrician's office.

"Can I help you?" she finally offered.

"I'm Dr. Williamson," Wayne said. "This is . . . Dr. Pauling. She'd like to see Dr. Frank if he's not too busy?"

She glanced from him to me and back again and said, "Just a moment, please." She vanished down the hall and a minute later a man who looked well past retirement age opened the patient door.

"Wayne! How are you?" His eyes were wary. The two men shook hands.

"Not too bad, I guess. This is Andi Pauling. She needed to talk to you. Sorry I can't stay, but I'll catch you later." He took off.

Frank's expression clouded at the mention of my name. He knew who I was, all right.

"I wanted to talk to you for a minute about Gilda Hopkins."

He stepped backward through the door, beckoning me to follow him into a vacant exam room. When we were alone he said, "I don't think that's a good idea."

"I know she asked you to talk to me."

"She is incapable of signing a waiver."

"I suppose that's true. How about informally?"

"What is it you want to know?"

"How bad is she? Is there more that could be done to make her comfortable?"

"Are you questioning my treatment plan?"

"Of course not. Come on! I'm in a very awkward position. I knew her years ago, and I think you realize why she contacted me. She's miserable, and she's dying, and a morphine rate of only twenty milligrams per hour seems low. I just wondered if there was something that might make things easier for her."

Indecision crossed his face. "The pain relief offered by narcotics is dose related, I'm sure you know. But in severe cases, the margin between therapeutic dose and toxic dose becomes perilously thin."

He was telling me the amount needed to control her pain could hasten her death. "I'm not sure I see the problem."

He cleared his throat and glanced at the closed door. Lowering his voice even further he said, "You've met the, ah, family?"

"You mean Alexandra? Her daughter."

He nodded. "Then you know."

I sighed. "She's talking about lawyers?"

Another nod, a helpless shrug. He probably dealt with such things daily. He was used to seeing things from others' perspective, but I had not been in his shoes so could not judge him for this.

"When did you last see Gilda?"

"A few weeks ago. Didn't think she'd last this long, truth be told."

"Maybe a visit would . . . change your way of thinking about her case."

He opened the door. "I can't fix all the world's problems, Doctor Pauling. When you're my age you'll have learned not to try."

He moved down the hallway, leaving me to find my own way out. The patients, still waiting, eyed me suspiciously as I left.

On the way back I stopped at Celebrity Used Bookstore to see what they had on the subject of voluntary death. I found the famous book by Derek Humphry, *Final Exit*. There was another, titled *Arguing Euthanasia*, a collection of essays on the subject by thinkers I'd mostly never heard of, edited by Jonathan Moreno. And my collection would not have been complete without *Dr. Death*,

Kevorkian's biography by Joan Brovins and Thomas Oehmke.

Gilda Hopkins occupied my thoughts, and I wanted to learn everything I could about what she was feeling. It didn't mean I planned to . . . *help* her.

I set the unopened bag of books on the treatment table and Wayne and I discussed the possibility of surgery.

"I've asked a couple of pediatric surgeons, but no one's got the time to come in and do this," he said.

I felt affronted, insulted, but fought it. An MD surgeon would be faster, surer, more experienced. Better. Wayne was right to try to arrange one. At the same time, I acknowledged a small thrill over the fact that he hadn't found anyone.

"The book makes it sound pretty straightforward," I ventured.

Wayne gazed through the Plexiglas and didn't respond.

"I mean, you basically just ligate the shunt, right?" *Sure, inside a chest the size of my fist. With the lungs popping into your incision, and the four great vessels in your way, not to mention vital nerves that absolutely must not be cut. No problem.*

Wayne said, "You almost sound like you want to do it now."

It was my turn not to reply. We both stared into the incubator, as if it were a crystal ball that could foretell the little chimp's fate. The *whoosh, sigh* of the ventilator continued, and the ECG proved her heart was up for the try.

I said, "Do you do much surgery in your practice?"

He shook his head slowly, while his face assumed a sad, condescending smile. "I might occasionally stitch up a minor skin wound." As if I should have known that. As if his profession had long ago outgrown the jack-of-all-trades approach to medicine still widely used by most veterinarians.

As if he didn't realize how lucky he was that I was even willing to try this.

"You're right," I said. "I want to do it."

After Wayne left I called Clay. The sound of him evoked thoughts of the rest of him. I wished for the night off, an evening of uncomplicated pleasures, the answering of simple needs.

"You sound blue," he said.

"Yeah, maybe. I miss you."

"Want to come up, later?"

So tempting. So damn late. Sigh. "Not tonight. You'll come down for dinner tomorrow?"

I heard the smile in his tone. "You're cooking?"

I laughed. Thought about the cat hair accumulating on every surface in my house, the weeks' worth of mail stored more or less permanently on my dining-room table. The August heat that made barbecuing miserable. "I was thinking in terms of an air-conditioned restaurant, dim lights, a nice Chardonnay."

"Mm-hm. That could be arranged. And later?"

"Later" either meant he came over for sex, then went home to sleep, or it meant I drove to Morongo Valley where he lived, spent the night, then got up early to go home, take care of my animals, and get ready for work. It was an increasingly sore point with me, but I didn't feel like fighting now. "Later could be negotiable," I said.

"Well, then, how about I pick you up around seven?"

I hung up already looking forward to seeing him.

Baby Andi had seven o'clock treatments, which I administered then noted on her chart, along with her temperature and pulse rate. Her lungs sounded slightly wet, so I turned her fluids down and noted that, too. I wondered if I should give her a little Lasix, but she looked so good otherwise and Wayne would not be pleased if I did so without checking with him first. I suctioned the mucus from her trach tube and decided to watch her awhile longer.

Wayne had removed the gauze gloves, opting instead for more tape around the trach tube. She was moving more on her own, in fact, her hand balled up around my little finger, just like a normal human infant, but much, much stronger. I wondered what that reflex was called and whether, in humans, it represented a vestige of evolution, when primate infants must either hold on or be dinner for a passing carnivore.

The tiny ape invited touching, and seemed to respond to it, so I spent fifteen minutes gently massaging her arms and legs, careful not to dislodge any of the equipment. Brad had offered similar contact earlier, singing to her and cooing. He called it bonding. Definitely the more maternal of her "parents."

I recognized that baby Andi was more than a patient to me. Trinka was right about that, but what she saw as a problem I saw as one of the perks of my job. It wasn't the first time I'd let an animal get through the professional detachment the practice-management consultants are so adamant about. But I'd never gone to such extremes before. The equipment, the twenty-four-hour watch, the no-holds-barred sense that one life was precious—all this was unique in my professional experience. Wayne and Brad might take my efforts for granted, but somehow that made me more determined to do everything right. I carried the burden of my profession's reputation on one shoulder, the negligible weight of little Andi's fragile existence on the other.

And I wasn't burned out. I thrived on it. Really.

* * *

Trinka arrived early, catching me off guard. I was curled up with my book, staring past it, fighting to stay awake.

She took one look at what I'd been reading and said, "Christ, Andi, are you still thinking of putting that old lady to sleep?"

"Of course not. I've been visiting her, that's all. She's lonely and no one comes around anymore."

"When do you have time?" Slightly accusatory, as if I'd been slacking off at work.

"I make time. In fact, I'm going over there on my way home. Taking her dog back. Glad you were able to get some rest." I began gathering my things.

"Hang on. We need to talk."

Again? I should have known she hadn't just wandered in an hour ahead of schedule. "We need to talk" was invariably Trinka's code for "I'm not happy about something so you need to change." The old adage came to mind, that a partnership was like a marriage, without sex to redeem it. What did it say about us that neither had ever been married?

She sat on the round stool that lived in Treatment, while I settled back in my office chair. I waited.

She squirmed slightly, as if wishing she hadn't started this. Then, "I checked with someone I know at CVG. Your pediatrician friend is on his way out."

I was out of my chair. "I can't believe you would—"

She sprang to her feet. "I had to! He's in here all the time, Andi, he's taking over! Will you just listen to what I found out?"

"I don't care. Whatever it is has nothing to do with us."

"It does if he can't pay his bill!"

"That's all you care about, isn't it? Never mind the professional challenge. This is the chance of a lifetime! If that ductus doesn't close by Thursday, we're going in."

"The guy's a—"

"He's a jerk, but—"

"He's a child molester."

As if triggered by our shouting, baby Andi's heart chose that moment to stop beating.

Chapter Nine

More than two years at the Animal Emergency Clinic gave Trinka an edge at resuscitation. The crash kit was out and ready. She had the incubator open and began delicate chest compressions while I reached for drugs. The ventilator kept her breathing, but oxygen was useless if her heart failed to pump.

Damn it, I thought. *Should have given her the Lasix earlier*. I'd thought she had fluid in her lungs and should have paid more attention.

Trinka called out orders. I drew up minuscule doses and injected them into the IV line, one panicked eye on the monitor screen. The belated diuretic first, then epinephrine and digoxin and atropine, and enormous—relatively speaking—volumes of sodium bicarbonate. The ECG line leaped randomly, deflected not by the little chimp's heart, but by Trinka's frantic activity.

We went on for what seemed like ages, though it couldn't have been more than a few minutes. Compressions, drugs, pause to watch the monitor for any signs of life. I fought to steady my hands, struggled to focus on the tiny lines on the syringes.

Trinka paused, forehead glistening. She'd felt something. We held our breath while the ECG line organized itself into a semblance of normality. Her oxygen concentration had dropped like a meteor, but now returned to the mid-70% range. Not great, but close to what we'd grown accustomed to. And, as we watched, it hit 80.

Trinka and I grinned at each other. We couldn't help it. The high of cheating death is rare and unparalleled. I was loath to break the spell by asking her what she'd meant before.

I fell back in my chair, while the monitor issued its reassuring series of beeps, and we savored the moment. "Damn, why did that happen?"

"I don't know, but it will probably happen again. Between her lungs and her heart, this kid doesn't have a chance."

It wasn't like Trinka to give up. I wondered briefly if she was jealous of my involvement in the case. Or was she letting her dislike of Wayne interfere? It would be hard not to.

"I thought she had some edema earlier," I said. "I turned her fluids down. Wonder if I should have started her on Lasix then?" Damn it, if I could have prevented this and didn't . . .

Trinka sized up my fears immediately: *Been there, got the souvenir tote bag to prove it.* She shrugged. "It's hard to tell. Wayne's already got her on dobutamine in the drip. You'd have just as easily screwed up her electrolyte balance as helped her."

Which had been my logic at the time. I let up a little. "Well, I'm glad you were here. And thanks for bringing her back."

She grinned again. "Couldn't have done it alone."

We shared another moment of partnership, but the strain between us could not be ignored. There was nothing to do now but watch little Andi, and hope her tiny body straightened itself out.

The monitor beeped, the ventilator whooshed, and I could hear Trinka breathing.

I waited, refusing to ask what she'd meant earlier and thereby admit she'd piqued my curiosity. Finally she spoke.

"A thirteen-year-old boy says he made a pass at him in the office." No need to explain who "he" was.

After a bit I said, "That's it? You heard a rumor? Don't they always keep a nurse or parent in the room? Just to avoid allegations like that." Thinking, *Why should I stand up for him? If what she says is true, he ought to be shot.*

"I don't have details. His parents filed charges. The hospital is considering canceling his privileges."

I digested this. "Who told you this?"

"Someone I met at rounds." Trinka had attended morning rounds at CVG for a couple of years to observe, and I knew she had contacts among the hospital staff. It just never occurred to me she'd use them this way. "She's a patient advocate."

Gossip advocate was more like it, I thought uncharitably. "What are you suggesting we do?" I kept my tone carefully neutral. If the hospital, knowing more details than we did, still had not made up their collective minds, I would not be led to conclusions. And whatever Wayne might have done, it shouldn't be taken out on little Andi.

But Trinka was not a moral militant, she was a pragmatist. "Get a deposit."

I nodded. I had to admit, I was a little nervous about the bill we were running up. Sure, I was having fun, but if we didn't get paid for this one it would devastate the staff's morale—as well as mine and Trinka's—for a month. Not to mention making it hard to pay bills for a while. "Don't you say anything to him about . . . that other thing, okay?"

Trinka looked hurt. She'd waited till now to tell me, in order to avoid Wayne hearing us talk.

"I'm going to call him now," I said. "Let him know what happened. He'll probably want to come down."

"No doubt. Want me to bring up the subject of payment?"

I hesitated, then agreed. Trinka, being more in tune with the business side of practice, was much better at broaching that subject. I picked up the phone, dialed the number on the chart. Thankfully, Wayne answered.

"It's me. She coded, but she's okay now." I could do better than that. "We brought her back. Trinka's here."

"I'm on my way." And the line went dead.

It would take him at least forty-five minutes to get there. We used the intervening time to record the drugs we'd given, arguing briefly over whether the second shot of epinephrine had gone before or after the third dose of bicarb. Wondering if the calcium gluconate had helped at all, predicting that Wayne would gripe about the lack of availability of blood gas measurement, when he arrived.

"He'd suck her dry, pulling blood every few hours." This from Trinka, who heartily believed in diagnostic tests. She often complained that I didn't do enough.

But she was right about the little chimp. Andi had gained weight, but still tipped the bird scale at under three pounds, with all her equipment attached. How much blood could she have in her? "We'll get chest X rays in the morning," I said.

Wayne thankfully arrived alone, in loose-fitting shorts and T-shirt, hair mussed and dark bags under his eyes. This ordeal was taking its toll on all of us.

Or was he worried about the boy Trinka had discovered? I would never be able to regard him in the same way.

He scanned the chart, not commenting on the list of drugs we'd given. "Damn it, I wish we could run gases," he mumbled. Trinka and I exchanged grins.

"You could take it to CVG," I said, knowing he would

reject the idea simply because someone other than himself had suggested it. “I’m sure they’d run it for you.”

Sure enough, he shook his head as if dealing with an incompetent nurse. “If half an hour passes between drawing a sample and running it, the results are meaningless.”

Trinka said, “I attended a conference last year, where someone presented a chart on that. Found out that if you store it on ice, results aren’t significantly altered for up to two hours.”

I hid my smile behind a cough. Trinka can pull trivia like that from her brain, dating back to vet school. I have to look up doses for drugs I use once a month.

Wayne was caught off guard. Possible responses flitted across his face: *How dare you contradict me!* battled with *Really? Do you have the article?* But Trinka had put him in the awkward position of feeling he had to argue against something he’d wanted in the first place.

Finally he said, “We don’t have an arterial line. Should have put one in the first day, but now the umbilical artery is closed.”

Trinka responded, “I could tap the femoral.” She was teasing him now, but he couldn’t see it.

“You don’t have blood gas syringes.”

“Heparinized TB syringes work fine.”

I kept my hand to my face, trying to appear thoughtful, afraid Wayne would see my grin and realize Trinka was toying with him. To be fair, he was tired and not up to the game.

“Too much time has passed since she coded. And the bicarb would mask any acidosis.” The note of finality in his voice indicated that should be the end of it.

“I pulled blood immediately after we got her back.”

I shot Trinka a furious glance. This was an outright lie, and if he called her on it our credibility was ruined.

But Wayne was rendered speechless. After a long moment he said, "Is there coffee made?" and walked out of the room.

Trinka and I shared a quiet laugh. "I'm so bad!" she whispered, and I nodded. Really, Wayne made an irresistible target sometimes. I wondered what made him so unreceptive to others' suggestions. Wondered if he'd really molested a young boy. If there had been others before.

"Well, it's not like blood gas results would change anything," I whispered back. After all, she was already on oxygen, ventilated, and pumped full of every drug we had to keep her blood pH stable. And to be honest, I wouldn't know how to interpret them if we had them. I suspected Wayne wouldn't either.

Wayne appeared to be settling in to stay. He returned with a cup of stale coffee, and I smelled a new pot brewing.

"You need an on-call room," he muttered, apparently lamenting the lack of a cot to rest on. I was perversely relieved to see that Trinka hadn't deflated him any. Could this man, so devoted to Brad and this baby chimp, really have done what Trinka and her unnamed source alleged? It didn't seem possible, but I knew pedophiles were often the most ordinary among us. And they frequently had jobs that brought them into contact with children. A pediatrician? Almost a cliché. Still, Wayne had been in practice for years without a hint of impropriety. I decided to reserve judgment.

"You don't have to stay," I pointed out to him. "Your shift doesn't start for another—" It was almost two. How had that happened? "Two hours."

"It's stupid to go home and have to come right back. I don't mind. I'll call Brad in a few, let him know she's stable."

I saw the objection rise in Trinka's eyes, and shook my

head fractionally. Not worth it. If he thought he could do a better job of watching the baby chimp, let him do it. I certainly wasn't complaining. I was leaving.

"Let's open her up in the morning," Wayne said.

I stopped in the doorway, his words echoing nonsensically in my ears. "Open what? You mean, her chest?" Thinking I should object in some way, maintain control.

"Of course, her chest. Repair the ductus, first thing in the morning. After this, I don't want to wait another day."

Oh, great. That was six hours away. I was sure to sleep well now.

But of course, he was right.

In the runs, Sally began shrieking, apparently having heard Wayne's voice. The boarding dogs started barking. Wayne went to get Sally. I took Frankie, now tended to. I was glad to go.

Worn out, I needed to sleep, but knew I would toss and turn, thinking about the potential for disaster the following morning.

As long as I was doomed to lie awake, I might as well get the Gilda Hopkins decision settled. If the house was dark, I could always turn away. But the family seemed never to sleep. I took Frankie and headed out.

Turning onto their street, I passed the pale Honda belonging to the nurse, Eva Short. And, as I expected, several lights cast their feeble glow from the house into the darkness. It was as if the structure were holding a vigil, waiting for Gilda to die.

I sat in my car for a while, gazing up at her window, considering what I was about to do. How would she react when I told her my decision? Her reaction was important to me.

A shadow moved across Gilda's window, moved back

again, and was gone. Perhaps Alexandra was checking on her mother. At any rate, someone was up.

If I didn't ring the bell now I would not be able to do it. With a sigh I shut the car door, stretched in procrastination, and slipped my purse strap over my shoulder. Then, a tired Frankie in one arm, I went to the door and knocked lightly. After a long time—I was ready to leave, calling it an honest try—Alexandra opened the door. She stood in the gap, staring at me.

"Alexandra?"

She didn't move.

"Please. I need to see her."

Nothing. Finally I pushed past her, self-conscious about asserting myself in her house but determined to get this over with. I lumbered up the stairs, my feet feeling heavier with each step. From a corner of my eye, I spotted the granddaughter standing in her doorway. Then I was in Gilda's room, with its oppressive silence and hulking machines. I deposited Frankie on the bed.

I sensed Alexandra in the room with me. I stood beside the bed, the lack of sound reverberating in the room. No wheezing breath, no cough, only the minute mumbles of the equipment behind the bed. How long had I been there? I was holding Gilda's hand—soft, bony like a malnourished kitten, still warm. But her eyes were dead eyes. And the wrist bore no pulse.

Frankie, on the bed, whined.

"Is she gone?" came a horrified whisper.

I glanced at Alexandra. Nodded, then stopped myself. "I'm not an MD, you'll want to call her doctor." But the truth was plain.

Alexandra held my gaze, fury burning in her eyes, undirected anger. If she wanted to turn it on me, that was okay, I thought tiredly. Whatever helped.

"Are you happy now?" she demanded.

I sighed, placed Gilda's unfeeling hand on the bed. Happy? I didn't want to be here, didn't want to bear the brunt of Alexandra's fresh grief. My emotions were used up, my energy quotient spent for the day. So why were my hands trembling?

Gilda's eyes bothered me. I closed her lids, the way I'd seen it done in movies, but they reopened when I took my fingers away. With pets I sometimes glued them shut, if the owner planned on burial at home. I wondered what they did with people.

"Don't you ignore me!" Alexandra shouted.

I spun and fell into the chair in time to ward off a fist that wouldn't have hurt. She attacked, with wild glancing blows, some of which landed on my head and shoulders. Shouting, "You bitch, how dare you!" Then a wild hand connected with my throat and I panicked for a second. I couldn't get out of the chair with her looming over me, and suddenly my eyes were tearing and I couldn't breathe.

When she stopped I found I had pulled my legs against my chest and wrapped my arms around my head. The day's frustration had culminated in this ridiculous fight, and I found my eyes were still watering. Alexandra was sobbing. As I began to relax she turned and ran from the room.

I started to follow, but it felt wrong somehow to leave Gilda alone. What does one do for the newly dead? Whom did one call? My mother had died in the hospital, with a phalanx of efficient staff to deal with the details. I had not been faced with this problem before.

I stood in the doorway, undecided, and wiped tears from my face. I really had no business here now, but no one else seemed to be doing anything.

Then a door opened down the hall and Rainie stepped

out hesitantly. She approached as if she were a deer and I a hunter. Frankie, clearly confused, went to her and the girl picked him up. “Is she dead?” she whispered.

“Yes, she is.”

She sighed, her shoulders slumped and she pulled the little dog’s ear so hard he whimpered. “Poor Gramma. I’m gonna really miss her.”

“Do you have her doctor’s phone number?” I asked.

“Dr. Frank. He’s on the auto dial.” She glanced over my shoulder, refusing to enter the room with the dead woman. “Hang on, I’ll give him a call.”

She stared past me for another long moment before returning to her room to make the call. I sighed, leaning against the wall, wondering at what point I could gracefully leave.

When Rainie returned she refused to come more than halfway down the hall, though she kept glancing past me as if expecting her grandmother to appear there. “He said to call the mortuary and they’ll come and get her.” She shuddered, hugged herself, stared at the floor. “I don’t want them to. I don’t want her to lie on some cold table all night.”

After what seemed like a long time it occurred to me that it was probably the first time this young woman had faced the death of someone close to her. Her own mother should have been there to comfort her, take over. “Where’s Alexandra?” I asked more impatiently than I’d intended.

She shrugged, still not looking at me. “Her room, I guess.”

I sighed, took a careful step toward Rainie, as if approaching a frightened animal. She didn’t draw back. I put a hand on her arm, as intimate a gesture as I was comfortable with. “She can’t stay here,” I said. “Her body . . .” *Great, Andi. What were you going to say? Her body will start to rot? Smell? Worse than it already does?* "I'll make the call if you'd like," I finished lamely.

She tensed, then nodded and retreated silently to her room. Mentally I kicked myself, both for handling her so badly and for offering to stay. I went back into Gilda's room and picked up the phone, with no idea whom to call. There was no phone book.

I glanced back down the hall, a long row of closed doors. Which was Alexandra's? Stifling my rising anger, I went back to Rainie's and knocked. "Do you know which mortuary your mother planned to use?"

She said what sounded like "Hang on a sec." I assumed she'd been on the phone, but then I thought I heard the murmur of a male voice. A moment later she opened the door, standing in the opening and blocking my view of the room. "Gramma wants to be cremated."

I digested this for a second, wondering how she'd come by this information. "Did she have a religious preference?" I asked.

Rainie stared at the floor. "There used to be a preacher who came and sat with her. I think he was Presbyterian? He quit coming, like, in May or something." She hesitated. "Gramma wasn't very nice to him."

I'd never had to handle arrangements like this either, and it wasn't my place to do so now. "Where's your mother?" I asked again.

Rainie stared at me with soulful eyes, needing comfort I had no way of giving. Then she pointed to a door next to Gilda's. I moved toward it while Rainie watched. I knocked, said, "Alexandra, please. You need to call the mortuary, so they can come and move her." Obsessed with getting this one thing done so I could put this oppressive house and the misery it held behind me.

The door flew open. "You're not taking her anywhere!"

Her face was puffy and red and slightly crazed. "The police are on their way. They'll do an autopsy and you'll pay for what you've done."

Instead of whatever reaction she expected, this news made me tired. Damn these people, why had I gotten involved with them? "Is that what she would have wanted?" I asked.

"It's what I want!" She was shouting, but backed up instead of coming at me with her fists again. "It's my turn! She always got what she wanted, now it's my turn!"

I gazed at her, feeling pity more than anything else. "Your mother is dead, Alexandra. She was at the end of her life. She was miserable. Let her go."

"She was murdered. You killed her. Like some animal."

I shook my head, wondering where this would lead. Knowing it was useless trying to reason with her. "Your daughter is very upset. You are, too, I know." I held up a hand, not looking at her. If I did, I was afraid I would start screaming back. I wanted to pull this woman's hair and poke her in the eye. "Instead of hiding behind closed doors maybe the two of you could . . ."

"Just shut up! Shut up, shut up, shut up!"

I stopped, turned, and headed down the stairs. I yanked open the door and found myself facing a fist, raised to knock on the door. I took a step back.

"Officer Jackson, ma'am. Did you call in a suspicious death?"

"No, she's upstairs. Both of them. The person who called you—Alexandra—and Gilda. Gilda died. Finally." *Stop it, Andi. You're babbling.*

I stepped back. Officer Jackson and another uniformed policeman entered. The second man's name tag said "Costello."

"Is anyone else in the house?"

I nodded, started to explain, but Alexandra already stood on the landing.

"She did it! She killed my mother! Arrest her, Officer!" Her hair stood out in disarray and her bathrobe threatened to fall open. Smudges of mascara made her eyes look hollow.

Jackson looked at me, an eyebrow raised in question. Then he and the other cop exchanged glances and the second man approached Alexandra.

"Who else is in the house?" Jackson asked me.

"Alexandra's daughter Rainie is upstairs in her room. I think her boyfriend is with her."

"And someone died here tonight?"

"Gilda Hopkins. Alexandra's mother." I waved a hand to identify Alexandra. "Gilda had terminal cancer, and she's been on life support for months."

"Why does her daughter think she was murdered?"

I hesitated. "I don't know. Denial?" I shrugged helplessly.

"Who was with her when she died?"

I sighed. This looked like it would take a while.

"I was."

Chapter Ten

An hour later I was in my car. Officers Jackson and Costello had called Gilda's doctor, who confirmed that her death had been expected. Dr. Frank may even have suggested a touch of hysteria on Alexandra's part. They called the coroner's office as well, explained the situation, and waited while someone there contacted Dr. Frank. Eventually they told Alexandra they were sorry about her loss but it appeared the older woman's death had been imminent and natural. Rainie stood big-eyed in the doorway of her room during much of this exchange. I felt worst for her—what must it be like to witness such behavior in one's parent?

But Rainie had lived with Alexandra her entire life, and seemed to have turned out all right. I reminded myself this was not my concern. It took some doing. I had given Rainie my numbers before I left, at work and at home, and encouraged her to call me if she needed anything. Naively, I thought this was my last dealing with the family.

Almost out of habit, I stopped in at the clinic before heading home. Passing the Dumpster behind the clinic, I took a 60cc syringe from my purse and tossed it in among the bags of fouled newspaper cage liners, little Andi's diapers, and other indescribable refuse. It's rare to find even the most desperate transients investigating this one.

"What are you doing back here?" Trinka asked when I got inside.

"Gilda died tonight. Finally."

She didn't respond immediately. Then, "You must be relieved."

I shrugged. "I'm just tired. The cops came."

Her eyebrows raised in alarm.

"They declined to get involved. I think it's over."

We didn't speak for a while. Trinka was undoubtedly wondering if I'd helped Gilda along. I knew she'd have to ask sooner or later.

We were standing in the office, which looked odd now that both desk chairs had been moved into Treatment. Wayne remained with baby Andi. Roosevelt, in his corner cage, muttered to himself. The altered schedule had disrupted his routine and he'd been irritable all day. Make that yesterday.

Damn, how was I going to perform surgery in a few hours?

"So why did you come back here?" Trinka didn't ask why I went over there at this hour to begin with.

It was a good question. I could not have articulated my feelings, but I needed to be with someone alive and familiar. I had watched a person die. I had seen dead bodies before, and I had stroked the ears of untold numbers of dogs and cats as they breathed their last. When my mother finally slipped away I had been at home asleep.

Now I felt restless, uneasy. I felt like talking.

"I don't think I can sleep. Alexandra insisted on calling the police. I don't understand what makes her tick."

"But they didn't do anything, right?"

I shook my head. "No, they called Gilda's doctor and the coroner's office and looked at her, all hooked up to those pumps. They told Alexandra it looked like a natural death. Coroner didn't even send anyone."

"So why are you here?"

Trinka has something of a bulldozer approach to life. Persistent. "I needed grounding, I guess. The whole chain of events was so unreal, I just felt like touching something familiar before I went home to bed."

Trinka didn't say anything but continued to stare at me. Her eyes narrowed. "Did you . . . make it happen?"

I opened my mouth and nothing came out. I closed it and almost smiled. "How can you ask?"

"I mean, it still would have looked natural. No one could tell by just looking."

I grabbed for the box of Kleenex on the desk, whipped out half a dozen, and sat on the floor. I expected tears but there were none. Trinka leaned against her desk and waited.

"What if I had, Trinka? What if I'd helped her? Would I be a different person?"

Her eyes held mine for a long moment. Gone was the mischievous attitude she'd displayed only two days ago when the question first arose. I wondered what she would have done—what she truly would have done—in my position. And I felt ashamed for having delayed my own decision for so long. *Two days. Has it really only been two days since that video showed up? That's not so long, is it?*

Trinka finally shrugged. "It's moot, right?" I didn't answer. Suddenly she had to check on our patient and I was alone in the office.

Eventually I dragged myself outside to the Miata, jammed my key in the ignition and went home. I let the dogs out, let Gambit back in, set the alarm for seven and lay down to sleep. Gambit came and rested his head on the comforter for a while, and I stroked his soft, old-dog ears. Clyde, Carbon, and Evinrude arranged themselves on the pillows, my chest, along my side, purring in their distinct rhythms, and I was grateful for their presence.

I did not dream at all.

Seven o'clock, predictably, came too soon. For a blissful minute or two it was any other morning, then last night's events crowded into my memory, casting their grim shadow over the prospect of the day.

I got up, made coffee, let the dogs in, stood in the shower and let the cool water do its best to wash away my anxiety. Gilda's death was now in the past, I told myself. Time to focus on the future. On a baby chimp named after me. I wondered if I should tell Wayne I felt distracted.

On the other hand, what options did he have? There wasn't a line of surgeons waiting to take my place. Trinka hated this stuff, preferring to use "brain over brawn," as she put it, using diagnostic tests and book knowledge and medical treatments to gain her objectives. If that didn't work it was my case.

And baby Andi was unequivocally my case today.

Wayne didn't need something else to worry about.

The procedure appeared very straightforward. Wayne had assumed he'd have to provide the surgical clips with which to ligate the shunt, and responded only with "Good" when I showed him our own. By now I felt immune to his casual insults, and actually swelled a little at this tacit approval.

Diane was late again. None of the staff had known we were operating on little Andi that morning. But it didn't matter. We'd tolerated too much and today meant a written reprimand. In the meantime I borrowed Sheila from the front desk and asked her to help Didi get the OR ready. That left Arlene, the new receptionist, alone. Trinka supervised the preparations. I turned my own attention to my patient.

There was so little hair, and her skin felt so fragile, I hesitated to use the clippers. "You don't have a razor?" Wayne muttered.

No one answered. I clipped her left side, delicately, wincing when the clipper blade cut her skin in two places. How would her tissue ever hold sutures? At Wayne's instruction, we administered warm-saline enemas, twice, suctioning gently the second time, hoping to staunch the constant flow of her bowels during surgery. Wayne had turned off the feeding pump a few hours earlier, and switched her IV to half-strength glucose in saline. Wayne hung over Didi while she swabbed little Andi's side with Betadine, rinsed, swabbed again.

I was leery of the effects of anesthesia on Andi's immature lungs. So, apparently, was Wayne, because instead of the isoflurane gas I would normally use, Wayne calculated a dose of Valium and a narcotic called oxymorphone. Both drugs had specific antidotes, should they prove too potent for her fragile system.

Using sterilized rolled cotton towels, Wayne positioned her on her right side and administered a local, numbing only the nerves that served our incision area. She did not flinch as the needle penetrated skin between her fourth and fifth ribs near the tiny muscles along her back. Wayne didn't speak, tension evident in the pallor of his face, the deepening lines there.

Brad waited with Sally in Treatment. Sally would be leaving when he did.

Wayne and I scrubbed and gowned silently, taking turns at the sink, me waiting patiently while Didi tied Wayne's gown first. Wayne had brought his own sterile gloves, as his hands were a size and a half larger than mine, two sizes larger than Trinka's.

That's when Diane arrived. Mumbling, "Sorry I'm late," she absorbed the poisonous glances from Trinka, Wayne, and me, and pitched in, opening packs and tying the backs of our gowns. The problem with Diane was that she could be a very good tech, but her performance was unpredictable.

Wayne helped me with the elaborate draping procedure. Actually, I helped him. Normally I would have simply cut a slice out of a sterile paper drape and anchored it with sharp skin clamps. Wayne, however, had obtained a huge sterile paper sheet, which Diane opened for us and which we arranged over the chimp and the table, sharply creasing it upwards at the level of Andi's neck, to separate us from Didi, who was monitoring Andi's vital signs. Or perhaps to maintain a barrier between our sterile field and our patient's undraped head. Then Diane handed him a delightful piece of clear, tacky material—an adhesive drape—which adhered to Andi's skin like a transparent sticky note. No clamps to work around, no holes to heal, no distortion of the site. We would incise the drape with the skin. Idly I wondered if we could afford more of these. I'd ask another time.

After that, I did most of the work. Here in the OR my relationship to Wayne altered subtly. I was the surgeon, he the assistant. He needed me, and his demeanor reflected this. Also, though he rarely ventured near an operating room, he had prepared as well as I had. As well as two people could without having actually done the procedure.

The initial incision was both enormous and much too small. I laid Andi's side open and Wayne spread her miniature ribs with a pair of smooth retractors—well, spay hooks, since that was all we had that would fit. Immediately, *whoosh,* a delicate pink froth filled the gap. Lung.

As the ventilator released air, the lung shriveled and I saw Andi's beating heart.

I wished fervently for one of those headlamps that "real" surgeons wore, some means of directing light into the tunnel in which I had to work. Not even on Trinka's list. Wayne, for all his preparation, was not a surgeon and had not thought about light. Diane adjusted the ancient overhead reflectors as well as possible, and I studied the anatomy.

There were structures everywhere. Wayne kept my field of vision free of blood, but was no better at sorting out vessels than was I. Okay, this was the left side therefore that—*whoosh, sigh,* the lungs filled and retreated—must be the aorta arcing out of sight against her spine. I reached in a finger and touched it: pulsations confirmed a thick-walled main artery no wider than a pencil. So the *(whoosh, sigh)* pulmonary artery had to be beneath it, with the shunt somewhere connecting the two. It was urgent that I correctly identify it; if I clamped the wrong thing I would kill her.

The incision, though extending nearly from Andi's spine to her sternum, wasn't large enough for my entire hand. Probing delicately with the blunt end of a thumb forceps, I tried to deflect the aorta to visualize the PDA. Everything moved—the heart jerked, the lungs filled my incision, every vessel throbbed and vibrated. I spotted the phrenic nerve, which told the diaphragm when to contract. Few other nerves travel through the chest cavity. The viscera do not sense pain. Baby Andi, unanesthetized, never twitched.

"There." Wayne couldn't point without letting go of one of his retractors, which would have eliminated half my field of vision. But knowing he'd seen the shunt made me pause and stare more closely.

Sure enough. It looked like a bit of connective tissue

rather than an artery, a few millimeters long, barely discernible between the arteries it connected. How was I going to get my clip around that without puncturing something?

We'd worked this out in advance, but putting it into practice was terrifying.

"Hang on," I said. "Diane, get me a Gelpi." She opened a package containing a self-retaining retractor. The sharp points made it less than ideal, but I needed Wayne's hands free. With the Gelpi in place, he moved one of the spay hooks to gently—oh, so gently—pull the aorta out of my field of vision.

I loaded a surgical clip into its applicator. The stainless-steel clip was open on one end, and when I squeezed the applicator handles it would smoothly close to form a permanent ligature. Position was crucial, so the steel would not irritate heart or nerve tissue. The applicator resembled a lightweight pliers with colored handles. Even the smallest size seemed too big for the job at hand.

Wayne said, "Turn off the vent."

The lungs lay flaccid.

I held my breath and slipped the ends of the clip around the ductus. It was do-or-die time. The shunt could rupture easily with pressure. If it did, she would bleed to death while we watched, helpless to stop it.

I squeezed the handles.

The tissue held.

I said, "Yes!"

Wayne said, "Vent."

Whoosh, sigh. Andi breathed again.

So did I.

Chapter Eleven

We moved the little chimp back to her incubator. The bandage masking her incision dwarfed her tiny body, and it would be a day or more before we expected the effects of the operation to outweigh the stress of surgery. But already her oxygen saturation had improved, now stable at nearly 90%.

I noted with surprise that it was not yet ten o'clock.

Every one of us was smiling.

Wednesday was Trinka's day off this week, but she had come in anyway, ostensibly to see clients while I was in surgery. But as there were no appointments scheduled before ten-twenty, I suspected she had gotten caught up in Andi's struggle and wanted to see how things went. I regretted our arguments and resolved to celebrate with her the day Andi went home.

If she went home. I had to remember, that was hardly a sure thing.

Diane, gazing into the incubator, said, "We should call the news. I bet they'd want to do a story on her."

Wayne blanched. "No media. This has been hard enough."

His eyes met mine and I saw his fear. I doubted it stemmed from concern over Andi's well-being, or even Brad's. If the news media started looking into the pediatrician's life, they might uncover the allegations against him. A simple human-interest story about a baby chimp undergoing life-saving surgery was unlikely to generate such scrutiny, but Wayne's concern was understandable.

I had my own reasons for saying no. Anything that might possibly remind Alexandra about me was to be avoided. But neither of us could explain this to the staff, all of whom were now excitedly arguing whether to call the local TV station, or the *Desert Sparkler*, our newspaper.

Trinka said, "You know, that kind of publicity would be great for business."

Too late I caught her eye, shook my head slightly. She shrugged. I said, "For now, let's respect Wayne and Brad's privacy, and leave it alone." It was lame, and the baffled disappointment on Sheila's and Didi's faces made me want to relent. But Trinka redeemed herself by suggesting we call them on the day Andi went home, and the subject was finally dropped.

Wayne eventually left, to see his own patients for the day. He'd drawn the early shift for that evening's baby watch, and would stop in during his lunch hour.

My ten-twenty appointment was one of my favorite patients. She's a miniature dachshund named Tammy, irrepressibly cheerful, and impossible to be grumpy around. She was in for her routine checkup and booster shots and to schedule some dental work, but I spent forty-five minutes with her reveling in the normalcy of my interaction with the healthy dog and her owner.

After that I saw a couple of other appointments, nothing terribly interesting. Didi had a poodle under anesthesia and was cleaning its teeth, leaving Diane to alternate between occasionally assisting me and keeping an eye on baby Andi. Trinka stayed in the office, catching up on bookkeeping.

My eleven-fifteen was an unpredictable gray tabby cat, Mortimer. At fourteen, he tipped the scales at around twelve pounds, and was quick to respond if something displeased him. Most things did. For some reason he tolerated me.

Because his nervous owner had lost another cat to kidney failure, and the one before that to leukemia, Mort had lab work every six months to screen for such things. Didi knew Mort but she was not available to assist. Diane held him and I warned her about the cat's temper. Didi had always managed to distract him while I drew the blood; Diane assured me she could handle him. We drew it in the exam room, to minimize excitement. Fortunately, his owner left the room as she always did. Diane got the cat in position. I chattered to him, a nonsensical stream of "Morty, Morter, good pudders, hold still, handsome kidders pudders," while I scratched the skin over his jugular and inserted the needle.

Mortimer left the table, clawed my arm on his way down, and made two circuits of the room before the syringe fell out. Finally he crouched in a corner under the client chair, hair on end, bottle-brush tail extended, teeth bared.

Diane started to go after him.

"Leave him! Damn it, Diane!" I went to the sink and ran cool water over the scratches on my arm. They were long and deep, and blood ran freely from one area. I dried it and applied surgical glue until it stopped oozing.

Diane stood sullenly near the door. "Guess he's tired of giving blood."

It was the wrong reaction. I glanced at her as I rubbed a steroid-antibiotic cream into the scratches. "How's your thumb? Did you ever see a doctor?"

A shrug. "No, it's okay. Still hurts a little. Guess it's not as strong as usual." Her only gesture of apology for letting go of the cat. I waited and nothing else was forthcoming. That irritated me more than the injury itself.

I opened Mort's carrier and showed it to him. He dashed inside and I secured it. We'd have to try again next week.

That was it for the morning. By eleven-thirty, it was quiet. I called Diane into the office and waved at Trinka's chair for her to sit.

"Diane, I'm sorry your thumb was hurt. You were definitely entitled to some time off on workers' comp while it healed."

"I just figured you needed me."

Uh-huh. "And we all appreciate your efforts. But if you're going to work, you have to be a hundred percent here."

"It's not my fault that cat scratched you!" A sullen whine.

I took a deep breath. Morty was a tough cat to work with. A blaming contest would not solve this issue. I dropped it. "You were late again this morning."

"Only twenty minutes. My son couldn't find his shoes."

"Last week he had a rash. The week before that you didn't have lunch food and had to swing by Circle K. I know you have your hands full, Diane, but we need you to be here on time and awake. Plan ahead, fix their lunches the night before, and lay their clothes out, if that's what it takes."

Her eyes teared. Damn it, I hated this. I'd stuck my neck out the previous spring and hired Diane over Trinka's objections. I knew things were tough at home—she was raising two young children alone—so I had cut her a lot of slack. In so doing, I had inadvertently encouraged her to think it was acceptable to arrive late, to avoid proper medical care when she was injured, and to feel she was entitled to a paycheck without having to earn it.

The most frustrating thing was that she had flashes of

brilliance. She knew how to be a good tech, but needed constant prodding to do it. She did not understand how her poor performance affected the dynamics of the practice. When one person on the team didn't pull her weight the stress level soared for the rest of us. Didi, who had never fully embraced Diane's presence in what she considered her workspace, grumbled about having to do more than her share.

Why couldn't everyone just do their jobs, so I would not have to deal with crap like this?

I handed Diane the reprimand I'd prepared beforehand. "Sign this and leave it on my desk. It's your last warning." I handed her a box of Kleenex and left the room feeling like an ogre.

The little chimp was moving more, but not strongly enough to dislodge the lines and leads. I wanted to believe she was fighting the respirator as well, or the endotracheal tube at least. I tried to imagine her without the tube protruding from her mouth and found I couldn't picture it.

As I watched her I thought of Gilda Hopkins and, inevitably, Alexandra. I wondered how Rainie was coping. Almost reached for the phone to call and check on her, but I stopped myself. It shamed me to admit that I was afraid Alexandra would answer the phone.

Why had she been so determined to preserve her mother's grotesque life? When Gilda was clearly dying in the most horrible way imaginable, why would a daughter wish to prolong the process? Did she suppress the normal empathy that should crave an ending to pointless suffering? Out of some misguided belief that one should not wish a parent dead? Could the power of guilt be so strong?

Of course it could. Guilt was perhaps the greatest—

and most twisted—motivator among human emotions. Alexandra had watched her mother's decline over a period of years, and still she wished to postpone her death. I recalled her accusations the previous night. Upon reflection, it seemed unlikely that I had truly heard the last of her.

It occurred to me that updating my lawyer might not be a bad idea. I called Lara. She'd left a job with a local firm about six months earlier to go out on her own. She kept busy. She was in court and her secretary didn't expect her back until late afternoon. My luck. I left a message, saying only that I needed to talk to her.

Brad arrived just before noon, wearing a reasonably normal outfit consisting of ordinary white shorts and a gold lamé tank top. He brought lunch.

And what a lunch.

From the astonishing array, I guessed he must cook when under stress. Little round puffy cheese-flavored canapes, tiny watercress sandwiches, sparkling cider in lieu of champagne, a tureen of vichyssoise, delicately flavored steamed vegetables, and a beef roast he'd somehow managed to prepare so that one end was cooked through, the other rare, to accommodate all tastes.

Except Trinka's, of course. Trinka hasn't eaten meat since she found out where it came from.

"More for the rest of us," Brad declared, unfazed. He displayed the pièce de résistance, a cake decorated to suggest our old incubator, with a delicately rendered baby Andi nestled inside. Except in this depiction there were no tubes, no wires, only an animated infant chimpanzee with wide, expressive eyes and a distinct bloom of health.

I blinked away tears. While we had been wiping the sweat off our brows, hoping the clamp would hold, Brad had the faith to spend his morning preparing this feast.

Of course I was starving. Of course I hadn't eaten that morning. How could I? I reached for one of the cheesy things. It virtually dissolved in my mouth.

Brad delicately tapped his champagne glass with a silver fork. "Okay," he said. "No more nibbles until I give my little speechie."

I withdrew my hand, resisting the pull of the food with effort.

"I just want to say that, no matter what happens after this morning, I'll never forget the care our baby received here. I've known a lot of vets, and I've worked with exotic animals all my life. I know how hard it is for you guys to work on them. I've seen wonderful feats of medicine, but I've never seen the devotion Doctors Pauling and Romanescu gave our little Andi, here at Dr. Doolittle's Pet Care Center."

I swallowed hard. "Thank you, Brad," I said.

He had one more surprise. It was a framed studio portrait of Sally with an actor whose name was a household word. Sally had performed with him in a jungle action movie a few years ago. The picture had been signed by the actor, and a bright splash of yellow-and-red paint represented Sally's signature.

Then Brad gave me a hug. That single gesture meant as much to me as all the rest. I hadn't realized how badly I needed a hug.

Which naturally made me think of Clay. I wished he were there to have lunch with us. But the thought was fleeting.

Wayne arrived, somewhat breathless. He received one of Brad's hugs, checked on Andi's progress and smiled. This was the closest I'd ever seen him come to enjoying himself.

The staff had gathered, and I heard snatches of phone conversations as lunch plans were hastily canceled. Brad had brought china, since paper plates couldn't possibly do justice to his production. The treatment table easily converted to a crowded buffet, and we all filed through the cramped space, filled our plates, accepted slices of tender roast beef from Brad, who had produced a toque from somewhere and was playing master chef with a flair, despite the gold lamé.

Because of the cramped quarters, our party spilled into the hall. I sat on the floor and gorged myself, then went back for cake. I hadn't eaten like this for a long time.

As I scraped the last crumbs of cake on my plate, Brad said, "Can I get you anything else?"

I shook my head until my mouth was empty. "That should hold me till dinner."

Dinner. Suddenly I felt the need to call Clay.

I excused myself to make the call. Clay answered on the fifth ring, slightly out of breath, and I knew from the background noise that he was in the barn.

"How's it going?" I asked.

"Not bad over here. How's your monkey?"

I couldn't remember if I'd told him the surgery was moved up. Then I knew I couldn't have. "We went in this morning. Ligated the shunt. It was actually pretty easy, and so far she's doing great!" My spirits lifted more as I spoke. We had done a good thing that morning. I had not allowed myself to celebrate it.

"That's super! Congratulations! So you've got your nights free again?"

I laughed, wishing it were true. I imagined Clay's gentle arms around me, his hands on my back, in my hair. Made myself stop. "No, we've still got to watch her. But with any luck she'll be going home soon."

We reiterated our dinner plans and hung up.

I wondered how much, if anything, I would tell him about Gilda Hopkins and her daughter. Surely it wasn't a good sign that I hadn't told him already. After all, we were in a relationship. That meant sharing, right? Why hadn't I thought of him first when I needed to talk?

I shrugged off the question and started back to Treatment, when Sheila's voice came over the intercom. "Dr. Pauling? There's someone on line one asking for you. Sounds real upset. Her name is, uh, Rainie Dixon?"

My skin went cold. *Damn, I knew it wasn't over with.* But I couldn't duck the call. It didn't even occur to me.

"Hello, Rainie. This is Dr. Pauling." Maybe I should have said "Andi."

"Uh, Dr. Pauling, could you come over?" Her voice was high and thin.

Whatever I'd expected, it wasn't this. "You want me to come to your house? Now?"

"Yeah. My mom's, like, talking about hurting herself. She has a gun. I don't know what to do!" She was holding back hysteria, but not by much.

"Why me?" I blurted. When was this family going to leave me alone?

"She keeps saying your name. Like, under her breath. I don't know who else to call!"

I started to point out that if Alexandra was muttering my name in a self-destructive rage, it most likely did not mean she wanted to see me. But Rainie needed support, and I mentally cursed Alexandra for putting her daughter in this position.

"Is anyone else there with you?" I asked.

"Uh, Eddie's on his way. My b-b-boyfriend." I thought I heard her teeth chattering.

Damn it. I liked Rainie, wanted to help. But my going over there was more likely to make things worse than to improve them.

"Please?"

Oh, hell. "I'll be there as soon as I can. Stay in your room. If anything happens, call nine-one-one."

On the way out of the parking lot, I almost sideswiped the truck that was emptying our Dumpster.

Chapter Twelve

Rainie met me on the stoop, dancing like a nervous colt. I followed her inside. She wore a black spandex crop top and biker shorts, her midriff as tan as her legs. She was so anxious she practically hummed.

"After I called you, she got real quiet. She's in her room and I don't know what she's doing."

"Did you tell her you called me?" I asked in alarm.

Rainie shook her head. "No-ooo." Teenage disdain. A spark of life, good.

"Did you try to talk to her?" I asked, glancing apprehensively up the stairs. I seriously didn't want Alexandra to even know I was there.

Rainie nodded. "She didn't answer. I'm, I don't know, kinda scared." She was hugging herself as if cold, her hands rubbing her arms. "I heard water running. Maybe she went in the shower. She always did that in the afternoon, while Gramma was asleep, but . . ." Her voice became a childlike whine at odds with the self-possessed young woman I'd met the day before. "It's like she wants everything to just, you know, be the same. But Gramma's dead. It's not the same. It's not."

I debated what to do. The crisis seemed to be over. I had no place here. But I wanted to find out what happened after I left the night before, and this might be my only chance.

"Let's wait awhile," I suggested. "She might not appreciate it if we barge in on her. Have a seat." I sat on the staircase and waited for her to do the same. Her hands moved from her arms to her hair to her bare middle. Hands that had no job, nothing to occupy them. Her eyes shifted from me to the step she sat on, to the landing above.

I studied her, unsure how to ask what I wanted to know. "Can I get you something?" I asked. "A glass of water?" Anything to make those hands stop moving.

She shook her head and absently braided a few strands of hair. Frankie climbed halfway into her lap and nudged her wrist. She slipped one hand over the little dog's shoulders.

"I thought when they finally came and took Gramma this morning, things would get better. I thought everything would be okay. Gramma got what she wanted, didn't she? That's what always mattered."

"Who came? Do you know where they took her?"

She shrugged. "Two guys in a hearse. It was, like, ten o'clock this morning. Gramma laid in there that whole time."

It bothered me, too, but I couldn't see that any harm had come of the delay. Gilda had waited a long time to die; it was hardly surprising that she would wait to be embalmed as well.

Rainie kept throwing glances upstairs. The sound of running water stopped.

"Well," I said, anxious to be gone before Alexandra emerged, "she seems to have settled down. Maybe she'll get some sleep and feel better afterward."

Rainie shook her head, reaching out as if to physically prevent me from leaving. "You should have heard her earlier. I know you think I'm, like, overreacting or something. But you didn't see her!"

I did think she had overreacted, but knew better than to say so. I sighed and sat back down. "What happened? It might help if you tell me about it."

She nodded abruptly. "She was on the phone practically all morning. Then she got all upset. That's when I called you. She was, like, storming through the house, slamming things. She spent a lot of time in Gramma's room and it was like she was talking to her."

"What did she say?"

"Some of it didn't make any sense. She'd go, 'You never even knew,' and then she'd, like, walk around in circles. She knocked over some of the stuff in there. On purpose! Then she went, 'How could you?' and 'What am I supposed to do now?' That's when she said your name. She'd go, like, 'Andi Pauling, that Andi Pauling, Pauling.' It was so weird, y'know?"

It did sound strange, but it could have been part of a normal grieving process. Especially if she truly believed I'd contributed to her mother's death. "That isn't why you called me though, is it?" She'd said Alexandra might hurt herself.

Rainie was shaking her head. "Nuh-uh. I saw her gun out on her dresser, but she was in Gramma's room. She kept opening drawers and slamming things, going 'Where is it? What did you do with it?' I went in and asked her, like, what she was looking for and she totally flew apart. Like it was my fault or something! She thinks Eddie stole Gramma's medicine."

Pills? Gilda couldn't have taken oral medication for months. "What medicine?"

"I'm not even sure. She wasn't making sense. Then she got on the phone some more, after I called you. And then she got quiet and went in the bathroom and I heard the water."

"Eddie's the guy who was with you the first day I visited?"

A nod, as she straightened and smiled proudly. "She doesn't like him. She thinks he's on drugs, or something. He's gonna be a doctor, then he's gonna join the Peace Corps and go to South America. But Mom thinks he just wants me for my money. I mean, I don't have any money now but, like, Gramma put everything in trust for me, for when I turn twenty-one. She liked Eddie, too. Mom never even gave him a chance." Her expression alternately softened and turned angry when she spoke about this.

I recalled that my own initial reaction to Eddie was less than admiring. The dreadlocks and baggy clothes triggered an instant negative reaction. Had I really judged someone so dismissively based on his appearance? I, who had Trinka Romanescu for a partner?

But I was getting distracted. What did Alexandra need Gilda's "medicine" for in the first place? "So your mom was looking for these, what, pills? She didn't find them, did she?"

A head shake. "Nuh-uh."

I chewed my lower lip, trying not to gaze upward. Should I announce my presence at the risk of upsetting her further? Or just get out of the house and hope Rainie knew not to tell her I'd been there.

"I wish she was like other people's mothers," Rainie said wistfully, but with more than a trace of annoyance.

"How is she different?"

A shrug, an upward glance. "She's just not, like, *there*." The hands now braiding, now unbraiding. "Eddie thinks Mom has, like, a borderline personality? It's like she doesn't really feel what other people feel. Or something."

I'd have to think about that. I was no psychologist—what I knew of borderline personality syndrome came from popular fiction. But it fit what I'd seen of Alexandra.

"I miss Gramma. Gramma always knew what was going on. She listened to me. You know?"

How much of this was a normal teenager's resentment of her parent? "She told me she'd had a difficult childhood. Maybe—"

"Hah! She grew up in San Francisco! I was, like, born there." Spoken with the wistfulness of a young person who wishes to live elsewhere. Anywhere. As if difficult childhoods could not occur in San Francisco.

Frankie, being ignored by Rainie, abandoned her lap for mine. Automatically I stroked his ears. "How old are you, Rainie?"

The ordinary question grounded her. "Eighteen."

I did some quick calculating. Gilda, undoubtedly, had been a strict mother. Alexandra had grown up in San Francisco during the hippie heyday. Some would have rebelled. I couldn't see her as one of them. "Does your father live up there? Can you go stay with him awhile?"

"He's dead. Before I was even born. He, like, jumped off a building or something. Mother always said it was 'cause of me."

Her simple, uninflected words hit me like a whip. Even if it were true, which seemed unlikely, what mother would inflict such knowledge on her child?

"What are you telling her?"

It was Alexandra's voice, and it held an undercurrent of the hysteria I'd witnessed the night before. She stood at the head of the stairs, her hair wrapped in a towel and a green mud pack drying on her face. An image to haunt one's nightmares. And a damned weird way to exorcise her grief.

"You little bitch! You ingrate!" Her fury was directed at her daughter, who flinched visibly. "Telling family secrets! After all I've done for you!" Alexandra turned on me. "You! You want to know all about our sordid little family? About how my Jeffrey was going to Stanford, until Mother wrote a letter to the dean? Dear, suffering Gilda. It was a lie! We were married! My daughter's no bastard! She thought she'd won, but we would have straightened it all out. He wouldn't kill himself over that, wouldn't have left me. It was only because of the baby! He couldn't face being a father." Back to Rainie. "He didn't want you. You see what I've been through? What I gave up for you? And see how you turn on me!"

Rainie's expression was resigned. She'd heard this before.

She'd grown up with it. I felt terrible for her but she looked like she'd be okay. She said, "I—I'm sorry, I was just—"

"How dare you come here, anyway! You killed my mother, and I'll prove it! I hired a lab. They'll test her blood, and you'll see. Everyone will see!"

That's when the front door opened, slowly, as if reluctant to admit the new arrival. Eddie stood on the threshold, looking very young.

Rainie swept down the stairs and met him a few steps inside. Unlike Rainie's California tan, his darkness was genetic—either Asian or Hispanic, I couldn't be sure. Today he wore loose-fitting shorts and a T-shirt advertising a rock band. He had a thin, adolescent beard that made him look like a wanna-be gang member, and the scraggly hair was off-putting. He was tall and lanky, awkward in his new role of protector, but clearly ready to stand his ground.

Alexandra barely glanced at him. She advanced to the head of the stairs, still pointing at me like an operatic caricature. "I've called the police, reporters, everyone. I'll get you! You wait and see, I'll get you!" I half expected her to finish with ". . . *my pretty.*"

Then the door opened again and Eva Short stepped in, stopping when she saw us.

All the usual suspects, I thought irrelevantly. Then, *This really has been one hell of a week.* How could it only be Wednesday?

"I need to get going," I said, and headed for the door. No one stopped me. To Eva I said, "Could I talk to you for just a second?"

She glanced uncertainly at Alexandra and followed me out into the heat. I wanted to leave, didn't even like standing on the front stoop, but it was the only shade around.

"Gilda died last night, didn't you hear?"

Eva nodded. "Some of the equipment is rented. Someone will be out later to pick it up. I'm just here to get a few things I left, and pick up the drips and stuff. What's going on in there?"

"Alexandra is convinced her mother was murdered."

Eva's eyes widened, but otherwise her expression didn't change. "That's ridiculous!"

I shrugged in agreement. "She's not exactly thinking logically. I just wondered, if she's determined to have Gilda autopsied, can she do that?"

Eva frowned thoughtfully. "I'm not sure, but I'd think so. She's the next of kin, and it's not hard to find a freelance pathologist if you know where to look. And Dr. Frank could tell her where."

I shifted my weight. I had to crane my neck to look up at her, and sweat ran down my back. "She must have died within minutes of your visit last night. Did you have any idea she was that close to death?"

She squinted defensively, and I regretted my question. She said, "I knew she could go any time. I think it was a blessing." Daring me to disagree.

I nodded. "Of course. I just wondered if anything was different last night."

She crossed her arms in front of her and took a step toward the door. "Are you suggesting I did something to . . . speed up the process?"

So that was what bothered her. "No! Not at all!"

"She asked me to, you know. Sometimes I wished I could help. When the pain would get so bad—" She stopped talking, bit her lip thoughtfully.

Of course, Gilda would have asked her first. And of course, she wouldn't want to discuss it with me. Eva had spent more time around Alexandra than I ever would.

"That damned Alexandra. Always threatening lawyers. Dr. Frank might have increased her morphine dose. Might have . . . made it easier."

"Look, I'm just trying to understand. I . . . I liked her." It was like an admission of guilt. What an odd woman Gilda had been. "Did she tell you why she got in touch with me in the first place?"

She held my gaze but didn't answer. Finally I dropped my eyes. I pulled my scrub top away from my skin in a fruitless effort to cool myself off. "Never mind," I said. "I'm sorry I bothered you." And I turned to go.

"Wait! I'd like to know. Did you . . ."

I looked at her, my expression blank. Neither of us spoke. Eventually we both smiled a little. She went inside and I got in the Miata and started the motor. I held the door open and turned the AC fan up full.

As I put the car in gear a large, moving shape appeared in my peripheral vision, then suddenly filled the doorway. I gasped and turned, an arm coming up defensively.

"Sorry," mumbled Eddie.

I lowered my arm. "It's okay. You just scared me. I didn't see you."

"Yeah, sorry. I, uh, wondered if I could, like, kinda talk to you a sec?"

"Sure, I guess so. Want to get in the car? It'll be cooler in a little bit."

He stepped around the back of the car. As he folded himself into the other seat—Miatas are not designed for tall people—I said, "What's up?"

He swallowed, and I saw him mentally change gears. "Rainie's mom is tossing a lot of accusations around."

The missing "medication." Rainie had said Alexandra thought he stole it. From Eddie's point of view that was a very serious charge. I put the car in gear and started moving. "She's having a hard time dealing with her mother's death."

"I guess."

I turned left and started around the block. Large, older homes sprawled on multilevel green lawns with mature trees casting their shade into the street. It could have been any affluent neighborhood anywhere.

Suddenly, as if he'd been working up his nerve, he said, "If you did what she said, I think it's totally cool. You know, like . . . gave her euthanasia. I just wanted you to know."

I couldn't think what to say, so I didn't say anything. After a few seconds he changed the subject.

"Alexandra hasn't been a very good mother for Rainie. No one ever really took care of her, you know?"

"She seems to have done okay."

"Her grandmother was the best thing in her life. Luckily she fixed her will before she died, or Rainie's mother probably wouldn't even let her go to college."

The will. If Rainie inherited, where did that leave Alexandra? With a motive for keeping her mother alive as long as possible? Was that what drove her?

"I'm going to med school, you know? Starting next month."

"Rainie told me. She's very proud of you."

"I work at a clinic in LA, after classes. Poor people, they don't do this stuff to them, you know?"

"Stuff . . . You mean like Gilda? Life support?"

"Yeah. It's weird. Most of the world, she would have been dead months ago, maybe years. You have any idea what it costs to keep someone alive like that?"

I reached another corner and turned left again. "Not really. But a lot."

"Huh. A lot, yeah. More than some countries could spend on their king. If it was even available. And for what? So they can lie there and suffer and wait to die."

"If you're going to be a doctor, you'd better get used to it."

"I'm not gonna stay here. I'm gonna join the Peace Corps. Go to South America—that's where my people are from, you know? On my papa's side. Mama's Japanese-American. Anyway, I want to help people, not like what we do here. I want to make a difference."

I wondered why he was telling this to me.

"You understand. You don't do this kind of stuff to animals. I bet that's why you went to vet school." It wasn't a question. I wondered what he would think of baby Andi in her incubator.

"We each have to answer to our own conscience," I said. I turned the last corner and pulled into the Hopkins's driveway. Eva was just stepping out of the house, carrying Gilda's biohazard container and a bag half-full of things she had carted out of her patient's room. She looked scared, and I couldn't blame her.

Eddie paused with the car door slightly open. "I just wanted you to know I'll back you up if things get ugly."

He seemed about to say more, but then he turned away, climbed out of my car, and went back inside.

I stared after him for a few seconds, then pulled the emergency brake on and got out of the car.

"Eva? Can you hang on a minute?"

She paused, towering over the Honda. Her posture bespoke impatience.

"When I asked you about her earlier, I was just wondering how she was, at the end. Was she. . . comfortable?"

"You were here after me."

"She was asleep when I arrived." Or comatose. Or in a morphine-induced stupor.

"She didn't say much. I just came in, cleaned her up, and changed her bags. The drip was set to run out around four." She gave a little laugh. "If I'd known I could have saved the effort."

"She got a new morphine drip just before she died?"

Her stance changed subtly, became defensive. "Yeah. So?"

So, indeed. "I don't know. What happens to the leftover when you start a new one?"

"It goes back to the office and gets disposed of." She tightened her grip on the bag.

"So you took it with you last night?"

Her eyes hardened. "Just what are you implying?"

The tone set me back. Surprised, I studied her. Wariness, defensiveness, a little guilt. "Nothing, Eva. I just wondered."

"I gotta go." She folded herself into her car, tossed a single scornful glance over her shoulder while she shut the door, and started the motor. I stepped away from the car and watched her depart.

Chapter Thirteen

Trinka had left, needing the rest of her "day off" for the usual errands. Wayne glanced at me, then pointedly at his watch, and left for his own office. Baby Andi slept soundly.

There were only minor appointments that afternoon—a nail trim and a suture removal, both of which Didi took care of, a first exam and vaccinations for a newly purchased basset hound puppy, and one health certificate for a lucky little dog who would be flying to Seattle until October. Wistfully I signed the form, wishing I was going, too. Green and lush and cool, it was exactly the place I dreamed of in summer.

With no urgent cases to keep my mind active, I found myself drowsing in my chair in front of the incubator. Little Andi fussed at her chest drain and pushed irritably at her endotracheal tube. Fortunately, both were well secured.

Sheila's voice on the intercom jolted me awake. It had that high-pitched, frantic tone it gets when she's on the brink of panic. "Dr. Pauling, there's a reporter up—Hey, you can't—!"

I was out of the chair, shaking the fog from my brain, before he reached Treatment. Recognizing him, I let out a groan. A scrawny, nondescript man, thirtyish, wearing khaki shorts and a polo shirt with a front pocket to hold his cigarettes. A 35mm camera dangled from a strap around his neck.

I pulled the Treatment door shut behind me.

"Dr. Pauling, we meet again!" He held out a hand as if this were a social call. "Bud Thorpe, independent journalist."

I put my hands in my pockets. "I remember your name. What do you want?" I could not help the hostility in my voice. This man haunted my life for several weeks the previous fall, after a friend was accused of murdering a polo player. The reporter probably still thought Ross had gotten away with it. I, on the other hand, knew Thorpe to be a mean little rodent of a man, not above making up a story if he thought he could get by with it.

"Now, Doc, 'zat any way to be? I got a real interesting call earlier, a Missus . . ." He pretended to consult a little spiral notebook he seemed to carry out of some preconceived idea of what a reporter should do. "Alexandra Dixon. Seems she's convinced you killed her mom."

Damn it. She'd found the one person who might take her accusations seriously, and delight in doing so. "So why aren't you over there interviewing her instead?"

"Been there. Done that." He flashed a smile I'm sure was meant to be intimidating. Instead he looked like a spiteful little boy who never got the toy he really wanted. Thorpe was Stephen King's take on Jimmy Olson. In my previous dealings with him, he seemed to derive a sadistic pleasure from causing misery to those whose lives he publicized.

Then again, it's possible I wasn't being completely objective. Last time our paths had crossed, I'd tricked him into reporting a death that never happened. He wouldn't have forgotten. Now he was back, as creepy as ever, no doubt with an agenda this time.

I said, "You know she's delusional. The poor woman needs help, not encouragement."

He shrugged, still grinning. "I'm helping. Just wanted to get your thoughts on the subject."

"What subject?"

His expression turned cagey. "You want to play it that way, huh? I'm talking about mercy killing. Euthanasia. That's what it was, right? Or, I could just tell the public you killed a helpless old woman in her bed." The implication was clear: *Cooperate. Or I'll make it even worse.*

"Oh, please. Gilda Hopkins should have died months ago. She finally did. She had terminal cancer, for God's sake!" Thinking, *Shut up, Andi. Just stop talking to him.*

"You denying she asked you to give her a push?"

"She asked everyone in hearing range. That doesn't mean any of them did it."

"Uh-huh. But you're the only one that's used to killing. Part of your job, right? Don't suppose you got a witness who could prove you didn't slip her a little something?"

"What, you're a cop now? I didn't kill Gilda. Happy?" Lara's voice in my head berated me for my lack of restraint. "Now please leave my clinic," I said. "I have work to do." The overall quiet made my statement a lie. I wished for an emergency to give me an excuse to hustle off, leaving him in my dust.

He ignored me, scribbling thoughtfully in his little notebook. I stood there, my frustration growing. I could hardly throw him out physically, and I didn't want to start shouting—though it was tempting, this would only give him more fuel for his "story." Would a responsible paper print this? Surely not, though I'd been surprised before at the carefully worded articles Thorpe had managed to get published. Now, standing in my hallway ignoring my demands for him to leave, he made me want to throw something.

I had to struggle against a need to open the Treatment

door to check on baby Andi. She'd been fine moments ago, but watching her had become an obsession. This was the longest she'd been left alone since her birth. But Wayne had been adamant about no publicity, and I felt I should honor that.

As if responding to my thoughts, the little chimp made a sound. Not a vocalization, impossible with the tube in her throat. It was a knocking, a foot against Plexiglas. Repeated. And again.

"Whatcha got in there?" he asked, his eyes narrowing.

"A very sick patient." I crossed my arms and stood firmly between him and the door.

"What kind of patient, Doc?"

"One who's probably contagious," I lied. "Now get out of my clinic before I call the police."

The kind of uncertainty crossed his face that laypeople get whenever confronted with medical scenarios. He seemed about to barge past me into the room, but hesitated a moment too long and his nerve failed. "So that's all you got to say about Mrs. Hopkins?" He couldn't simply walk away.

"That's it." I didn't move. Kept my arms crossed. His stance had relaxed and he finally turned to go.

Then Wayne Williamson entered the hallway.

He glanced curiously at Thorpe and the other man paid him little attention at first. I held my breath, hoping Wayne would simply go in and sit with Andi and keep his mouth shut. Instead he saw the closed door and panicked.

"What happened?" His hand on the knob.

Thorpe perked up, took a step toward the door.

"She's fine, Wayne. This man's a—"

"How could you leave her alone?" He barged through the door, leaving it wide open, the incubator and its contents in full view.

Click-POP-whir. Thorpe had his camera in hand and had snapped her picture before I even saw him move.

"What—? Who the hell are you?" Wayne turned on Thorpe, only to have his outrage immortalized on film.

"Thorpe, *get out of my clinic!*" I advanced on him, blocking his view as well as I could, crowding him physically and standing too close for him to take my picture. He shot one more over my shoulder then backed away. "Don't know why you're so jumpy about a sick monkey, but I'll find out!" he said cheerfully, turning and snapping one final photo of me, furious, standing by the open door to Treatment.

Wayne started after him, then wheeled abruptly. "How could you?" he demanded. "How could you let a reporter in here, after everything we've been through?"

"I didn't 'let' him in! Damn it, why couldn't you pay attention for once? I tried to tell you—"

"You left her alone! You stood out there jawing with that little shit, while my baby was in here unattended!"

"Will you shut up for one second?"

He did, his mouth still open in protest.

"I did not invite him. He showed up and I didn't have time to get someone else to watch her. Under the circumstances it seemed better to leave her alone than to let him see her. I stood out there trying to get rid of him, because I knew you wanted to keep the media away."

"But why did he come in the first place?"

"Not to see your chimp. He showed up out of the blue, about . . . something else." I hesitated, my anger used up, a bone-numbing fatigue in its place. Wayne had his secret; for some reason, I'd kept mine. I owed him nothing more than competent veterinary care, yet he'd virtually taken over my clinic and rearranged my life without giving me any options. And I had let him do it. But it was time to change that.

"Look," I said more calmly, "I know you didn't want the media to find out about little Andi. But now they have, so you might want to get ready to make a statement. Or give Brad a call—he seems good at that sort of thing."

"I told you I didn't want them involved."

"Yes, you did. But they are, and you'll have to deal with it."

He held my gaze, still furious. "Why did you have a reporter here, if not about Andi?"

"It has nothing to do with you. I really don't feel like explaining." *Just wait for tomorrow's paper. You'll know more than I do.*

I filled him in on the afternoon's vigil while he listened silently, fuming. I asked how Sally was doing, and he said she was almost back to her old self, but had very little milk left. He'd brought some of it, to mix with Andi's formula. He settled himself in for the evening and I went home to change.

I had the midnight-to-four watch again that night. Wayne would stay that evening, Trinka coming in early again. It was odd not to have to visit Gilda, but it was also a relief. I had seven hours of freedom, and I planned to make the most of it.

I dashed home, greeted the dogs and let them out, filled their food dishes, and the cats'. I rubbed ears and stroked sleek coats for those who wanted attention, promised a rain check for more. I jumped in the shower, letting the cool water run over my head and down my back and making a conscious effort to let my worldly concerns trickle with it down the drain. It was Wednesday night; I had Saturday off. Two more days—and I couldn't remember needing a day off more. I would sleep and sleep.

Get up and eat, read awhile, go back to sleep. With luck, we'd even get little Andi home by then.

I made an active decision not to think about Bud Thorpe and whatever story he was inventing at the moment.

After drying off, I sprayed Safari into the air and walked through it, catching the faintest trace on my skin. I'd already decided on what to wear: mint-colored silk, loosely draped in a lightweight sleeveless pants suit that flattered my waist and felt sexy against my skin. I hadn't seen Clay for two weeks.

I laughed at the thought. Before we'd gotten together it had been nearly two years since my last date. But now, seeing him had become almost a need. I didn't know how long it would last, but I planned to enjoy it while it did.

The dogs, still outside, announced Clay's arrival while I was applying mascara, the last touch of makeup which brought out my pale eyes and added shape to my oval face. My blond hair gets both darker and grayer with time, but my lashes and brows have stayed fair. Unlike most desert dwellers, I don't tan—I have neither the time nor the patience for basking in the sun. So the makeup, however inconvenient, is necessary.

Clay greeted me with an enthusiastic hug and I soaked it up. His solid body marked a contrast to those who filled my life lately. He was *there*, I could touch him, hold on to him, wrap my arms around him and squeeze. Gilda would have disintegrated under such contact. Baby Andi could barely be picked up.

"Let's skip dinner," he joked into my hair.

I laughed. I'd been thinking the exact same words. "No way. I'm hungry!" Surprisingly, it was true.

It was a restaurant we hadn't tried before, a new Japanese place on Palm Canyon, in a storefront which had clearly held a succession of restaurants. Some of the decor showed signs of deterioration, and the whole place had the feel of a neighborhood diner. An attempt had been made to create an Asian ambience by placing fragile bamboo-and-paper decorations here and there, and what had once been a dining counter had been converted to a sushi bar. The menu was full of delightful misspellings: *a god white wino.* And interesting descriptions: *Please not to order if you should not take salt.*

The middle-aged Asian couple I assumed owned the place were polite but slow moving. She wore a threadbare kimono; he some loose-fitting cotton Dockers and a polo shirt. She took our orders; he prepared food while watching a baseball game on television.

We ate; we talked of his most recent show; we talked about baby Andi. I managed for much of the evening not to think about Gilda Hopkins or Bud Thorpe or Alexandra Dixon. I had not mentioned any of them to Clay. I wasn't sure why, except there had not been a good opportunity. They were downers, and I didn't want them in this part of my life. But how long could I keep them separate? I knew I should tell him before tomorrow's paper gave him Thorpe's view. But the food and the "god white wino" came and we ate and drank and I never said a word.

Chapter Fourteen

I had to get up soon and take my shift watching Andi; Clay would go home to sleep and I wouldn't see him until the following week.

Candles burned and cats sprawled around us on my king-size waterbed. In the afterglow of lovemaking I lay drained, sated, ready for sleep. Still my mind jumped like a budgie in a cage, topic to topic, day to day.

I thought again of mentioning Gilda. Her death, her daughter, the reporter with too much free time. It bothered me that I hadn't told Clay about all of it. But I resented Gilda and her intrusion into my life. The only way I could keep her out of my bed was to shove her out of my thoughts. And how exactly would I bring it up? *"By the way, Clay, if I call you from jail, would you come and bail me out?" Smooth, Andi.*

I knew he would find out. I did not know how he would react. I had the sense of spinning through the dark on a roller coaster waiting for the next unexpected switchback, helpless to predict or alter its course. In this one moment of normalcy I just wanted to revel in Clay's presence.

I recalled wistfully the early days of our relationship, when we spoke almost daily. He called from other towns on weekends, to tell me how he'd done, catch me up on gossip, and inquire into my own day. We'd only been seeing each other four or five months. What happened? It wasn't the gossip I missed—I didn't know any of the horse-show people—it was the inclusion. One Saturday night he'd called and I'd gone to a movie with Lara. After that he didn't call anymore from the shows. He'd fill me in when he got back, but I found myself less interested in his monotonous stream of wins.

I snuggled closer to him, felt the solid warmth of him, the dampness of our lovemaking, the rise and fall of his chest as he breathed and the reassuring rhythm of his heartbeat. His body was familiar, his moves and responses predictable without yet being boring. But a certain connection was lacking, and I had no idea how to make it happen.

"I'm thinking of going back," he said.

"Back?" I felt I should immediately know what he meant.

"To South Africa. For a visit, I mean."

"Oh. How long has it been?"

"Almost six years. With Dad gone, it's not the same. Hell, nothing's the same, the whole country's changed. But it was home, once."

I didn't say anything.

"Want to come along?"

That surprised me. It shouldn't have. I thought about it—taking a few weeks off from the clinic. I hadn't taken a real vacation since graduating vet school. Longer—when Ma got sick she and I spent a week in Florida, two tourists in a herd of tourists. Cheap hotel, crowded beach, Disney World. Thirteen years ago. I hope Ma got more out of that trip than I did.

Trinka thought I was burning out. Maybe she was right. Maybe getting away, to a place completely new, would help.

"I don't know," I said. "When were you thinking of going?"

"October, maybe. Springtime, there."

I reflected on how little I knew about Clay's homeland. Thought about Christmas in the middle of summer. "Do you really have winter?"

He laughed, a spontaneous sound that made me smile and feel closer to him. "Not like here in frigid Palm Springs."

"Point taken."

"If you mean, do we have snow and pine trees and blizzards, then no, not anywhere on the whole continent. We have a wet season and a dry one, though from what I hear it's been hard to tell one from the other for the past several years."

"What made you decide to go back now?"

"I've a cousin getting married, girl I grew up with. Seems like a good excuse."

We didn't speak for a while.

"I'll think about it," I said, picturing vast plains, enormous herds of wild animals. Chimps, the few remaining wild ones. No, that was Kenya, but didn't the Kalahari extend into South Africa as well? "I've always wanted to visit Africa."

The next thing I was aware of was the shrilling of the telephone in my ear. I jumped, unsure for a moment where I was, then reached automatically for the receiver as Clay groaned and rolled over.

"Yeah?" I mumbled, glancing at the clock. I had to push Carbon out of the way to see that it was almost twelve-thirty. I'd slept almost an hour. "Oh, shit."

"Don't worry about us," Wayne's irritable voice came over the line. "Feel free to sleep in."

"Thanks," I said. "I think I will." And I hung up.

It rang again before I'd pulled my hand under the covers. "I'm coming," I snarled into the receiver. I decided baby Andi was definitely going home before the weekend. That, or to the emergency clinic like any other case.

"Time izzit?" Clay muttered.

I fought an urge to lie back down, skin to skin, and say, "It's early. Let's go back to sleep." Instead I stretched and extracted myself from the tangle of sheets and cats. "Time for me to go back in. Stay if you want."

But he roused himself, joined me in the shower, got dressed, and went home. I got to the clinic at twelve forty-five.

Wayne barely spoke, other than to tell me that Andi had slept throughout his shift. I gathered this whole adventure was wearing thin for him as well. He left and I curled up in my chair with a cup of coffee and the mystery novel I'd managed twenty pages of so far.

This shift really sucked. Nothing happened, and I dozed off several times, jerking awake guiltily to refill my coffee cup and vow to stay alert. Several times I paced the clinic to get blood flowing. Fortunately little Andi barely stirred.

Trinka showed up at four o'clock sharp, making me feel even guiltier. The fact that she appeared well rested and ready for the day did not make it better. I filled her in, went home, and crawled into bed.

And could not sleep. Not for anything.

Clay's scent clung to the sheets, and I missed him. At that insane hour, I regretted not confiding in him. He was a good man, a sensible person. And he would find out soon anyway.

My brain, buzzed on caffeine, returned to Bud Thorpe's gleeful face as he finally left Dr. D's. I should have been relieved to see him distracted from Gilda's death by the little chimp. After all, baby Andi represented potential good publicity, which no one in any business should turn away from. But Wayne had been so adamant: *No publicity. None.* Given the allegations Trinka had discovered, I could see why.

Was that really *our* problem? If Wayne had made sexual advances toward a teenager, why should I take his side?

But I didn't know if he had. I only knew he'd been accused. And I had no right to know that much. The whole mess was nothing to do with my own life, except where mine intersected Wayne's. I wanted Wayne and Brad and their primate to go home and let me sleep. Let me deal with the other issues in my life. Let them deal with theirs. For now, they were clients and would receive the same discretion and confidentiality as any other client.

The best I could do was a restless drowse, interrupted again by the too-soon buzzing of an alarm clock I was growing to hate.

I dragged myself back to the clinic at around eight-thirty, suspecting the touch of makeup I'd applied did not make me appear alert or any less pale.

Diane smirked. "We were getting worried about you," she said. I did not reply because it wasn't worth it.

The dark expression on Trinka's face as she passed me on her way into an exam room could not be explained by my lateness. Sheila stared at me with big, apprehensive eyes, like a spaniel about to receive an injection. The rest of the staff seemed to be avoiding me.

The newspaper story. A cold chill climbed my spine. I did not want to read it; I could not wait to read it.

I glanced into Treatment, where baby Andi slept. The remarkable thing was, nobody sat watching. So I did, but just for a minute. I could put it off no longer. With a sick feeling unrelated to fatigue, I headed for the office.

The *Desert Sparkler* lay open on my desk. The photo was remarkably flattering, given my exhaustion and the fury on my face as Bud Thorpe had shot it. Next to it was a picture of Gilda that must have been ten years old.

The headline made me tremble. EUTHANASIA: NOT

JUST FOR ANIMALS ANYMORE? And below that, smaller: *Local Veterinarian Accused of Easing Client's Death.*

Damn, damn, damn. My hands trembled as I smoothed out the paper, tried to focus on the print beneath.

Palm Springs. Prominent local philanthropist Gilda Hopkins died early yesterday in her home. She will be remembered, perhaps, not only for her work with various local charities, including, ironically, Coachella Valley Hospital's Cancer Center, but for the way in which she apparently died. Bedridden from terminal cancer herself, unable to move or even swallow, Gilda Hopkins died of an overdose of morphine.

Her daughter, Palm Springs resident Alexandra Dixon, has accused a local veterinarian of taking her job too far. Dr. Andrea Pauling, of Dr. Doolittle's Pet Care Center, visited Dixon's mother several times this week. According to Dixon, the purpose of these visits was preparation for the mercy killing of the older woman.

Dixon claimed her mother had contacted the veterinarian, who treated her dog several years ago for a similar condition. According to Dixon, her mother was depressed and asked to be put out of her misery. "But she didn't want to die," Dixon insisted yesterday morning. "She was just lonely because no one visited anymore. She called her old friend, someone who could have helped her. And now look what happened."
see Vet, A10

My hands shook as I turned the section over and found the story's continuation. I got up, poured myself a cup of coffee, and took a deep breath before plunging ahead.

It is not clear what did happen. Dixon has a laboratory report that indicates that the morphine level in her mother's blood at the time of death was higher than would be expected. A spokesman for the lab indicated the level was high enough to be toxic.

Hopkins's geriatrician, Dr. Alan Frank, contacted at his offices on Palm Canyon, declined to comment.

However, Coachella Valley Hospital internist Dr. Vincent Jones said, "When a patient is dying of protracted disease, commonly he or she undergoes some degree of organ failure prior to death. This can result in reduced metabolism of drugs, such as narcotics. If she had been receiving the drip for months, and her tolerance was very high, it can be almost impossible to give enough morphine to ease the pain without eventually causing toxicity."

Dixon insisted her mother was comfortable and had not shown signs of overdosage prior to Pauling's final visit, which coincided with the older woman's death. "That bitch killed my mother," she said. "I know she did it, and I'll prove it. You just watch."

Pauling, contacted at her Palm Springs office, denied causing the woman's death. A spokesman for the Palm Springs Police Department stated that the allegations were being investigated, but that no charges had been filed to date.

"It could have been worse."

I turned my gaze from the blurring page to the doorway. My hands shook and my mouth felt dry. Trinka stood, arms crossed, small but formidable.

"It probably will be," I said.

"At least he interviewed that doctor. And didn't mention Kevorkian once."

"Hmph." I suspected I'd be hearing enough about Kevorkian over the next several days.

"They can't prove anything, can they?"

I put the paper down, looked at Trinka. "You still think there's something *to* prove."

She held my eye a moment longer. "The chimp's looking good. Have you seen her this morning?"

"I checked on her when I got here. We'll turn off the ventilator as soon as Wayne gets here. Think we can send her home tomorrow?"

We talked about Andi a little more, then discussed a couple of other cases we'd worked on together. It was my day in surgery, but there was only a tomcat neuter, which took all of a minute and a half. Just as I finished, Sheila buzzed me to say the owner was on the phone. I picked up in Surgery.

"Good morning, Mrs. Baker. I just finished Troller's operation."

"Is he dead yet?" She sounded like she was crying.

"Dea—? Of course not. He's just waking up from—"

"How could you? Here I drop my precious baby off, all innocent, how could I know?"

"Know what?" But the chill was back.

"I just read the paper! We're Christians! I'm coming to get my Troller right now!"

"Mrs. Baker, he's fine!"

"I don't believe you!"

This ranked among the more bizarre client phone calls I'd received, but the circumstances were unusual. "He'll be awake in a few minutes, and you can take him home."

She'd hung up.

Okay, I should have expected this. Clients would see the article, and would react in different ways. It would be hard on me, hard on the staff. But we would deal with it.

I carried the young cat into Treatment and sat with him on my lap while the gas anesthetic wore off. I had the sense of waiting for events to come to me. Most clients would be more rational, but I really could not predict what their reactions would be. Would the police really "investigate"?

The staff gazed at me silently, Sheila big-eyed with wonder, Diane wary and angry like a child. Arlene, the new receptionist, was harder to read. She practically worshipped Trinka and would doubtless follow her lead. Didi, who had been with the practice longer than I had, seemed to be reserving judgment. This was not the first time I'd been in the paper.

Mrs. Baker made record time, and refused to pay her bill until she saw for herself that Troller was really alive and well, if groggy and missing certain parts. She stared at me suspiciously as if I had secretly replaced her cat with an imposter. Ruefully I watched her go, knowing we'd lost a client but not sure that was a bad thing.

By now the image of Gilda suffering in her lonely bed had faded from my mind. She had finally gotten her wish. I wondered if she'd have been at all sympathetic if she knew what her humble request might now do to my own life.

Chapter Fifteen

A roving reporter for one of the local TV stations showed up at around eleven. The reporter stopped at the front desk and asked to see me. Over the intercom I told Sheila I had no comment. The other TV station and two radio-show representatives called asking for interviews. Sheila and Arlene, however they felt personally on the issue, obviously enjoyed fielding these calls.

I had left two messages for Lara, who was in court that morning. On the third try I caught her.

"Did you see the paper?" I asked.

"Yeah." She sounded distracted.

"Well?"

"Well, what? I told you not to do it."

"Lara, come on! That's hardly—"

"Look, gotta go. Jail to meet a client, then Rob Sherman for lunch. I'll call you later. Don't say anything to the cops or the media."

"KPAR was already here."

"Don't talk to them. Later."

Damn. I stared at the dead receiver for a moment before replacing it. Now what?

The intercom clicked on. Sheila. "Clay Tanner on one."

Clay. Oh, damn. "Hi."

"Andi. What is this?" I heard a note of betrayal.

"I'm sorry, Clay. I was going to call you. I'm a little overwhelmed right now." *Lame, Andi.*

"But what *is* this?" A rustle of paper in the background.

"Pretty much what it says. An old client asked me to put her to sleep like I did her dog. She died a couple of days ago, and her daughter can't handle it."

"Then you didn't—?" He sounded almost disappointed.

"Oh, God, Clay. What do you think?"

He didn't say anything for a long time. No doubt he was wondering just what sort of woman he'd gotten involved with. "I won't ask, then. But, Andi, once this sort of thing hits the news . . . It won't go away, you know."

The concern and confusion in his voice touched me in a way no amount of Trinka's or Lara's irritation could. Tears welled in my eyes and I was grateful for one person who cared about what I was going through. "I'm sorry I didn't say anything, Clay. This all happened so fast. I don't know what to do, I'm just so tired." My mouth wanted to ramble but my throat was closing.

"Hey, now. Don't worry." He seemed to realize how inane that sounded. "I'm sure things will turn out okay."

I didn't answer. I couldn't.

"This old woman, what was she like?"

"Gilda? She was . . . she was strong. She was . . . strong."

Our silence stretched.

"I miss her," I said.

"But you . . ."

"Yeah, I didn't know her all that well. But I admired her and now she's gone. She didn't give a damn about anyone, you know?"

I wasn't making sense but Clay was kind enough not to point that out. "Can we talk later?" I said.

"Of course. Are you free tonight?"

"No, little Andi still isn't ready to go home. I've got first watch and then I'm going home to sleep."

"Of course. You must be beat. I'll call you tomorrow."

As soon as I hung up I missed the connection. I felt isolated, helpless against the unknown future. I wanted to go to sleep and stay there until Gilda was buried and the media had had its excitement and Trinka had decided to get over it.

Didi glanced through the door. "New client in Two." I stood up and took a deep breath, walked down the hallway and into the room, zipping up my white coat as I walked.

Inside an elderly man waited. He was stooped and jaundiced, looking more in need of medical attention than his pet. A scruffy terrier wandered the room, sniffing the corners and ignoring her owner and me alike.

I introduced myself to the man, Archie Phelps, then glanced at the chart and said, "And what brings Beulah in today?"

The terrier glanced up briefly when she heard her name, then resumed her explorations.

"She's getting old. I want you to look at this lump on her side and tell me if it's cancer."

I tried not to sigh. It's a rare malignancy that announces itself so clearly. A lump is a lump is a lump, until it's been biopsied.

I scooped the dog onto the table and began my systematic examination, so ingrained it was almost unconscious. Checked her eyes, face, ears, and throat—all normal—and her teeth, which definitely needed work. I was sliding my hands down her neck, checking the lymph nodes, when Mr. Phelps interrupted.

"It's on her side, there."

He stood and tried to point it out. He checked first her right side then her left, then went back to the right, digging through her wiry brown hair with shaky hands and increasing frustration. "It was there this morn . . . here it is."

It wasn't a skin lump. It was a mammary lump. Breast tumor. Common in female dogs, the last thing I wanted to deal with today. "Is she spayed?" I asked.

"What?" The apparent change of subject seemed to confuse him.

"Did you have her fixed so she can't have puppies?"

"She's never around other dogs."

Which both did and did not answer my question. "So she's never been spayed?" Early removal of the ovaries prevented almost one hundred percent of such tumors.

"No," he finally said, slowly, as if speaking to someone a little dense.

The lump, about the size of a pea, did not seem to bother Beulah. "She's got a tumor in her breast. When did you first notice it?"

He peered into the distance, face creased in thought. "A few months ago. I don't know. It's cancer, isn't it?" Prepared for bad news. Almost begging for it.

"Probably. But I only find the one. We might—*might*—be able to keep it from spreading."

"Do what you have to. I don't want her to suffer."

I stepped back and looked him full in the face. "Okay, the best treatment is removal of all the glands on this side. We'll need to spay her, too, of course, to remove the hormonal stimulation. But the first thing is to x-ray her chest to look for metast—"

He waved a hand. "No, no, I don't want to put her through all that. Just put her to sleep."

That stopped me. I glanced down at his pet, now investigating the surface of the exam table with the same intensity she'd brought to the floor earlier.

"Now?"

"I don't want her to suffer."

Those words are often genuine and painful; other times they spell a euphemism for "I don't want to spend any money on my pet." But in this case it was grossly premature, at best. I thought carefully about what I would say next. "Mr. Phelps, what makes you think she's suffering?"

He wouldn't meet my eyes. "I don't want to put her through all that. She's too old."

The notation on the chart listed Beulah as thirteen—geriatric, but not ancient. I placed the bell of my stethoscope against her chest, buying time. Her heart clopped along, and air moved smoothly in and out of her lungs. I set the instrument aside and ran my hands over the solid little body. Finally I leaned against the sink behind me, crossing my arms over my chest. "I don't see any indication that she's in pain."

"You said yourself, she's got cancer."

I'd said no such thing, and I couldn't even know if it was true without a biopsy. Dogs can have benign lumps, and even the other kind can be removed. "But you seem to have caught it in the early stages. Surgery could save her life. Fairly routine surgery at that. And even without it, she could easily live another couple of years." I tried to hold his eye, but he kept glancing around the room.

"She's too old! She won't make it through the operation!"

"You're sure of that?"

"Well, I . . . She . . ." I realized he was crying. "Why are you doing this to me?"

Doing this to *him*? "Doing what, Mr. Phelps?"

"You're making me feel like I don't care about my dog."

I took a deep breath and let it out slowly. *Don't start, Andi. You are not responsible for what this man feels.* It was his decision to treat or not to treat, but ethically I could not justify killing this animal on this day. "I don't want you to make a decision you'll regret later." I handed him a box of Kleenex, standard furnishing in the exam room.

A niggling voice wondered if I was being selfish. I'd had enough of death. Was it affecting my clinical judgment? But I really didn't think so.

Beulah hunched herself up to leap off the table. I caught her and placed her on the floor. She lay down next to her master's foot, panting quietly, waiting patiently for him to be ready to leave. To take her home.

"Look at her," I said. "Tell me why you think this dog should be put to sleep."

"You're making this so hard." He yanked half a dozen tissues from the box. His arms were thin and did not match his bloated torso. "Be—because, she's old and—and I can't stand the thought of her being cut open."

Something was off. "Mr. Phelps, I just can't—"

"What's the matter with you?" he suddenly demanded. "You did it for that Hopkins woman! It's because she's rich, isn't it. How much did she pay you? I'll find the money! I'll find it!"

Oh, shit. "We're not talking about Beulah anymore, are we?" I was shivering. How many such encounters would I have in my lifetime?

"It's in my liver. Some days it hurts so bad. I don't want to leave my Beulah all alone. We want to go together. Please, I'll . . . I'll get the money."

I shook my head. "Please tell me exactly what you're asking."

He nodded, his yellow skull bobbing as if palsied. "I want it. I want the shot. Me and Beulah. I want us to go together, cause there's no one else to take care of her. Put us out like you did that woman. Put us to sleep."

I wanted to run from the room, get this man from my sight, with his yellow face and his swollen liver and his plea for mercy. I hugged myself to lessen the shivering. "Who is your doctor?"

"What does it matter? It's my decision."

"I'd like to talk to him. Him?" He nodded. "I need to talk to him."

At least I'd given him something to do. With obvious effort he tugged a worn-out wallet from his pants pocket and began fishing through the myriad cards and papers protruding from it. Finally he offered me a gray card, so battered I couldn't tell if the marbling on the paper was intended or not. Vincent Jones, MD, diplomate, American College of Internal Medicine. An address on Palm Canyon, a Web page, phone and fax numbers, and an e-mail address. I wondered if all those choices would make it more or less difficult to reach Dr. Jones.

Almost certainly, this was the same Vincent Jones that Bud Thorpe had interviewed for his article. He was someone I wanted to talk to anyway.

I copied down the information on the margin of an instruction pad for canine ear care. "Thank you," I said, and handed back the card. "I'll give him a call right away. And I'll be in touch. You take care of yourself, okay?" It was pretty lame, as was the smile I put with it. He hesitated, wanting an answer, but inured to the delays of the medical profession and resigned to wait. Shoulders folded in over his protruding belly, he tried to hook Beulah's leash to her collar. After a few fumbling attempts, I did it for him. Without another word he shuffled from the office. I handed the chart to Sheila through a window, wondering what I would write on it when it came back.

The next client was one we saw roughly every fourteen months, for checkups and vaccinations. Marin Connor usually waited until the third reminder card to make her appointment. This time it had been just ten months. But the chart said only "checkup."

She had a whippet on a leash and her Siamese cat in his carrier on the floor. The whippet cringed against her legs; the cat noisily demanded to be let out.

I smiled—this was getting harder to do and I couldn't be sure how it came off—and asked Marin how she was. She said, "Fine." I asked if either of her pets had any health problems she wanted me to check out. She said, "No." She looked a bit flushed but I attributed that to the heat. We chatted about the weather while I lifted Wispy, the whippet, onto the table.

Wispy appeared to be as healthy as ever. Ditto the cat, Sampson. We discussed dental care, which was an annual topic, and breathlessly she agreed to make an appointment to have both pets' teeth cleaned. Honestly, her attitude reminded me of a high school girl meeting a celebrity. I shrugged it off and returned Sam to his crate. All this had taken maybe thirty minutes, during which Marin occasionally giggled and seemed on the brink of hyperventilating. After my encounter with Mr. Phelps, I was afraid of what was coming.

"Okay, see Sheila up front about that dental appointment," I said, moving to open the door for her.

"Okay." She got up, but didn't move. "I just wanted you to know, I think it was incredibly brave, what you did."

"What's that?" I asked. Thinking, *No, please, don't do this.*

"For that old woman. She must have been suffering terribly. You didn't think about yourself at all, did you? You just did the right thing with no regard for the consequences!"

She was almost gasping by now, and her eyes shone with a sort of excitement I can only describe as sexual. I absolutely could not form words. I edged toward the open door.

She leaned forward conspiratorially. I pulled away, until my back collided with the door frame.

"Death is such a blessing sometimes," she whispered seductively.

I glanced toward the front desk, where Sheila watched with wide eyes and a smirk.

"It's okay," Marin said. "I know you can't talk about it. But I just wanted you to know, you're not alone." She slipped something into my hand, which gripped it reflexively, then she left without a backward glance.

I looked at the piece of paper I was holding. It was a business card. "Humanity for Humans," it read.

There was a post office box in Berkeley. And a Web page.

I slipped through the hallway into the office, crumpling the card in my hand.

Chapter Sixteen

At least there were no other appointments for a while.

I checked baby Andi, who was sleeping, then slipped into the office and sat down at my desk. I dropped the Humanity for Humans card on the desk and dialed Vincent Jones's number. When the receptionist answered I told her I was Dr. Andi Pauling calling for Dr. Jones. As I'd hoped, she didn't recognize my name and was too well trained where doctors were concerned to question my right to speak to hers. She said he was with a patient but would be out shortly. Would I prefer to wait, or should he call me back?

"I'm between appointments myself. I'll hold for a minute," I said.

"Thank you." I was serenaded by lite rock for a lot more than a minute, before a harried voice came on the line.

"Dr. Jones."

"Dr. Jones, thank you for speaking to me. I, ah . . ." Now that I had his ear, what exactly did I mean to say? "This is Dr. Andi Pauling. I saw a patient of yours today, Archie Phelps. He, um, he . . . expressed a wish to die."

There was a pause. "Have we met, Andi? I can't place you, must be getting old. Heh, heh. What's your specialty?" The voice still friendly, but wary.

"I'm sorry, I didn't mean to mislead you. I'm a veterinarian."

Another hesitation. "How did you come to 'see' my patient?"

"I didn't mean in my professional capacity. I mean, I did mean that. . . . Okay, let me start over. Mr. Phelps brought his dog to see me today. He wanted me to . . . Did you read this morning's paper?"

"What? No, I rarely have the chance. A couple of patients mentioned that I was quoted. What in the world has that got to do with Mr. Phelps?"

He doesn't know! What a thrill it was to encounter someone unfamiliar with my sudden notoriety! Unfortunately, I would have to bring him up to date. "Look, could I possibly stop by your office? After you've had a chance to check the front page?"

Again he didn't answer immediately, probably wondering if I was some sort of kook. "Can you come between five-thirty and six?"

It would be awkward, but I could arrange it. "I may be a bit late."

He laughed, revealing a sense of humor I hadn't expected for some reason. "I probably will, too," he said. "See you then."

It was nearly five now, and I had only a cat vaccination scheduled at five-twenty. But Wayne wasn't due until six, at which time we planned to wean baby Andi off the ventilator. I called his office and asked to speak with him. When he picked up the phone the terror in his voice sent guilt waves through me.

"What happened?"

"Nothing, Wayne. It's okay. I have to leave a little early, so I won't be here when you come. Diane will watch her."

"Okay. Okay. Jesus, I thought something had happened. Or those damned reporters were back."

"Oh, they've been here. I'm sure the story will be picked up all over now. But I haven't talked to anyone."

"That Thorpe . . . He's poison."

"I'm not a fan, either. I take it you read the article this morning."

"Article? . . . oh, that. Thorpe dug up something, I . . . he was here this morning. You must have wondered why I was so opposed to publicity. He . . . this is all going to be made public. It could ruin me. I . . . I . . ."

"If you mean the boy you . . . who claims you molested him, we already know a little about that."

After a moment of silence he said, "But how—?"

I almost told him. "Does it matter?"

A stunned silence. "Of course, it matters!"

I sighed. I wasn't getting anything right. "We'll talk later, okay? I'm sorry, I have to go." I hung up before he could protest.

I found Diane sitting in my chair in Treatment, wrapping Vetrap around her hand.

"How's the thumb?" I asked.

"It's getting better." Her words were a bit slurred. Her pupils were constricted.

"Are you taking something for pain?"

She grinned up at me. "Yeah, I had some Vicodin left over from when I had a tooth pulled last year."

"Just be careful, okay? That stuff can seriously slow your reflexes." I didn't like her working that way at all, but the weekend was coming up and surely she wouldn't need it anymore after that. I decided to let the subject go.

Dr. Jones introduced himself as Vinnie. He was a little under six feet tall, a little bit overweight, but it softened what could have been a severe bearing. His crisp white coat and disciplined graying hair bespoke an exactitude I could only envy.

I pushed my own wispy blond hair out of my eyes and made a mental note to get it trimmed. He led me into an impossibly tidy office of neutral tones, and sat behind his sleek, whitewashed oak desk. I sat in a buff-colored chair across from him, picturing Archie Phelps in the same chair. I wondered what awful news had been received by others in that very seat over the years. How many people who had sat there were now dead? Or wished they were? "I'm really glad I treat animals," I said.

"I beg your pardon?"

I shook my head. "I met Mr. Phelps and his dog, Beulah, for the first time this afternoon." I told him about the visit in detail. When I finished, he sat quietly for what seemed like a very long time, his hand absently stroking his perfectly cropped gray beard.

"Would it surprise you to learn that I support his right to decline further treatment?"

"No, but that's not the same as asking for euthanasia."

"True." He nodded slowly. "I find myself in an awkward position regarding your inquiry."

I waited.

"Ordinarily, the fact that Archie elected to consult another physician would enable me to discuss his case in detail with that doctor. But a veterinarian . . ." His hand moved in a helpless gesture. "It's hard to justify."

I leaned forward uncomfortably. "I'm not sure I want to know any more than I do. Please understand, I have no intention of carrying out his request." He didn't answer but held my gaze. "Just in case you were wondering."

"So why are you here?"

Why indeed? "I thought you should know."

That slow, sage nod. "I do know."

How could he be so unaffected by this? Then I pictured my own demeanor when I knew an animal was terminal. It did no one any good for me to break down. I was the professional and both my clients and I expected me to act like it. But I had the option of ending my patient's misery when it became too much for the animal, or for its owner, to bear.

As if picking up an echo of my thoughts, he said, "Do you realize that responsibility for that dog might be the only reason he hasn't done away with himself? Certainly he has, shall we say, the means at his disposal. But who would take care of—Beulah, is it?—if he were gone?"

I didn't answer. Neither of us spoke for a minute. I studied the sand-colored carpet and the matching wallpaper. I felt his gentle, detached eyes watching me, waiting. Finally he broke the silence. "If that's all?"

I shook my head. "You were quoted in that article."

"Ah, yes. I wondered when you would get to that."

"The article is why Mr. Phelps came to see me. It just came out this morning and already it's making my life weird. I need to know more about the immediate causes of Gilda's death."

"I never knew the woman. When that reporter called, it was with a theoretical question."

"It doesn't matter. Tell me about morphine metabolism."

He nodded again. "Unlike some, I won't assume you did what the article claims."

"I appreciate that. But she did ask, and her daughter is making a big stink. She hired her own pathologist. I don't know much, but apparently the morphine levels in her blood are pretty high."

He paused before answering. "Certain cases are undeniably terminal, and quite painful. Patients might be provided doses of narcotic that ordinarily would not be considered safe."

"Ordinarily?"

His head bobbed a bit lower. "Perhaps 'safe' is not the correct word. The doses I refer to are not exactly 'safe' under any conditions. But there comes a point in the treatment of debilitating terminal illness where all we can offer is relative comfort."

I waited. None of this was new.

"The patient's system learns to metabolize morphine faster. The pain, sometimes it's almost as if the pain were a living thing, with its own increased tolerance. We must increase the dose proportionately. Tolerance increases and so must the amount of drug required to provide relief."

"Yes, but at some point the organs can't keep up, right?"

"Concisely put. At some point the organs can't keep up."

As I drove away, an unexpected wave of depression washed over me. Everything in my life, every goal I ever set out to achieve, felt exposed as a futile joke. What had I hoped to accomplish, coming over here? I had angered Wayne and possibly broken a client's confidence, and done no one the slightest bit of good.

There was entirely too much misery in the world.

And nothing I could do to change it.

I headed back to the clinic, and it was an effort of will to go inside. Wayne stood by the incubator, while Brad had both hands through the portals, tickling the little chimp who clung tenaciously to his fingers. Brad's wide grin and sheer enthusiasm went a long way toward making the upcoming shift bearable.

"Ready?" Even Wayne couldn't hold on to his lousy mood.

"Yeah, thanks for waiting."

An air of anticipation charged the room. First, Wayne set the ventilator control to two breaths per minute. This was slower than normal respiration, but it would still kick in if Andi's body failed to take over the job.

I don't think any of us took a breath while we stared through the Plexiglas. Waiting, hoping, willing her diaphragm to contract.

After thirty long seconds the ventilator filled her lungs. I let out a groan.

"Shh," Wayne said. "Sometimes it takes a minute." Of course I knew that. We'd discussed it before. But I wanted her to breathe *now*.

Another long half minute ticked by. Baby Andi kicked and squirmed, but her chest did not rise. My eyes flickered from the chimp to the second hand of my watch. Twenty-eight seconds.

Twenty-nine.

And she breathed.

"Yes!" Brad shouted.

Wayne sighed with relief. My face stretched in a wide grin.

Baby Andi's second breath came twelve seconds after the first. Wayne disconnected the tubing from her endotracheal tube and loosened the tape. As if in agreement, little Andi grasped the tube herself and pulled it from her throat.

Wayne smiled indulgently. I laughed. Brad practically roared.

The rest of my shift was filled with wonder. I spent half the time with my hands through the portals, the baby chimp's fingers gripping mine with their astonishing strength.

Once in a while we do get to make a difference.

Chapter Seventeen

It was after lunch on Friday when the detectives came.

Trinka and I were sitting in the office. She was doing something on her computer while I sorted through the detritus on my desk. Roosevelt perched on a piece of PVC pipe Trinka had glued atop her computer monitor for that purpose. Trinka's workspace was, as usual, pristine. One day I'll catch her clearing her desk onto mine when she thinks I'm not looking. How else could I explain the piles of papers reproducing there?

Calling Mr. Phelps had been incredibly difficult. Ashamedly, I ducked and dodged the overt question of euthanasia for dog or owner. I gave him a phone number for a client who'd gotten a Westie from a rescue organization. She, or the organization, would ensure the little dog would be taken care of when her owner could no longer do so. I didn't know if he would call or not. But Beulah would have a home should her owner predecease her. Now, sorting journals, I was glad to put my brain on hold for a few minutes.

Sheila brought in the day's mail, handing an obvious ad flyer to Roosevelt, who liked to chew paper. I got the rest. Two pieces caught my eye immediately, but I sorted through the whole stack. The bills went to Trinka—she insists, really—as did three that looked like payments on account. I stacked two journals on top of a pile that already threatened to topple, dropped the offers for magazine subscriptions and catalogs from grooming supply houses into the trash. Finally it was just the two items.

One was an ordinary white legal-size envelope, with a local postmark. It had been addressed in a shaky scrawl, in pencil. The other was pale blue, almost square, the kind greeting cards come in. Clients sometimes sent thank you cards or photos of their pets in such envelopes. It was stiff enough to hold pictures. But both had return address names I'd never heard of, so they did not appear to be from clients.

I opened the blue one first. Inside was a note card with a daisy on the front, and a photograph of a woman I didn't recognize. She sat in a wheelchair, dwarfed by a mound of afghans and sweaters. Oxygen tubes trailed from her nostrils over her shoulders and disappeared behind the chair. She may have been attempting to smile, but all I saw in her face was resignation.

I knew what the note would hold. I read it anyway.

Dear Dr. Paulling,

I am righting to take advantige of your service you provide, to put old ladies like me out of there mysery. I am alone in all the worl. My children are scatered to the fore winds and they never visit there old mom. I wait for the Lord to take me away. I have sickness in my bones, and in my lungs from before we ever knew how bad it is to smoke cigarettes. I am on social security, I am no rich lady but I am hoping you will take mercy on my poor soul. I have that anteak cherry rocker that was my granmamas and I supose I coud offer that but I am hoping to have that for my great granbaby to have when she is of age. I dont spose you woud want my old TV, which I wont need any more

when I am called home. The wheelchare and all belongs to medicare. Well, you call me and I hope we will work somthing out.
Sincerely,
Dorothy Whetson Daniels
(909) 555-8136

I gazed at the photo for a long time, a lonely old woman who thought she wanted to die. The postmark was San Bernardino, the return address in Rialto. I would contact Social Services and see about getting someone to visit her, maybe take her on outings to the Senior Center. The decision made me feel better. A little.

I handed the letter and photo to Trinka. She read quickly then said, "Christ. I've got to visit my mother this weekend." Not that her mother would notice. The last time she had recognized Trinka was four months ago. My partner's descriptions of those visits were painful to hear. But I understood the impulse.

The other letter waited. I took a deep breath and slit it open. Inside was a page torn from a Big Chief tablet. What had not been as obvious on the envelope was that the handwriting belonged to a child.

Dear Dr. Vet,
My name is Dack. I am nine. I saw about you on TV. I think you can help me. I have leukemia. My mom cries all the time. When I am dead she could afford to take my sister to Disneyland instead of the hospital all the time but now there is no money. I hate the hospital. I throw up all the time and hurt. So I think if I could die that would fix a lot of things. I promise I won't tell my mom if you say you will help me.
Your friend,
Dack Adams

The return address was Desert Hot Springs. But the Palm Springs postmark most likely meant he was at Coachella Valley General Hospital. I had no idea who should see the letter. Thank God there was no photo with this one.

Roosevelt said, "Cool!"

"Trinka, I can't stand this." I handed her the page.

"This is just the beginning."

"That's what I'm afraid of."

"I didn't even know kids could still write letters. And look, not one misspelling. This is a kid the world needs to hang on to."

"Damn it, Trinka, this isn't funny!"

She was silent until I looked at her, then said, "Am I laughing?"

Roosevelt was, a deep roll he'd learned from Trinka's father. But even he seemed to pick up on my somber mood.

I sighed. "What am I going to do?"

"Write back and tell him no."

It wasn't that simple, of course, but I considered my options. I could ignore the letter, I could try to visit the kid. I could write back but the letter would most likely be opened by his mother or sister, and he had seemed to beg for discretion. I could turn the letter over to someone at the hospital.

I could ask Wayne. I would see him later. The thought of turning it over to someone else was so irresistible I was tempted to drive the letter to his office.

My thoughts were interrupted by Sheila's voice on the intercom. "Dr. Pauling? There are two cop—uh, policemen, up here that want to talk to you."

It was bound to happen soon. "I'll be right up."

I met them at the front desk. They weren't wearing the navy PSPD uniform, but no one would be surprised to learn they were police. One wore khaki chinos and a blue polo shirt, the other blue chinos and a tan button-down over a white T-shirt. Both clean and crisp, but not new. Mirrored sunglasses. Short, generic haircuts. Black shoes.

"I'm Andi Pauling," I said, unsure whether to offer my hand.

"Hi, Dr. Pauling," said the one in the polo shirt. "I'm Detective Majors, this is Detective Suarez." Majors removed his sunglasses and slipped them into his pocket. Apologetic. Respectful. Authoritarian.

I said, "What can I help you with?"

"I guess you know why we're here?"

"I assume it has something to do with Alexandra Dixon's ridiculous allegations."

"We're following up on that, yes."

Sheila and Arlene sat listening. "Want to come into the office?" I suggested.

"Sure. We have a search warrant to exercise, too. We need to look for a syringe that might have been used to administer morphine."

I stopped, looked at them. Their expressions did not reveal whether they knew what they were getting into. "Sure," I said, unable to suppress a tiny smile. "I'll show you where the syringes are." I detoured through the first exam room, pointing out the contaminated-waste box and the drawer full of new or resterilized syringes. I led them into the second room, with a similar setup. Into Treatment, and Pharmacy, and Surgery, each with its supply of syringes. "There are probably some in Lab, too. And most of the used syringes are recycled, after being thoroughly washed and resterilized. The rest go in the trash, without needles, of course. But help yourself. Just leave us a few so we can function."

Again, their neutral expressions didn't tell me much. I proceeded to the office, where Trinka was still doing something on her computer. Roosevelt, who had been dozing on her shoulder, started awake.

"This is my partner, Trinka Romanescu. Detectives Majors and Suarez."

"Hi."

"Ma'am."

"Dr. Roma—nescu?"

"Cool." The last from Roosevelt. It's his favorite word.

"I'd offer you a seat," I said, "but . . ." I gestured to show there was only one unoccupied in the room, the one behind my desk. The other was in Treatment. During staff meetings we would pull in the rolling stools and the two chairs from up front. But it felt counterproductive to ask these men to wait while I scouted places for them to sit.

Majors shook his head. "That's okay. We shouldn't be here long. As we said, we're looking into the death of Mrs. Gilda Hopkins. We have a complaint from a family member."

"Her daughter. No kidding."

"We just have a few questions. For now."

"Fine."

"What was your relationship with the deceased?"

Relationship? "I was her vet."

"But you visited her frequently?"

I shook my head. How many times qualified as "frequently"? "A few times, when she first got sick. A few more at the end."

"What caused you to visit her after so much time?"

"She asked me to." I leaned against the desk, then stood again. Neither of the detectives said anything. I glanced at my watch, wished another client would come in. Knowing Trinka would take them if they came. "I only recently learned that she was so sick. She was lonely, and paralyzed, so she couldn't write. She sent me a videotape. She wanted . . ." I bit my lip, knowing they had used silence to compel me to talk, resenting it, wanting nonetheless to talk.

"Did you visit Mrs. Hopkins on the night of her death?" Suarez spoke for the first time. He was attractive in a paternal way—I'd have bet he had children, and they didn't lie to him. He'd taken off his sunglasses and the blue of his eyes stood in stark contrast to his Hispanic features. They were kind eyes. Eyes that invited confession.

"Yes, I was there that night. I was with her when she died. I was there when her daughter called the police, and I was still there when they decided there was nothing for them to investigate." It was already a matter of police record.

"So she was still alive when you arrived?"

I stared at him, wondering if they really believed I'd slipped Gilda a lethal dose of morphine, or if they were just going where they were sent.

"Look, I can see where this is heading," I said. "And I think I should consult my attorney."

The detectives exchanged glances. Majors shrugged and sighed. "Does that question bother you?"

I reached behind me for the phone, punched in Lara's number, left another message. "She's in court," I said to the men. "And I'd like to get some lunch before my next appointment. You can wait, or . . ."

Majors produced a card. "Call us when your lawyer says you can talk," he said with only a trace of sarcasm. "Meanwhile, we'll be exercising that search warrant."

As if bidden, two more officers arrived, preceded by Sheila. They didn't look at us. One handed Majors an official-looking piece of paper. Trinka stood up, outrage on her face, mouth open to protest.

"It's okay, Trinka," I said. "They need to check out our syringes."

"And your narcotic supply," Majors amended. "This is a search warrant authorizing us to search for syringes and missing or unauthorized narcotic drugs. I need you to show me your records and supplies."

The hairs prickled along the back of my neck, and I could see Trinka was scared, too. It didn't matter if we had nothing to hide; it was suddenly clear that any territorial illusions we may have had were exactly that—illusions. These people could legally enter our place of business and do whatever they liked—if they were polite and respectful while they did it, which only contributed to my sense of invasion.

They allowed us to follow them, but they were four and we were only two. Trinka stuck with Suarez, I trailed Majors. Wordlessly, Majors signaled the others into sections of the building, and he started with our drug cabinet. I produced the keys from my desk drawer and opened it for him. I got the log book and showed him how we kept track of scheduled drug usage. Every bottle of every controlled drug had a number and was accounted for, since the day I'd gone to work at Dr. D's.

Oxymorphone, butorphanol, these and others he ignored. He picked up the only bottle of morphine sulfate. According to the log, it should have been nearly full—and it was. But as Majors wrote a receipt for the bottle, I noticed the rubber stopper was riddled with needle sticks. We'd opened it for Sally, and only used it twice. There should not have been so many punctures.

Lara called while they were still in the clinic. I handed the phone to Detective Majors. He seemed to know her a little. Her tendency to speak in short, clipped phrases often leads her conversation partners to do the same. Majors's side went like this: "Detective Majors. That's correct. We need to interview her. ASAP. Fine."

He handed the phone back to me. Lara said, "Meet you tonight at PSPD. Lobby. Six-thirty."

It pissed me off that she and Majors had made the appointment without even consulting me. "I have the early shift on chimp watch tonight."

"Change it."

I stomped on the urge to argue. This was not a time to dig in my heels. Trinka would switch with me. Gladly, since she had the midnight-to-four A.M. shift. Sigh.

"Okay, Lara. I'll see you then."

Roosevelt said, "Baaaad bird," and whistled the first bar of "How Dry I Am."

After they left, we held a brief, impromptu staff meeting. For two days I had fielded questions with abrupt comments. My irritability, coupled with the odd events of the past two days, on top of baby Andi's ordeal, had disrupted the atmosphere of our normally congenial workplace.

They gathered around on rolling stools and exam-room chairs. They sipped Diet Pepsi and bottled water. They waited.

Trinka left it to me. I cleared my throat and dived in.

"You all read the article in yesterday's *Desert Sparkler*. And you saw the police who were here just now. You may have figured out they were exercising a search warrant." I paused, tasting the words. How had my life changed so drastically in less than a week's time? "On Monday, I received a videotape that I think you all know about, even though you didn't see it. Detective Majors has the tape now." He'd asked, I'd given it to him. Lara would kill me when she found out, but they would only have gotten another warrant. Refusing to cooperate just didn't seem worth the effort. It's what guilty people do.

"What was on it?" Sheila asked.

Didi said, "We know what was on it. I remember Mrs. Hopkins, too." Didi had helped me with Maui's surgery.

I said, "I'm sure there has been some speculation, and it's been a weird week so I haven't really talked to any of you about it." Trinka, obviously, had. But I was the focus of attention at the moment. How else to say it but to just say it? "A former client asked to be put to sleep. Euthanized."

"Jesus."

"It's really true?"

They commented to each other and to me. Sheila's eyes might have belonged to a startled rabbit; Didi's were resigned to yet another episode in the continuing saga of my life. Arlene peered at me through narrowed slits. She had the smallest investment in the practice, but she was older than the others and needed the job. I wondered if she would quit. Only Diane seemed not to care.

"So, like, what's gonna happen?" Sheila asked.

I had no answer. "I wish I knew."

Chapter Eighteen

Lara arrived ten minutes late. I waited in the police station lobby. I hadn't thought to bring anything to read, and the three worn and stained orange chairs did not invite sitting. I read the Law Enforcement Code of Ethics *("... to serve mankind, to safeguard lives and property, to protect the innocent against deception ...")* a dozen or so times, and studied a photograph of a smashed police car above the caption, "No one is safe from drunk drivers." Yet none of it really registered. I wondered what the coming hour would bring. I was scared. No amount of self-justification could change that.

Lara's arrival did not help. She swooped in with her usual intensity, in a white rayon suit and unscuffed white pumps. Her thick mane of deep auburn hair was pulled back and braided, a concession to the heat. She did not apologize for being late, and I thanked her for coming. Our relationship had subtly changed. Today, friend or no, I was her client.

She whispered, "Just answer their questions unless I jump in. Answer slowly. Give me a chance to interrupt. Ready?"

Somehow I'd imagined lawyers spent a little more time prepping their clients for such interrogations. *Just an interview*, I reminded myself. It didn't help.

Five minutes later Detective Majors escorted us to a

small interview room. The room had pale carpet that extended up the walls, four folding chairs on either side of a scarred table. There was no space for anything else in the room.

Lara said, "You're not taping, right?"

Majors raised his eyebrows but didn't answer.

Lara said, "If you're recording, this interview is over now."

I glanced around for a tape and realized with a creeping sensation that the walls were bugged.

Majors sat diagonally from me, across from Lara. Under the harsh florescent lights, his eyes looked too old for his face. The room smelled of stale sweat and fear. "We are not taping. Happy?"

I imagined a disappointed rookie turning off the recorder in another room.

Lara had a notebook out and jotted something down. I tried to get comfortable.

" 'Kay, let's get started," Majors said. He turned to me and said, "You know why we're here."

I nodded and glanced at Lara. "You want to know about the night Gilda Hopkins died."

"Right. You've already told us you were there."

I glanced at Lara, who didn't say anything. "Yes, I was there."

"Please describe what happened."

Again, Lara remained silent. "Okay." Where to start? "It was late, around two in the morning." Andi had arrested that night. I'd left Trinka and Wayne at the clinic. "The nurse was just leaving. I went up and sat with Gilda for a while." *The dead silence of that sick-stink room, when she wasn't breathing anymore. Her breath had sounded like the death rattle it was. Still, when it stopped all I could think was, so quiet.*

"How long were you there?" Majors prompted me.

I shook my head. "I really don't know."

"Give me an estimate. Three minutes? Ten? Thirty?"

I thought. "Closer to ten than thirty. Maybe even less. I'm not really patient about things like that, so it probably seemed longer than it was."

"What did you do during that time?"

"What did I—? Oh." I felt Lara growing edgy beside me. "I was surprised to find her so out of it. On other visits, no matter what time I showed up, she'd always been awake. The night before, she was listening to a tape. I figured she'd wake up anytime. I sat by the bed like I always did when I visited her."

"What else happened while you were there?"

"Not much. Her daughter, Alexandra, seemed to resent my visits. She didn't try to stop me, but it was clear she wanted me to stop coming over."

"How did she make it clear?"

Interesting question. I tried to explain Alexandra. "The first time I went to the house, it was like I was the second coming. She'd been effusively glad to see me, then she suddenly turned . . . I guess 'mean' is the only word that fits. That first visit, she was more interested in telling me about herself. She never offered to show me Gilda's room, until I more or less insisted. When I left she was just outside the door. I had the feeling she'd been listening in the whole time."

"Had you known the deceased well?"

"Not really."

"How did you meet her?"

"She was a client."

"So the family had pets?"

"Yes, a King Charles spaniel. Gilda used to have a sheltie. Maui. But I . . . It died."

Majors's eyes did not change. "When?"

August seventh, nineteen— "A few years ago."

"How did the dog die?"

Lara finally spoke. "What does this have to do with anything, Detective?"

He shot her an irritated glance. "I'm just trying to understand the history between them."

"Please try to get to the point, then. My client is a busy professional."

With exaggerated casualness he turned back to me. "How did Mrs. Hopkins's dog die?"

I'd barely noticed the exchange between them. I was remembering my first year out of school, and the woman who had placed such faith in my abilities.

"Hemangiosarcoma," I told her. "It's one of the worst, most insidious cancers there are. He's bleeding from a ruptured tumor on his spleen." "Do whatever you can." It was my first splenectomy, a wreck of an operation that left the OR looking like a murder scene. Transfusing what I could salvage, because Philip, my employer at the time, did not think stored blood was worth the trouble, and there was no time to find a donor. Clamp, tie, cut, clamp, tie, cut, my unskilled fingers awkward with the instruments, made clumsier still by the terrible urgency that filled the room. Before the pulse oximeter, with only Didi to ensure that the dog continued to breathe while I fumbled with his organs. Maui. Miraculously he survived the procedure. Months of chemotherapy did little to dampen his spirit. When the seizures started, Mrs. Hopkins accepted the inevitable with an enviable stoicism. She was right, but it was so hard. Tears in my eyes, but none in hers.

"How did the dog die?" Majors's voice had an edge to it.

"He had cancer. It spread to his brain."

"So he died of natural causes."

"I put him to sleep."

Lara shifted in her seat. Majors remained silent. I felt myself growing defensive.

"He was seizuring almost constantly. In between fits he probably had horrible headaches. We'll never know for sure, since he couldn't tell us. But he wasn't the same. His quality of life—" *Eyes glazed, barely responding to his name. Too tired to lift his head, merely grunting when moved.* "It was the right thing to do."

Lara said coldly, "Detective, this is a dog we're talking about. Dr. Pauling was doing her job. Where are you going with this?"

"Did the nurse say anything to you when you arrived at the Hopkins residence?"

"What?" I'd been distracted by the memory of Maui's endurance. Thinking how my surgical skills had developed since. Remembering thoracic surgery on an infant chimpanzee. Wondering if I'd have attempted that without having known Maui.

"When you got to the house that night, you said the nurse was just leaving. Do you know her name?"

"Eva Short. We'd spoken before." I grew nervous. Good interrogation involved jumping around, changing the subject a lot. I couldn't tell if it was habit, or if he really thought I'd done something.

"Did you speak that night?"

"No. She was driving away when I arrived."

"But you said there was a change."

"I did?" Was he trying to trip me up?

"You said you were surprised she was so out of it, compared to the night before. Was she awake or comatose?"

I glanced at Lara, feeling the fear grow in my gut. She nodded her head slightly. I watched her as I answered. "As far as I know, she was sound asleep. She was heavily medicated, and each time I visited, she seemed more depressed. That was the first time I'd come when she didn't respond to me at all."

Lara's expression softened a tiny bit.

"But she was alive when you got there."

"Yes." Technically speaking.

"And dead when you left."

"I . . . yes."

"Who was in the house at the time?"

Again, that disorienting change in direction. "As far as I know, Alexandra and myself, Rainie—Alexandra's daughter, Lorraine—and her boyfriend, Eddie."

"Where were they when Mrs. Hopkins died?"

"How would I know?"

"They weren't in the room with you?"

"No. I was there alone with Gilda."

"Did you kill her?"

I jerked at the abruptness of the question, despite the gentleness of his tone.

His voice had grown imperceptibly quieter with the last few questions. Now he all but whispered. "I know she wanted you to. She was in terrible pain. You wanted to help her, didn't you? A little push, that's all it would have taken. Just a few extra milligrams."

"I—"

Lara glared, leaned forward. "Detective, do you have an accusation to make?"

His expression hardened. "Does your client have some reason not to answer my question?"

"You bet she does! She won't answer because she's too smart not to take her lawyer's advice! And I'm advising her in the strongest terms not to answer your question! Now, unless you're planning to arrest her on these bizarre charges, this interview is over."

She picked up the file in front of her, which could have

been for show to begin with, and stuffed it into her briefcase. "Come on, Andi."

We both stood, she in apparent fury, me slightly dazed. I followed her out, not sure who my friends were at the moment. Because only one thing was clear to me: No matter that Lara was here as my advocate, she believed I had done it.

Chapter Nineteen

Outside, Lara asked if I wanted to go for something to eat. The suggestion had an obligatory ring, as if she thought I needed to talk and as my friend she felt she should listen.

I shook my head. "I'm exhausted, and I have to be back at the clinic at midnight."

She raised her eyebrows in question. I hadn't had time to tell her about the chimp. I did so now, a very short version. Her lawyer's eyes flickered with the briefest trace of envy, which I found perversely satisfying. I love Lara, and she has been a very good friend, but she is harsh and rigid in every place I am soft. She makes three times my income, lives in a condo decorated in shades of white and cleaned by someone else. She wears expensive white clothes and at the end of the day is still presentable. I envy her these things but would not trade places.

I collect strays. My house, with its mismatched furniture, is never really clean. I buy my clothes at discount stores and know better than to get attached to them, because the array of body fluids they collect is truly astonishing, and not everything washes out.

My clients are pet owners who mostly appreciate my work, even if they don't say so. Some of those who appreciate it most never pay their bills.

Lara helps scumbags avoid prison sentences. She usually

has to demand cash up front, and her clients take her for granted. They assume her fee guarantees acquittal. Anything less is sneered at. Though she has a few long-term clients, none are people she looks forward to spending time with. Sometimes I think all that clean whiteness in her life is an antidote to the filth that fills her days. Other times I wonder if it's how she really sees herself.

My work is infinitely variable. Medicine changes daily. I look forward to continuing education conventions, a chance to learn new techniques and spend time with colleagues. Lara gets her thirty-six hours every three years because if she doesn't, she will lose her license.

And I know some part of her envies the immediacy of my work, and the satisfaction of making lives better, of occasionally making life possible.

But right now I needed her talents. Nothing could express my fear of losing everything in my own life because of the ravings of a confused and angry woman. It had not been real to me until I sat in that stuffy room facing a cop who wanted to know if I had ended the life of a human being.

I took a deep breath. "So what happens now?"

"Can't tell. Need to find out what they have. I'll work on it tomorrow."

So offhand. Tomorrow. *Her* liberty wasn't at stake.

She sighed. " 'Kay. It won't go to trial. Far as I can see, they've got shit for evidence. Plus, no jury would convict. Like you said before, she was suffering. Might take a while, but you'll be fine."

Fine. She didn't have reporters camping on her door and children writing asking her to help them die.

Andi? Quit whining. Listen to your lawyer and rejoice. "Thanks, Lara."

"I'll call you, okay?" She headed toward her white

Porsche, which was parked near the front door in the small lot.

As she aimed her remote key I called, "Lara?"

She turned, backlit by a streetlight.

"I didn't do it."

She showed no reaction.

"I wanted to. I had the syringe with me when I went over that night. But she didn't need me. I was too slow."

Her expression, in the shadow, did not visibly change. After a beat she said, "Okay, Andi. We'll talk later."

"Yeah." I watched her go. After a long time I got in the Miata and left.

Baby watch was pretty much a formality, and I dozed through most of my shift. Wayne brought Sally when he came. She looked tired, holding his hand. She saw me sitting and climbed into my lap, hugging a stuffed gray rabbit like an infant.

"She was restless, didn't want me to leave, so I brought her with me."

I said I didn't mind.

"It might even be a good time to introduce them, let her hold her baby. See how she acts."

Baby Andi slept on. Sally stared at her, pointed, said, "Hoo, hoo, hoo."

Wayne said, "Sweetie, do you know that's your baby in there?"

It was the first time I'd heard him speak to her. Brad did, constantly. But I'd never heard Wayne address either chimp. I liked that he did so now. It made him seem more like a client and less like a doctor.

Though of course, I spoke to my own patients all the time.

"I thought Brad said you were going to keep them apart, so Andi would grow up bonded to you two."

"It's not fair to keep Sally from her baby. She'll be okay."

Sally, still in my lap, looked me in the eye and seemed to realize I was not one of her family members. Her lips puckered, relaxed, puckered, relaxed, as if she couldn't decide what to do. Finally she held out her arms, and as I leaned forward almost automatically, she gave me a hug. I wrapped my arms around her and experienced the disorienting sensation of being hugged by a patient. Her hand, patting me on the back, was not quite human. It felt very good, just the same.

Sally lost interest quickly, however, and by the time I pulled back she was reaching toward the plastic seals on the incubator.

"No, no, baby," Wayne said, pulling her hand back and giving her the stuffed rabbit, which had fallen on the floor.

"How's she doing?" he asked, nodding toward the incubator.

"No change," I said. "Sleeping like a baby."

He smiled weakly. "This is our last night. I'll bet you won't miss this."

"You're right about that. But it has been interesting. I'm not sorry we did all this." I started to get up.

"Anything new about . . . you know, the article?"

He hadn't been there all day, hadn't seen the letters, the police search, any of it. "I really don't feel like talking about that now."

"That bad?"

"Bad enough. For what it's worth, I haven't seen or heard anything about our patient. It's all been Gilda. The reason I'm on this shift instead of Trinka is that I had an interview with Palm Springs' Finest last night."

He flinched. "How did it go?"

"I'm not sure. My lawyer is optimistic. I'm not in jail, so I guess that's a good sign."

He wanted to ask if I'd done it, I could see the question in his eyes. Instead he said, "It's not going to go away, is it?"

"I don't think so. Hang on." I went to the office and retrieved the letter from Dack Adams.

Wayne read it while I looked on and his expression grew pained. I thought about how certain animals' deaths—and the misery in their lives—affected me, and considered how much worse that would be if my patients were human children.

Wayne folded the letter and put it in his pocket. "Tomorrow I'll find out where he is and speak to his doctor."

My sense of relief was enormous. And whatever the next day's mail might bring, I would not have to be here to read it.

I said, "There's a lot of despair in the world, you know?"

"And not a damn thing you can do about it."

"So don't even try?"

A shrug. After a beat I moved toward the door. Then, I couldn't help myself. "You of all people know what it's like to be falsely accused."

His eyes lost their expression. Sally picked up on his change in attitude, glancing anxiously at him, then me. "Hoo, hoo, hoo." She reached up and picked at his shirt, wanting to be reassured. Almost absently, he laid an arm around her shoulders.

"Somehow I don't think the letters I would receive if this got out would carry quite the same flavor as those you got today."

Of course, he was right. On the other hand, if the charges were true . . .

"I didn't—" He seemed to think about what had already been said. "What makes you so sure the charges are false?"

I thought about that. "Wishful thinking, maybe. It's naive, but I can't believe someone I've worked with would do such a thing. And the fact that it seems to be the first time. You've been a pediatrician for years. You have a successful relationship with another adult. It just doesn't sound right."

He laughed silently. "You don't know much about pedophiles, do you?"

I thought about a little girl I knew named Nikki who'd been abused so badly she'd lost her own identity. She thought she was a dog because she was treated like one. "More than I ever wanted to."

He ran a hand through his hair. "He . . . the kid . . . he's pretty confused. I may be the only gay adult he knows. We talked a little. When he put his arms around me, I should have expected it, but I was just stunned. I didn't push him away, I didn't do anything. I just stood there. And his father walked in."

Sally took his hand, led him to the incubator. She peeled one of the plastic sleeves away and thrust her hand through the opening. She grasped baby Andi by one arm and tried to pull her through the hole. Andi awoke and began shrieking.

Wayne gripped Sally's hand, saying, "No! No!" Sally pulled harder, baring her teeth and screeching. Andi reached a hand out, clutching the hair on her mother's arm. Her head, turned sideways, would not fit through the orifice.

"Sally, no!"

She pushed him away with her free hand. He fell against the treatment table, which tilted and hit the sink, then slid until it wedged against the cabinet.

I barely saw Wayne's hand move to his belt. But suddenly Sally let go of the infant and dropped to the floor, where she crouched, hugging herself.

The harness. He'd pushed a button that delivered an electrical shock through the receiver she wore like a backpack. It seemed like a brutal way to counteract the chimp's natural defenses, but once I'd accepted the fact of chimp ownership I could hardly dispute this as a means of control. Chimps are physical creatures, and the instinct to use violence is deeply ingrained. No amount of logic or reason would prevent her from going after what her maternal instinct said should be hers. The physical jolt of electricity was an immediate and effective deterrent. She was so well conditioned that it rarely required more than a warning, in the form of her handler's hand moving toward the remote, to work. That she'd required the jolt tonight spoke of the enormity of Sally's maternal bond with baby Andi.

I just hoped its use tonight hadn't wiped that out forever.

Wayne ignored her to check on the baby. She still held a few strands of Sally's hair in her tiny fist, and cried weakly.

I wanted to approach Sally, comfort her. But I'd seen her casually shove Wayne, and I'd seen her almost break Diane's thumb. It wasn't my comfort she wanted now. I righted the treatment table, keeping one eye on the frightened chimp.

"Are you all right?" I asked.

"I'm fine." Flat.

"How's Andi?"

"I think she's okay. The incision's intact. Look at her heart!"

I knew he meant the ECG, which beeped along at nearly 250 beats per minute.

"I guess Sally recognized the baby as hers," I said.

"Yeah, I just hope she's not terrified of it from now on. Damn it, that should not have happened."

"I don't know what else you could have done."

"Why'd you let her get her hand in there?"

"What?" I thought I'd heard wrong.

"You were sitting there with her. Why did you let her get to the baby?"

My jaw hung open. I started to protest: *How was I supposed to stop her?* But I realized there was no rationalizing with Wayne. He wanted to blame someone, and I was handy.

Furious, I left.

Wayne and his chimps and his whole irritating personality would be out of my life the next day.

But as I drove home I thought about the "false accusations" against him. And I thought about how he'd blamed me for Sally's normal, natural maternal action. And I wondered what had really happened with the boy.

Chapter Twenty

At home, my answering machine blinked red: three blinks. Three messages. But when I hit the playback button, each was an identical few seconds of dead air followed by the sound of a phone being hung up. Phone solicitors, most likely. At any rate, I was relieved not to have to return calls later that day.

I slept until almost noon. I awoke drenched in sweat, heat radiating from the east window near my waterbed. I had pushed the covers aside while I slept, my legs tangled in the top sheet. Carbon stretched next to my leg, his fur sticking to my skin. Clyde and Kiri regarded me from vantage points atop the bookshelf headboard, and Evinrude, seeing me stir, leaped down from the scratching post–jungle gym to greet me, purring and drooling as if her life depended on obtaining my affection before someone else got to me.

The dogs, except for Gambit, had opted to stay outside, but that was hours ago. I opened the slider in the kitchen before making coffee, and the three of them tumbled inside, panting and vying for attention. Gambit hobbled outside, relieved himself, and hobbled back in, stopping for a brief ear rub on his way back to his cedar bed in the corner. The Ayatollah snubbed me from atop the microwave, and Hara dozed on a chair in the dining alcove.

The phone rang. I answered. Heard the silence of an open line, breathing, then, "Murderer. Next time you'll be on the receiving end." A flat click as someone hung up.

I stood holding the receiver. The voice had been a harsh whisper, a little muffled. I couldn't have said if it was familiar; I couldn't even tell whether it was male or female.

A dial tone sounded. Numbly I hit the off button. Undoubtedly the same person had left the hang ups on my answering machine the day before. How serious should I take the threat? The most frightening thing was how quickly they had obtained my unlisted home phone number.

I debated reporting the call to the police or phone company, but what could they do? The very normalcy of my surroundings finally convinced me to ignore the call. Wait and see if any more came. Maybe order Caller ID on Monday.

Coffee brewing, I turned my thoughts away from the call and hit the shower. Half the day was gone, and I was tempted to waste the rest. I could drink my first cup over the paper—scratch that, I didn't even want to open my paper this morning. I could pick up the mystery I'd started days ago, read and sip, then nap. Later, if I felt like it, I could vacuum and mop and run the dishwasher, wash a load of clothes. Brush the animals and play with them. Maybe even watch some TV, or rent a movie. A very attractive proposition.

But I had realized driving home that it would take more than my indignant protestations to convince people I was not a murderer. There was a good chance the coroner would rule the death natural, the cumulative effects of metastatic cancer and morphine which Gilda's bankrupt liver could no longer process.

But if her death was determined to have been anything else, I had to be ready with a defense. I needed to speak with everyone who had been in the house that night, determine every detail of every event leading up to Gilda's death.

Who was the caller?

I wouldn't think about that.

While the water ran down my body, I tried again to picture the house that night, and Gilda. A shadow passing the window—Eva? No, she had already left. How much time might have elapsed between a bolus of morphine and the end of Gilda's life? Minutes, at least. Narcotics kill gently by slowly numbing the brain, first to outside stimuli, then to impulses originating within itself. Depending on the dose, and the existing blood level, and her body's condition, quite a bit of time could elapse.

I visualized the IV tubing that led from the central line in her neck to the pump behind her head. Her IV ran at 20 milliliters per hour, the morphine pump added five more. The tubing held perhaps thirty, over an hour's worth. Along that tubing were two rubber injection ports.

The IV extension set I'd noticed was similar to those we ordered for the clinic, so I surmised there would be around five milliliters between the most accessible injection port and Gilda's bloodstream. Theoretically, it would take fifteen minutes for an injected substance to travel that distance. But that depended on the volume of substance. A bolus of, say, twenty milliliters would be more than halfway there before the injection was completed.

I needed information that might be hard to come by on a Saturday afternoon.

Quickly I dried off and donned jogging shorts and a T-shirt. I poured my coffee and sat down with the telephone directory. First I tried Dr. Jones's office. I left my name and number with his answering service and dialed Gilda's number. Alexandra answered and I hung up. It was a childish impulse, and I knew it, but I wasn't ready to deal with her directly. It was her daughter I'd hoped to speak to.

Wouldn't she have her own line? I checked the directory and found "Dixon, L." Dialed again and was rewarded by Rainie's voice.

"Rainie, this is Andi Pauling."

She was silent.

"I'm sorry to bother you, but I really need some information. Will you help me?"

"Um, I guess. If I can."

"You probably know what's been happening to me since your grandmother died."

"Yeah, it was, like, on TV and everything! Mom talked to those news guys practically all day, but they only showed her for a minute."

"Do you know who your mother called Wednesday to get Gilda's blood tested?"

"God. She called all over! Hang on." Then silence, as I thought, *Me? Did she call me and whisper death?* Finally Rainie came back on. "Eddie thinks she would have gotten a private pathologist to order the tests to be performed from the mortuary. It was Eternal Spring Mortuary; you could check with them."

"I'll try, but I doubt they'll give information to just anyone. Would you do me a huge favor?"

"Well, I guess. What do you want me to do?"

"I'm going to call them and find out whatever I can. If I give them your number and they call, will you confirm that I'm asking on behalf of the family?"

"Um, sure!" She sounded happy with the idea. Like she hoped someone would check up on me so she could help.

"Thanks, Rainie." There was more I wanted to say. I hesitated.

" 'Kay, like, see ya."

"Okay. And, Rainie? I'm sure sorry things turned out like this. You grandmother didn't deserve this."

"Oh, I know. You were just doing what she wanted. Bye!"

"Rainie, wait! I—" But she was already gone.

I looked up Eternal Spring Mortuary and dialed. A calm female voice answered. She sounded young, which I decided was to my advantage.

I pitched my own voice up a few notches, somewhere between Rainie and Sheila and said, "Hi! I'm calling for Dr. Pauling's office? About a patient you picked up Wednesday morning, Gilda Hopkins? He's really upset with me, cause I, like, lost the lab report. Could you tell me which lab it went to?"

"One moment, please." And I was on hold. I knew it couldn't be that easy. She was probably turning me over to the boss, or tracing the call or something. I wondered if I should just hang up.

"Thank you for holding. I have her papers right here. A blood sample was submitted to All-Valley Medical Lab at the request of Dr. Rodney Carmello. The body was released to the coroner's office. But there's no Dr. Pauling listed."

"I know. We were called in late. Thanks, you saved my butt!" I hung up before she could ask any more questions. My hand was shaking. I wasn't good at lying. I couldn't help picturing the young, somber receptionist suddenly placing my name and calling some tabloid to try to sell her "story." What would the suddenly hungry media think of my calling around trying to get information?

Knock it off, Andi, you're not that hot a ticket.

I refilled my coffee cup, paced from the kitchen to the table and back again. Gradually it penetrated that I'd gotten some useful information, taken my first step in actively investigating what may or may not be a murder.

"Why do these things keep happening to me?" I asked the dogs, who always crowded around me when I entered the kitchen. They offered no suggestions but wagged their tails eagerly. I realized their bowls were empty and refilled them. Gambit got a special diet, lower in protein, which of course he didn't like much, and naturally the other dogs wanted his food just because they weren't allowed to have it. So I stood and watched while he ate, then gave him his chondroitin sulfate for arthritis, and his geriatric vitamins. The others got regular vitamins, so they wouldn't feel left out. And each got an essential fatty-acid supplement. After which I had no excuses not to make my next phone call.

Fully expecting the office to be closed on Saturday, I looked in the book anyway for Dr. Rodney Carmello. There was no such person listed.

It was like hitting a wall. How could someone not be listed? How would his prospective patients find him?

No, wait a sec. His prospective patients would all be dead.

I refilled my coffee cup and thought about it. Who would his clients be—the people who actually hired him to perform autopsies on other people's bodies? Distraught family members, perhaps those contemplating medical malpractice suits or the rare one, like Alexandra, who saw murder where no one else did. Imagining myself in their place, I wondered how I would go about finding such a person. I knew more about medical specialists than the average person, and assumed Dr. Carmello would be a pathologist. Somewhere in the world there was undoubtedly a list of such persons. Trinka would know how to find it on the Internet, but I did not.

Back to the phone book. I left a message for Gilda's Dr. Frank, a logical choice for Alexandra to have consulted in her search for postmortem tests. After that I didn't know who else to call. Decided to call Trinka at the clinic.

The phone rang in my hand, and I nearly dropped it. I almost answered, then let the machine get it. Fully expected a hang up. When Trinka's voice spoke I interrupted. I was embarrassed to note that my hand was shaking.

"Think of the devil," I said, not as lightly as I meant to. "I was just about to call you."

"What? I'm getting ready to send Andi home. Want to come down and say good-bye?"

I glanced at the clock—it was almost two o'clock. "I'll be right there." The clinic would be closing. Trinka would have her computer on. There could be no harm in asking.

Wayne's eyes were sullen and bloodshot. He cast a resentful glance my way when I arrived, but didn't say anything. I couldn't tell whether he was still blaming me for Sally's actions that morning, or for the media attention, or if it had something to do with the bill I was sure Trinka had insisted be paid before discharging the chimp. I chose to ignore him.

Brad hovered anxiously, holding the baby. That was something to see—little Andi clutched his finger, and he could extend his hand and move it up and down and she held on. In quiet moments I caught him doing just that, his entertainer's face lit up in exaggerated glee, saying, "Whee-eeee!" I half expected to hear a laugh out of Andi, and in fact, she did hoo-hoo as if enjoying herself.

Sally, thankfully, was not present. I did not know if she would be able to accept her baby now, or if Wayne and Brad would raise her themselves. I suspected the latter. It surprised me how much it mattered to me, and I had to remind myself that Brad was the expert on primate behavior and must be the one to work with her later. This would be possible only if the chimp grew up respecting him. If she were raised by another chimp, there would be a subtle boundary that would alter the working relationship. Given the events of the past week, I thought that if Sally succeeded in getting her baby, she would be very reluctant to allow her human handlers to take it away from her again—that is, if she wasn't afraid of it now that she associated touching it with receiving an electric shock.

I said to Brad, "Isn't it about time for your USDA review?" Twice a year he was required to have a veterinarian visit the premises and confirm that the animals were being housed properly and fed appropriately. As if I knew better than he did. This was one of many hoops he had to jump through to keep primates. But it gave me an excuse to drive up.

"Oh, anytime," he said, still not taking his eyes off the baby.

"How about this afternoon? I'd like to see how Andi settles in."

"Great! Want to follow us home?"

"I've got some things to do here first. How about if I come up in an hour or so?"

"No prob. Is it, baby? No, no, no, that's just perfect-wee okay!" Of course he was addressing the chimp, but his words were meant for me.

I walked with them to the front door, which was locked since we closed at two on Saturdays. I pulled it open and nearly walked into a woman in a blue silk suit, her hand reaching for the doorbell. She recovered first.

"Andi Pauling? I'm Krystal Grant, with KFMZ-TV. We're here to—oh, how cute! Is that a monkey?"

The skinny woman behind her moved in closer, zooming her video camera in on baby Andi. I stopped, undecided whether to try to shield her and her owners. Not that Brad wanted to be shielded.

"This is a chimpanzee baby," he said, expertly stepping into camera range. "Her name is Andi, after the wonderful doctor who saved her life." He demonstrated how she could be suspended by holding on to his finger.

Andi blinked at her first exposure to sunlight. Her tiny face crinkled and she said, "Ee, ee, ee." If she'd been human I'm sure she would have cried.

Krystal Grant, however, was transfixed. My namesake completely distracted her from the story she'd undoubtedly come for—Gilda Hopkins. I even saw a smile on the face of the woman behind the camera. I stifled my own grin, lest it be misconstrued on whatever story finally aired, and imagined a headline: INFANT CHIMP STEALS SPOTLIGHT! Brad held her for the video, showed them the stitches from her operation, gave Krystal his card, and told them the story about her delivery and subsequent care. Once in a while the enchanted reporter turned to me, saying, "You operated on her?" or, "You stayed up all night with her?" or, "Do you treat very many monkeys?" But it was Brad's show. Wayne went virtually unnoticed.

I almost enjoyed it. Unfortunately, just as Brad was saying, "Chimpanzees are humans' closest living relatives," Bud Thorpe drove up in his brown Chevy. Seeing us, he leaped out and rushed over. He quickly sized up what was happening and said, "So you place this animal's life above that of the human being you murdered in her bed?"

That jerked Krystal Grant back to her original purpose. She cast a vicious glance at Thorpe, who was crowding me. Shoving her microphone in my face she demanded, "Did you do it, Dr. Pauling? Is it true you euthanized Gilda Hopkins?" At least she made it a question.

I said, "No, I—"

"Have you been arrested yet?" Thorpe interrupted, making sure he was in camera view. "Are you out on bail? What are the charges?" He kept moving closer, making me want to step back. Or shove him. He'd have loved it. So I held my ground mutely.

The camera moved in closer, Krystal stepped in front of Thorpe, who leaned close enough to me to kiss, trying to keep his face in video range.

Finally furious, I picked up one foot and brought it down slowly on his instep, where the camera couldn't see. I leaned my weight on it until he pulled back, almost jerking my foot out from under me. I saw Krystal's mouth twitch but she jammed the mike in my face and said, "When you decided to help Mrs. Hopkins, did you expect it to change your life?"

"Excuse me," I said. "My patient is getting tired, and we need to get her home."

Chapter Twenty-one

I saw them off and told Trinka what I needed from her. She found Dr. Carmello's e-mail address in a matter of minutes, and I sent him a request to telephone me the following Monday. It was the best I could do for now, so I headed up the hill.

I caught up with them just outside of Yucca Valley. Brad's "compound" was an hour's drive away, near the High Desert town of Joshua Tree. The ten-acre property backed up to the national park of the same name. If I looked in the right direction, all I saw was wilderness.

The house was an interesting composite. There had been a small cabin originally, which Brad reinforced and connected to a sixty-foot trailer. Some years later he and Wayne added on a large porch, then converted that to two rooms and added a covered deck. The result was about what you'd expect from the outside, but inside surprisingly inviting. The redwood deck gave way to quarry tile, then carpet. The original cabin had been converted to chimp quarters, and a large network of cages had been added to the side opposite the house. The shrieks of chimpanzees at play emanated from that direction.

"Come on," Brad said, carrying baby Andi toward the back of the house. "Let me show you the nursery-boo. Dis poor widdle baby is wipered out. Yes, her sure is!"

He had set up a crib with a Plexiglas cover. The cover,

hinged on one side, was open. A teddy bear and a Kong toy—a sturdy dog chew toy—waited inside. The rest of the room looked not unlike any other baby nursery, with bright colors and a mobile hanging above the crib, but well out of reach. A tray near the crib held pacifiers, a stack of disposable diapers, and various baby-anointing substances.

He had to peel her clenched fists from his shirt in order to lay her in the crib. He hummed gently as he did so, murmuring nonsense syllables from time to time. She opened her sleepy eyes briefly, clutching at air. He placed the teddy bear where she could grasp it instead, and she relaxed back into sleep.

"You'll be a terrific mom," I said.

He flushed proudly.

Wayne, who had done so much to get her to this point, seemed lost. "You, too," I offered. But the description didn't fit. "We did good," I amended.

Brad stepped in with one of his periodic bouts of sensitivity. "Andi wouldn't be here if it wasn't for the two of you! I just can't believe she's really home! Andi, thank you so much for everything! And Wayne, I can't—we have so much—oh, honey, I'm just so happy!" He teared up and the two men embraced.

Feeling slightly uncomfortable and distinctly superfluous, I moved toward the door. "Call me if anything new happens, okay?"

Once outside, I stood for a few minutes gazing into Joshua Tree National Park. Miles and miles of open desert, the thousand-year-old yucca "trees" that gave the park its name, cactus and wildlife, and jutting boulders that drew rock climbers from all over the world. Even now, in the ungodly heat of August, there might be an occasional climber. The openness served as antidote to the claustrophobia of the past week. I was tempted to go for a hike, but it was well over a hundred degrees and I had no water bottle with me. People had died of dehydration out there.

Then I realized I'd forgotten the inspection that had been my excuse for coming. Knocking quietly, I reentered the house. "Brad? Do you want me to sign the USDA form?"

I didn't hear Sally, but suddenly there she was, rushing at me on her bandy legs, knuckles hitting the floor every other stride, teeth bared. I couldn't have run. I had no time to even think. Used to dogs, my brain assumed that since I was now on her turf, she was coming to establish her right to it.

"Sally! Chill!" Brad's voice.

She stopped just short of barreling into me. Suddenly the grimace looked more like a smile. She tucked her head and looked behind her.

Brad, standing in the doorway, said, "Friend."

Sally turned back to me, opened her arms, and wrapped them around me.

A chimp's strength is difficult to comprehend. Sally stood four and a half feet and weighed right at a hundred pounds. Yet she could have snapped my neck. I knew chimps were prone to biting as well, and their large jaws made that a formidable proposition. Yet she hugged me gently and my arms slipped around her shoulders almost of their own volition. My heart still pounded. But my wonder at the interaction with this closest of evolutionary relatives overwhelmed me.

Brad said, "Sorry, I didn't know you were coming back."

"I didn't sign the USDA form."

"Oh, right. Come on back and inspect the facilities."

As I followed him, Sally took my hand and walked with me. Now and then she would glance up, her lips moving, or her other hand touching her face, scratching her side. I had the sense that she was trying to communicate, if only I had spoken her language. I'd read about chimps learning sign language and wondered if Brad taught Sally.

As we entered the chimp quarters, the two males scrambled into their cages from outside. The young one was about seven, still cute and inquisitive. The old man, nearly forty, was a fearsome dude. Spotting me, he picked up the heavy plastic fifty-five-gallon drum in his cage and hurled it effortlessly at me. It slammed off the cage wall and bounced on the floor. He caught it, jumped on top, pounded the cage with his fist, and screamed.

"Don't mind Jimbo, he's always like that when someone he doesn't know comes in. Especially women."

I knew that, but it was always a little frightening. I hoped Jimbo never got sick.

"You've seen most of this before," Brad was saying. "Sally's bedroom." He gestured to an open cage, strong black steel with a sleeping platform to one side. A hinged door opened to the big outside exercise area, so she could swing or climb or just rest in the sun. I cast my eyes around for protruding wires or anything she could hurt herself on, but the inspection was a formality.

As I stepped out of Sally's cage I was suddenly drenched with water.

"Jimbo, no!" But Brad was laughing.

"Got me again." The big male liked to fill his mouth with water then wait for me to pass close enough to splash. It was a favorite trick, and once I got over the shock it actually felt good.

"You haven't seen Timmy since last year." He opened the cage on the end and the little male waddled directly to me and climbed into my arms. Seven years old, still sweet. He'd already learned to give kisses, and planted one on my cheek. I stood holding him, all sixty pounds or so, charmed but not sure what to do next.

"See that? He likes his Auntie Andi."

Jimbo slammed his barrel against the cage, breaking the spell. As I put Timmy down I noticed he had an erection. I stifled a laugh but felt my face flush.

"Just ignore him. You know how teenage boys are! Want to see what we do in our spare time?"

"Sure, why not?"

He led the young chimp into the next room, where a desk was set up with what I'd taken for a computer. He moved a joystick to get rid of the screen saver, then hit ENTER and a video game booted up. Timmy's eyes got bigger and he said, "Hoo-hoo-hoo!" He climbed into the chair and gripped the joystick, hardly able to wait for the game to start. In seconds he was clearly immersed in flying artillery, using the joystick with the enthusiasm of any youngster, to destroy the "enemy."

Sally pulled my hand, clearly torn between wanting to be the center of our attention versus competing against her brother for video access.

I watched in slack-jawed amazement. I was vaguely reminded of a scene from *Planet of the Apes*, but this was real.

"How did you teach him to do that?"

"I didn't teach him anything. Just sat down and started playing. Next thing I know, he's pushing me out of the way. It's his toy now."

"Unbelievable."

Sally gave up on me and joined Timmy, pushing her joystick impatiently while she waited for the next game to start.

I could not tear myself away. The young chimps were indeed like teenaged children, and showed no signs of tiring of the game when I left nearly an hour later. I drove away finally, feeling privileged to have seen what I did.

It was early evening by the time I got home. I didn't see the paper taped to my door until my hand touched the knob. I gasped and stepped back.

It was a picture ripped from a magazine, then torn in half. A doctor, white lab coat, stethoscope—an ad, no doubt. Red ink or paint spattered the fractured image.

It was in my hand and crumpled before I thought to save it for the police. Scotch tape—that was likely to hold fingerprints!

I turned on the television, the KFMZ channel, and kept one ear on the news while I called PSPD Watch Command. Amazingly calmly I identified myself and told a lieutenant what had happened. He promised to send someone to collect it as soon as possible.

"Do you think they mean it?" I asked.

"No telling. Can you stay somewhere else for a few nights?"

I thought instantly of Clay. Then of my pets, home alone, too easy a target. "I'll try to figure something out."

As I hung up, the TV caught my attention. "When is life not worth living? Who makes that decision?" The slim, perpetually young anchor had his serious face on.

"Should the standards be different for humans as opposed to our four-footed friends? A Palm Springs veterinarian proves there's little she won't do in the struggle to save her own patient, but police are suspicious she may have practiced an act of euthanasia, normally used only on animals, for a human being. Krystal has that story of a medical double standard. Krystal?"

Cut to Krystal Grant in her blue silk suit.

"Hi, Bob! I'm standing in front of Dr. Doolittle's vet clinic on North Palm Canyon. We came here to find out more on the controversial allegations surrounding veterinarian Andi Pauling, under investigation for the possible mercy killing of a former client, Gilda Hopkins. Now, as you may know, Mrs. Hopkins had terminal cancer. Some have said that what Dr. Pauling allegedly did was actually a kindness and shouldn't be considered murder. Today we got a little insight into what makes this Palm Springs veterinarian tick."

They must have filmed that segment after we drove away. I wondered how she'd managed to get rid of Thorpe. Maybe she tied him to the steering wheel of his car.

The scene cut to Brad holding baby Andi. Krystal's genuine fascination with the little chimp came through, as did Brad's showmanship and Andi's tenacity.

But it was Bud Thorpe who worried me. How far would he go to make this story? Had he made the threatening phone call? As a reporter, he could have the connections to get my number. He knew where I lived. He certainly had time, while I was watching chimps play video games, to find the picture and deliver it to my door.

I actually sighed with relief. Because as much as I loathed the man, if he was making threats that was as far as it would go. He wanted a story even if he had to make it himself.

Time to get back to work. I doubted I'd hear from any of the doctors involved in the case before Monday, but there was nothing stopping me from talking to the other people who had been in the house that night. I decided to start with Rainie, because she seemed friendliest.

I called her direct line and got a machine. I almost hung up, but instead said, "Rainie, this is Andi Pauling. I wonder if I could talk to you when you get a chance—"

"Hello? Hang on." She sounded breathless. " 'Kay, I'm here."

"This is Andi Pauling. You said you'd help me. I'd like

to talk to you again about the night your grandmother died, if you have time."

"I guess. What do you want to know?"

"I'm not sure, exactly. Could we meet somewhere?"

"Eddie's picking me up in a little while and we're going to Beaches. Wanna come?"

I was vaguely aware of Beaches as a hangout for twenty-somethings. Loud music, black walls papered with weird photographs and original art no one ever bought. Exactly the sort of place I might have hung out in in college; exactly the worst possible place I could think of to go tonight.

"Don't you have to be over twenty-one to get in?"

"Well, aren't you?"

I laughed.

She said, "You only have to, like, *prove* you're over twenty-one. That I can do. Want to meet us there?"

"Sure," I said. It wasn't like I'd gotten her the fake ID. Or even suggested the meeting place.

We arranged to meet there at, "I dunno, around eight I guess." That gave me time to make a few more calls. Putting Alexandra off as long as possible, I looked in the phone book for Eva Short. There was a "Short, E" in Palm Springs and a "Short, R&E" in Cathedral City. I tried the Palm Springs number and thought I recognized her voice on the machine. No one picked up as I left a message. I tried the other number for good measure and a male voice answered.

"I'm looking for Eva Short?"

"Not here." And he hung up. Which left me wondering, was she "not here" because she'd gone out, or was this the wrong number? I redialed. Same voice, irritable this time. "Yeah?"

"Excuse me, but can you tell me if Eva lives there?"

"You again? Like I said, not anymore." And he hung

up again. An ex-husband? Father? Another call wasn't likely to help my cause.

Who else should I talk to? I jotted down names, starting with Rainie and Alexandra and Eddie and Eva. Then I added Dr. Jones and Dr. Frank to the list, and checked them off, too. Carmello's name joined them, and I was out of ideas.

I still had over an hour before it was time to meet Rainie. I considered calling Lara to see if she would go with me. But she'd hate the whole idea. Likewise Trinka, who didn't drink and refused to enter a bar because of the secondhand smoke.

But I needed a friend. Someone who would not be judging me or ignoring the whole thing. It was asking a lot, because I still didn't want to talk about what had happened.

I called Clay. To my surprise, he answered.

"You're home?"

"Yeah, um, I was going to call you."

I digested that. "Ah, do you feel like going with me to Beaches tonight?"

A pause ensued. "You want to go to the beach? Tonight?"

"It's a nightclub. Kind of a kids' hangout, really."

Again he didn't answer right away. "Does this have anything to do with . . . you know, that article in the paper?"

How had he made the leap? And I realized then that the article was the reason he hadn't called, hadn't mentioned that he would be in town this weekend. I hadn't asked, either. There had been a time when I knew which cities he would be in on which weekends, and what rare Saturday night we might spend together. When had I stopped knowing? I was losing him, could feel whatever held us together slipping through my hands, and I had no idea how to hold it.

"Clay, I'd really like to see you tonight. I promised Gilda's granddaughter I'd meet her there at eight or so. It would mean a lot to me if you came, too."

After a moment he said, "I'd love to be your escort tonight. And this Beaches, it would certainly be something different."

We chatted a few more minutes, then the doorbell rang and we hung up. It was a policeman to retrieve the torn paper. He had not been involved in the case thus far, but knew who I was from the publicity. "Do you have any idea who left this?" he asked.

"No."

He helped me narrow down the time to between two and six, in other words, broad daylight. I pictured a presentable person who appeared to have legitimate business, but in truth I live in a scruffy neighborhood, and strangers of any ilk go unremarked.

"Is there someone who can stay with you till we get this sorted out?"

"My boyfriend will be here in a little while."

Satisfied, he marked a paper bag, then swept the message into it. He shined his flashlight out front looking in vain for footprints. He seemed to think the culprit was a right-to-life activist. Someone not even involved with the situation. I grew anxious all over again. That was the unknowable, the unpredictable.

After only a few minutes he left.

I showered and selected jeans and an oversized T-shirt. I had no intention of trying to blend in with the crowd. What I'd seen that age group wearing lately gravitated to extremes of tightness or bagginess. And, while some of the clothes in my closet had grown unaccountably snug, I rejected them in favor of more comfortable duds.

I moussed and dried my hair, dusted my cheeks with blush, applied mascara, and donned my favorite earrings: gold cats that peered coyly from my lobes while their bodies dangled behind, loose-jointed tails swinging. Clay rang the bell just as I was regarding myself in the closet-door mirror and second-guessing my choice of T-shirts.

As I let him in the phone rang. I hesitated, then answered. Eva Short. She sounded nervous.

"What do you want from me?" she asked.

Instinctively, I held back. "I'm trying to talk to everyone who was involved with Gilda. This whole thing is threatening to ruin my life, and I need to find out what people are saying."

"Well, I'm not saying anything. You don't have to drag me into it."

"Eva, I can't help it. You're in it. You were at the house the night she died. You saw her more than anyone outside the family. You knew her well."

Her voice rose. "I did not! I was just her nurse; I didn't do anything!"

Interesting. Why did my call panic her? "I know that," I ventured. "I know you didn't do anything. I just want to learn as much as I can about her life and what really happened that last night."

"I . . . But I . . . What do you want to know?"

I really wanted to talk to her in person, see her face. I wanted to do it right then, before she had a chance to compose herself, but I had to meet Rainie, and I wanted to spend some time with Clay. No telling when we'd get home. "Could we meet for coffee tomorrow morning?"

A hesitation. "What time?"

"Ten o'clock at Starbucks? If that's convenient."

I sensed a reluctance to just agree. "Make it nine."

Chapter Twenty-two

Beaches was all I'd expected, and more. Smoke clogged the air, colored spotlights zigzagging through it making eerie patterns in the space above what first appeared to be a solid, throbbing mass of youth. There weren't that many people, but the space was a small storefront between a bikini shop and a store selling crystals and incense and New Age compact discs.

I'd assumed the music would be live; instead it was at the opposite end of the spectrum: computer generated, soulless, mechanical. Young people with rings in their nostrils and lips and tongues, and with gold protruding from every millimeter of their earlobes, writhed with the beat, faces carefully devoid of expression. These were white and Hispanic kids for the most part, middle class to wealthy, with bright futures for the asking. After all, a beer here cost four bucks. Yet with their torn clothing and pale makeup they strived to appear street-smart and tough and without hope.

I glanced at Clay. His smiled his amusement and said something I didn't catch.

"What's that?" I shouted.

"You sure we're in the right place?"

I smiled and nodded. Wondering how I was supposed to find Rainie and Eddie in this crowd, looking forward to getting the interview over with. It had been a mistake to agree to meet her here. Not only did the noise level make conversation impossible but it was her turf.

A hand grabbed my sleeve. Rainie had slipped up beside me. She gestured with her head and moved away.

I reached for Clay's hand and followed. She led us into the far corner, where a black-painted staircase had blended into the wall. Up the stairs, through an open door, was an open-air patio lined with black benches and some mismatched lawn furniture. The music, still loud, was somewhat muted up here. There was still enough daylight to see well, despite the shadow cast by the mountain to the west.

Eddie sat on a wrought-iron chair in front of a plastic table with a round hole in the middle meant to hold a beach umbrella. A pitcher of beer and three glasses sat in front of him. "Hey, Doc," he said. "Didn't know you were bringing a date. We need another glass."

"That's okay, Clay and I can share."

"No prob, there's a waitress." I looked around but couldn't pick out which of the black-clad young people might actually have worked there. It was easier to let Eddie go ask one for another glass than to argue.

"So, like, what did you want to ask me?" Rainie said, pouring beer into the three glasses.

Mentally I kicked myself for not controlling the surroundings better. But we were here now, so I tried to think how to find out what I wanted to know. Decided bluntness was best. "I'm trying to find out exactly what happened the night Gilda died."

She shrugged and lifted her glass as if in a toast. Clay and I did the same, clinking them inanely before taking a sip. The beer was warmer than I liked it. It took me back to countless beers in countless bars when I was closer to Rainie's age.

"Nothing happened," she said. "I was sitting with her

before Eva came. Eddie wanted to say 'hi.' Then you came, and Mom got in one of her moods. Then Gramma was dead."

I glanced around for Eddie, wanting as much time as possible to talk to Rainie alone. I didn't spot him, and assumed he'd gone downstairs to retrieve the elusive fourth glass. "Do you remember exactly what order each of you went into the room with her?"

"Hm. Okay." She frowned thoughtfully, then seemed to get into it. "Eddie came over around nine, and we came out here for a couple of beers. But nothing much was happening, so we went back home. Mom doesn't like Eddie, like I told you. So I didn't tell her he was there, and we just went in my room. Then—"

"What time was it when you got home?"

"Oh, it was early. We, um, went to sleep, okay? Sometimes we did that—he'd come over and stay. But his parents worry if he stays out all night, so we'd get up real early and he'd take off. But anyway, ever since Gramma got so bad, the lights were always on so sometimes you couldn't tell what time it was. So, like, I woke up really, *really* early, but Eddie wasn't up yet, so I went in to see if Gramma was awake. She got more and more so she'd stay up all night and just nap during the day. She was awake, but real groggy. I couldn't tell if . . . you know, if she was getting worse or if she'd been asleep, or what. You wanna know what we talked about, too?"

"Sure, if it's not too personal."

She considered. "Nah, she wanted to know my plans. Like, had they changed. About marriage and stuff. She kinda seemed to like Eddie, at least a little bit, you know? She thought it was good that he wanted to be a doctor. She told me to keep him away from Mom and not let her hold me back." She stopped, her eyes gazing past me. "That's what she said. It's kinda scary; she never told me anything like that before. You think she knew it'd be her last chance?"

"We'll never know." Again I scanned for Eddie. He'd been gone a long time. It crossed my mind that he knew why I was here and had left to avoid being questioned.

"Rainie, the story your mother told me when I came over later . . ."

"About the supposed letter to Stanford? Yeah, I've heard that one since I was born. I asked Gramma. She said she wrote a letter but she never mailed it. She called it 'a sordid, shameful affair.' I feel bad for my mom, and I wish I got to know my dad. But how could it be my fault? I wasn't even born yet!"

I digested this. Felt relief. It was important to my image of Gilda that she had not sabotaged Alexandra's life. At least, not in any deliberate way.

"Did your grandmother ask you to help her die?"

Her eyes moved to the tabletop, and she took a swig of beer. "Yeah. 'Bout once a week or so. A couple of times she asked me to get those little gray cassettes out of the plastic thing after Eva left. There was always a little bit left over, but she was too crippled to get it out and use it. I never did get them for her. I saw her cry a couple of times."

"By plastic thing, you mean the contaminated-waste bin?" I pictured the open biohazard can on the table behind Gilda's bed. She couldn't see it, but must have known it was there. "Eva would change her morphine cassette and throw the leftover into the red container?"

"Sometimes."

"What did you do with those?"

Eddie dropped into the fourth chair. I jumped, not having seen his approach. He held a glass in his right hand, and it was half-full.

Clay said, "Hey, we thought you had to wash the glass first!"

"Ran into Butch and Billie. It's her birthday. I told them we'd be back down in a few."

" 'Kay." Rainie grinned. "We were just talking about the night Gramma died."

"Yeah, I figured. I read about it in the paper, and saw something on TV. It's too bad American society is so anal about death."

"Did you get to speak to Gilda that night?" I asked.

"Yeah." He glanced at Rainie, who watched him curiously. "I was about to leave, and Rainie was in there. So I went in, too. She was pretty out of it, but she asked me to stay with her while Rainie went to get my backpack."

I waited, thinking he'd tell me what was said.

Rainie misinterpreted my silence. "She did! Really! I heard her ask him to stay!"

Her need to defend him was interesting. It had not immediately occurred to me Eddie might be lying, but I realized it was possible. He had been honest in his scorn of the extreme measures used to keep some patients alive. Did Rainie think he'd seen an opportunity to act on his beliefs? Working at a clinic, planning to attend medical school, he might have access to the information needed. Rainie had just told me the drugs were at hand. I smiled reassuringly at her, then turned back to her boyfriend.

"When she asked you to stay, was it because she wanted to talk to you specifically? Or do you think she just didn't want to be alone?"

"Did she think it strange that you were there so late?" Clay interceded.

Eddie glanced at him. "I don't think she had any idea what time it was. She was used to people coming and going at all hours."

"What did she say after Rainie stepped out of the room?" I was genuinely curious.

He put an arm around her, ran a finger through her hair, and she kissed him. They made an attractive pair, despite his weird appearance. "She asked me to take care of her granddaughter."

"Take care of her? In what way? I mean, Rainie seems pretty sharp." *And she'll inherit money.* "Why would she need anyone to take care of her?"

They gazed at each other, two young people with love and their whole lives stretching out ahead. Then Rainie answered.

"It's my mom. She, you know, has problems. Gramma and I were always close, and I think she was afraid of how I would be without her. I went to COD"—two-year College of the Desert— "last year, and I'm transferring to UCLA this year. Eddie and me are gonna live together. Mom doesn't want me to go."

That certainly was consistent with what I knew about Alexandra. "But why that night? Do you think she knew she was going to die that night?"

Eddie hesitated. "It's possible. No one else was surprised."

There was something in the way he paused before answering. I phrased my next question carefully. "You knew Gilda wanted to die, right?"

He nodded.

"Had she approached you about helping her?"

"Not directly, but we used to discuss the . . . well, the philosophy of planned death. In fact, I did a little research on the subject."

"Really? Like what?"

A shrug and a self-deprecating smile. "Oh, you know. I read Kevorkian's *Prescription: Medicide* and his biography. Then there was a series of articles I found on the

Web. And Derek Humphry's books, and a series of essays and letters called *Arguing Euthanasia*. All available in the library or bookstores." Most of the same books I'd found.

I wanted so badly to just come out and say, "Did you do it? Did you give her the shot?" My lips parted slightly, the question formed. He'd been so honest till now, and the wry amusement in his eyes seemed to beg me to ask. *Did you do it?* If he had, if he told me, it would ruin his career before it started.

If he had, shouldn't that be the case? No matter how much I believed in Gilda's power to choose, if Eddie confided having done what they accused me of, I would have to tell someone. He was to start medical school that fall. I did not want any part of ending those dreams. But could I send him off to become a doctor, knowing such a thing?

I wanted to ask. Needed to ask. Opened my mouth, phrasing the question. Rainie and Clay leaned forward, anticipating it.

"Hey, dude! Rainie, wha'ss doin'?" Two young drunk people came bearing a fresh pitcher.

"Billie, Butch! Eddie said you were here. We were just gonna come and find you."

She raised her eyes in question to me. I glanced at Clay. "We were just leaving," I said. My burning question would have to wait for a quieter day.

Chapter Twenty-three

"You spared that young man," Clay said in the car.

We'd taken my Miata. Driving it gave me release. "Not necessarily."

"I think he euthanized that old woman. You think so. He was practically bragging about it."

"I think he feels the same way I do. I think he would like for people like Gilda not to have to suffer. For him there's more. He sees people in developing countries dying of treatable diseases because there's no money for medicine. He sees third-world sick made sicker by unsterilized needles reused from one patient to the next. All the while, in America we expend hundreds of thousands of dollars keeping a person alive while she begs to die."

"He's the only one who sees this?"

"Yeah, I see it, too. But he sees it through the idealism of youth, and the promise of a career in medicine. For me, it's theory. Wishful thinking. He's fresh enough to think he can fix things."

"Maybe he can."

"Maybe so," I said. "But not by committing murder before he even starts medical school."

"True. Not if he's caught."

"He wouldn't even have to be convicted. Just the kind of publicity I've been getting and he might find his slot suddenly unavailable."

"I'm not sure that's a bad thing."

Nor was I. I turned on the stereo, tired of talking about Gilda and the events surrounding her death. I'd left a Craig Chaquico CD in, and as the rhythmic guitar music filled my tiny car I reached for Clay's hand. His fingers twined with mine, and stayed that way even when I shifted gears. I took him home and took him to bed, and there were no messages taped to my door and only one hang up on my answering machine. For the rest of the night I did not think about Gilda.

The phone rang as early-morning light streamed in the windows. I grabbed it without thinking. Clay awoke, glancing at the clock as I said, "Hello?"

"Andi? This is your father."

"Pop?" Since I'd left home for vet school I couldn't remember him calling me. Ever. I managed to look at the clock, propped on one elbow and craning my head around. Six-thirty A.M. "Are you okay? Is something wrong?"

"Of course something is wrong!" His voice on the edge of hysteria. "I just saw the news! How could you? How can I hold my head up in church now?"

Oh, damn, I'd made national headlines. "When did you start going to church?"

"It's a figure of speech. I don't have to actually sit in a pew to know people are talking! If you'd gotten married, nobody would know you're my daughter!"

Clay was looking at me, a combination of inquisitiveness and concern on his sleepy face. I knew he'd get up and go home to feed his horses soon. This was the latest I remembered him ever staying. I put my hand over the mouthpiece and said, "Could you make coffee, please?"

He kissed me silently and went. I watched his naked, muscled backside while my father said, "Well? Now that you're in trouble I suppose you'll be needing my help?"

"What?" It had never occurred to me to ask him for anything. "What kind of help?"

"Not that I can afford much. But you are my only daughter."

"Don't worry about it. I don't need your money. I have a good lawyer. The whole thing is bound to die down soon. I'm sorry you had to hear about it this way."

The silence on the line was palpable. I wanted to reassure him, but found I lacked the words.

"Why *did* I have to find out this way?" he finally asked. "Why didn't you at least call?"

Damn, I'm dense! But finally I caught on. He was my father, he wanted me to need him. He'd been lukewarm about my going to college, adamantly opposed to vet school: *"What do you need all that school for? You'll just quit when the first baby is born!"* And when I moved to California I thought he would disown me. Not that there was much to own.

"I'm sorry, Pop. I thought . . . I'm really sorry."

I smelled coffee, heard the toilet flush and water running in the spare bathroom. I wasn't sure I wanted Clay to hear this.

"What really happened, Andi? Was it like they said? A mercy killing?"

I could have given him a simple answer, but instead I said, "Pop, do you remember when Mom died? How awful it was, how she begged every day for a cigarette?" *The hollow cheeks, sunken eyes, foul, rotting breath. "Please, Andi, honey, I can't stand it. (Cough, cough.) Please, make it stop!"*

"Remember when she saved up her sleeping pills that time? If she'd just been a little more patient, just waited a couple more days, she would have had enough. Remember?" My voice sounded high pitched, foreign to my own ears. It sounded like a little girl's.

Clay handed me my favorite mug, filled with coffee fixed just the way I like it. I mouthed "thank you" and sipped.

My dad cleared his throat in southern Illinois. "Is that what this was all about? Some kind of payback?"

"I wanted to help her, Pop. She begged me. Put a pillow over her face, get her some pills. I wanted to help. But I couldn't! I didn't know how! I didn't know how."

"That's okay, Andi. It wasn't your job."

"It wasn't anybody's. But when I'm sick . . . I won't go like that. You don't hear about doctors suffering long, miserable deaths, do you? It isn't fair that some people have to suffer like that."

Clay's hand stroked my hair, then my cheek. I realized I was crying and wiped the tears away with an edge of the bedsheet. Hid my face. Sipped my coffee. I wanted to shrug Clay's hand away. And I knew that wasn't a good sign.

"I know, I know," my father was saying. "But, Andi, you've got too much to lose. This isn't your crusade! Kevorkian, he's a lonely old man! Let the lonely old men of the world fight these fights. We don't have anything to lose."

"It's not a crusade, Dad. Not for me. The whole thing touched a nerve, is all. I think it will blow over soon." My voice under control again. "I didn't do it." *But I wish I had.*

After what felt like a long time he said, "I was thinking, every year it gets colder here. What would you say to a visit from your old man this winter?"

I sat up, leaned against Clay. My pop, in Palm Springs? "Well . . . sure! That would be great!" It had been over five years since I left, and I hadn't been back. I called on Father's Day and Christmas, and he wrote to me on my birthday. But in truth, I had never felt I'd known him. We talked about his visit for a few more minutes and I hung up feeling pretty good.

"You're not close, are you." Clay wasn't asking.

"It's almost seven. You don't have to rush home?" Why was I pushing everyone away?

"Rick will feed the horses." Rick was his groom. "He was expecting me to be gone this weekend. I canceled at the last minute. I'd like to talk, if you don't mind."

He'd pulled on his jeans and I was still nude. Feeling at a disadvantage, I went to the closet for a lightweight caftan and retrieved my coffee. "Sure," I said, and drained the mug.

"This . . . this thing with the old woman. It's a big deal, Andi. But you act like it's not."

He followed me into the kitchen, where I refilled my cup. "I know it's a big deal. I know it could ruin my life. I'm doing the only thing I can think of, trying to find out everything that happened that night."

"But you never said a word to me!"

"I know. I'm sorry. I didn't know how to bring it up."

"I'd like to have thought you'd talk to me first."

"First? Before what? Before I gave her the morphine? Is that what you think? Do you think I knew she was going to die when she did? She'd hung on for months, Clay! I visited her the last few days, trying to think. What exactly should I have talked to you about?"

I let the dogs out. Della glanced nervously over her shoulder at Clay as she went.

"We're supposed to be having a relationship! I'm trying to understand how something like this could happen in your life, and you don't even mention it until I see your face on the front page!"

I sat at the dining table, and Evinrude immediately jumped into my lap. Absently I stroked her fur and she purred and massaged my leg. "I . . ." What could I say?

"I'm sorry, Clay. I thought about it. But I don't see you very often, and . . . It was just so sad. I didn't want sadness when I was with you."

"Andi, I sat there just now listening to you talk to your father. He's the only member of your immediate family, right? I was sitting right there and you never even mentioned me. Does he even know you're involved with me?"

I considered. "I'm not sure."

"Not sure he knows? Or not sure we're involved?"

I stared. "We're involved. At least I am."

"And just how am I supposed to be able to tell?"

I let Gambit back in. The other dogs chased each other through the yard. I'd have to go out and clean it up later. A never ending job.

"Please, Andi, talk to me."

"You're scaring me, Clay."

"I don't mean to scare you. I'm trying to find out how you feel."

"About you? I . . . I care a lot. I admire you. I like having you in my life."

"But?"

"But what?"

"But when someone asks you to put an end to her life, you don't think to mention it to me? Maybe what I should be asking is, what do you want from this relationship?"

I sipped my coffee, but it had grown cold. I got up, put it in the microwave. Thinking. Buying time. Took it out again, warm. "I need you right now."

"Right now you need me. But what about next week? Next year?"

"I think . . . I don't know. I'm thirty-three years old, Clay, and I've been alone the whole time. My parents weren't communicators. I never came close to a serious relationship with a man. All I wanted was to get through school and move to a place where it never snowed, where my car would never freeze up, or be iced in. Where I could look outside my door and see mountains." I paused. This was difficult for me, mostly because I couldn't believe anyone would want to hear it. "I never thought in terms of 'me and someone else.' My mental images, my dreams . . . always had just me in them. If I'd gotten involved it would have been too easy to give up my dreams, get sucked into someone else's plans, and before you know it, there I'd be, pregnant and supportive and postponing everything that had to do with myself."

"It wouldn't have to be like that."

"No? Maybe not." I thought about it, tried to make the lights come on in that gloomy picture. "Sometimes, like when I was driving out here from Illinois and I'd come up over a ridge and there would be this incredible valley, or just an interesting tree . . . I wished I had someone to share it with. And yes, I've had problems in my life I wished I could unload on someone. But it was never anyone specific. And after a while I just got used to dealing with things on my own."

"But what about now, Andi? How do you feel now?"

That really was the question, wasn't it? "Like most people, I grew up thinking I'd get married and have kids one day. I just kept putting it off. I haven't dated much since I came out here, which was right after graduation. There just aren't a lot of single men our age, unless they're gay." Suddenly I laughed.

"What's so funny?"

"My pop said that lonely old men should fight the battles in society, because they have nothing to lose. Typical sexist remark. But if things keep up like this, in a few years I'll almost qualify."

"Oh, bloody hell, Andi!"

"Sorry. I guess I've just never learned to really include another person in my life."

"Remember our first night out together?"

"Yeah. Sushi." He'd charmed a little girl at a table behind us, leading to my briefly and erroneously suspecting him of being a pedophile. I'd never told him. Never would.

"I told you then I wanted children of my own. That won't change. I'd thought . . . Oh, hell, I've entertained notions of our getting married. Not right away, of course. But I need to know if you consider it a possibility."

"Clay, you're not even looking at me."

He did. I thought again what gentle blue eyes he had.

"What about you?" I said. "You've never mentioned any serious relationships, either. You rarely talk about your family, and you left your native country six years ago. You're home on a Saturday night and you didn't even tell me. This has to work both ways."

He smiled. He had a very nice smile. "Touché."

"We have lousy schedule conflicts and very little in common professionally. We're both independent as hell. I'm attracted to helpless creatures—animal and human. That carries a risk."

"Yeah, I've noticed that. Guess I'm a bit scared of giving up my freedoms, too. And I admit it would be easier if you liked horses more." He laughed. "Maybe I'm just not helpless enough."

"Oh, please." I pretended to shudder. "That's all I need."

We sipped our coffee and gazed thoughtfully at each other. I took my hand off Evinrude and reached out to stroke Clay's arm.

"I don't want to lose you, but I'm not ready to make any promises, either."

"Fair enough." I wasn't sure he really agreed, but both

of us had run out of new input. He glanced at his watch. "I'm headed home. Want to go riding later?"

I didn't. I needed the time to clean house. I wanted to think some more about the night Gilda died. "Sure."

"Right. See you around two?"

"Right. See you."

He kissed me before he left. And I headed for the shower. I still had to meet Eva Short for coffee.

Chapter Twenty-four

She was late.

The sleepy hum of an off-season resort town surrounded me. Locals with copies of the *Desert Sparkler* under their arms popped in for an espresso on their way to work, with maybe a muffin to go. A few weekenders and budget tourists sat at the tables scattered on the sidewalk outside, sipping iced cappuccinos that would taste the same at any Starbucks anywhere. The only people inside other than me were a very young couple with the bleary-eyed look of having been up late the night before; perhaps they had been partying at Beaches with Rainie and Eddie.

At fifteen after nine, I was buzzed from too much caffeine, and ready to give it up as a good try, when I spotted her in the doorway.

Her height did not make her elegant, nor was she gawky or stooped. She was merely tall. She seemed to take it for granted. She acknowledged me with a tired nod, headed for the counter, ordered, and stood waiting while the high schooler behind the counter created her mocha. I felt mildly surprised, having thought of her as very businesslike, not the kind of person to drink something so frivolous.

Finally she folded her long body into the chair across

from me. Gone was her nervous defensiveness of the night before; this morning she merely looked tired.

"Thanks for coming," I said, trying to hide my irritability.

"Another patient died last night."

"I'm sorry. It's been a lousy week for you, hasn't it."

She glared at me. "If that's supposed to make me sympathetic to your cause, forget it."

I blinked. My statement had been only a gesture of empathy. Every health-care worker of every stripe deals with death, and the bad days often seem strung together like beads on a string. "Look, I'm just trying to find out what happened that night."

"Yeah, well, I might not remember exactly. I have a lot of patients. And they're all terminal."

I couldn't think of an immediate response. What would draw a nurse into such a specialty?

"It pays good. Most of them don't drag on as long as Mrs. Hopkins. Most of their doctors give them enough morphine so they aren't in such horrible pain."

"Why didn't Gilda get more?"

"That daughter of hers. When I first started coming in, you'd have thought I was her savior. She'd want me to stay, drink coffee, listen to her life story about how much she'd sacrificed to take care of her mother. I couldn't stay; I had patients. So after a few visits she started in accusing me of not taking proper care of her. Questioning her meds, was I giving her too much morphine or not enough antibiotics. Asking me to check the feeding tube or the IV. The calls would come in at all hours, and I always knew they were bullshit, but I had to go see. Anyway, every time she had a question she had a threat to go with it. How she had a lawyer, how she was checking the morphine doses to make sure we didn't OD her. It was crap. I'll bet she never even talked to an attorney. But you want to scare a doctor, just say the word 'lawyer.' Dr. Frank's a good guy, but he's not stupid."

"Meaning he kept the morphine dose low enough so as not to hasten her death."

"Meaning he was scared shitless to give her any relief at all. A couple of times I thought he was going to cut out the morphine altogether. He didn't have to look at her, hear her begging!"

"I'm going to talk to him, too, tomorrow."

"Oh, hell, are you threatening me?"

"No!" Why was she so jumpy? "I was just making a statement. I talked to him once a few days ago. But a lot has happened since then."

"Oh. Yeah, it has."

"In the meantime, can you help me understand a few things?"

A shrug as she sipped her frothy chocolate coffee. With cinnamon and nutmeg on top, no less.

"How often did you normally change her morphine cassette?"

"As often as it needed it." She smiled. "About every three days or so."

"Was it always empty when you changed it?"

She shook her head. "No, sometimes it would be scheduled to run out over the weekend, or in the middle of the night. Despite what you saw, I try not to work at that hour. So I'd change it when I was there."

"What happened to the excess?"

"It got tossed."

"But how did you dispose of it?"

"Threw it in the biohazard container. Every patient has one."

"How often did you change the biohazard container?"

Her face froze. "Oh, no, you don't. You're gonna say I kept it, or sold it, or something. Nuh-uh. I'm out of here."

"What? Eva, wait! That's not what I'm getting at at all! Damn it, I think someone got the leftover out of the box and might have used it to, uh, you know." We were in a public place. "I'm trying to get a feel for how much might have been available."

The few people in the room turned to stare. Eva glared. "What do you think I'm supposed to do with it? Burn it? Take it back to the pharmacy? How would you dispose of it? Huh?"

"I don't know! That's why I'm asking."

"Well, I told you everything I'm going to. You're in big trouble, lady, and don't you try to drag me down with you."

She stomped out. People glanced nervously at me, then resumed their conversations. When I was sure she was gone, I left, too.

I hadn't gone riding with Clay for some time. Once there, I was glad I'd come. He loaned me a young gelding named Johnny, a former racehorse he was turning into a jumper, who had a lot of energy and truly seemed to like people. Trail riding, Clay insisted, did a lot to condition him to the movement and noise of a show crowd. I wasn't sure how jackrabbits and cars would inure him to blowing paper and crowds of people, but I enjoyed riding him. He'd calmed down a lot since the first time I'd been on him, and I felt reasonably comfortable on his back.

We traveled the back roads behind Clay's house in Morongo Valley, then followed a coyote trail along the foot of the mountain, and wound a big circle back home. We untacked and washed them down, then hung them on the automatic walker to dry. Johnny kicked up his heels and spun around his tether as it led him in big circles. Clay's mount, a new horse he'd taken in for training, hung her head lazily and followed the trail worn into the ground.

I felt talked out from that morning, like I couldn't handle another attempt to define our relationship. Clay didn't try, either. I helped him with a few chores, then afternoon feeding. He invited me to stay for barbecue—symbolic of an earlier date, the first time we'd slept together. I wanted to get back to work on Gilda's death, but there wasn't much I could do before Monday, so I stayed for dinner. As I watched Clay work it occurred to me that we'd reached our peak and started down the other side. He was a good man, as good as I was likely to find. But tying myself to him, or anyone for that matter, meant too many changes in a life I was content with.

I was losing him and I wasn't sure it mattered.

I should have stayed. He expected me to stay. I used the dogs as an excuse; I'd left them inside and unfed. I left as soon after eating as I could.

There was another message on my door. It was crumpled, as if the author had thrown it away then changed his or her mind. A few lines of computer-generated printing: YOU WILL NOT GET AWAY WITH THIS!!!! YOUR DEATH WON'T BE EASY!!!

Again I called the police, again the same young officer came to retrieve the note. The first note, he said, had not yet been tested for fingerprints.

I almost called Clay, knowing he would insist I come to stay with him. In the end, that's exactly why I did not call. Instead, I gathered the dogs into my bedroom and double-checked the locks on every door and window. It took a while, but I got to sleep.

The clinic felt empty without Andi.

After the usual Monday morning rush of clients who were waiting for us when we opened—minor emergencies and perceived emergencies—I decided to check on her. When I called, Brad answered.

"Oh, she's just doing so well! Want to talk to her?"

"Um . . . Brad?"

I heard the somewhat muffled cooing and gurgling I knew were his. But mixed in was an occasional "ee-ee-ee" that might have been an infant chimp responding to a colorful mobile rattling above her crib.

"Did you hear? Isn't that adorable?"

I had to laugh. "I'm so glad she's okay. We miss her."

"Well, maybe when she's bigger, she can come and visit. I bet she'd just wuv dat, wudn't her, Bo-bo?"

"Well, you're obviously busy. Tell Wayne I called. Talk to you soon."

At least something was going well.

Roosevelt, in his corner cage, said, "Come here, pretty bird!" His cue to be let out. I ignored him and put in a call to Dr. Alan Frank. His receptionist told me he wasn't expected before ten. I looked up All-Valley Medical Laboratory and punched in the number before I had time to lose my nerve. It was picked up by a professional-sounding woman.

"Ah, yes," I said, "this is An—gela, from Dr. Pauling's office? I wonder if you could fax over the results on a Gilda Hopkins? It would have been last week, Wednesday."

"Dr. Who?" Suspicious. My hands began shaking.

"Dr., ah, Pauling." My voice sounded nervous, too. I'd been stupid to use my own name. Perhaps to have made the call at all. "Do you need that fax number?"

"Is he one of ours?"

"No, I don't think so. I'm, um, new, can you tell?" I giggled, and it wasn't an act.

Behind me, from his cage, Roosevelt said, "Hello? Cool!"

I froze. There was no way he hadn't been heard over

the line. Then he launched into an elaborately whistled rendition of "America the Beautiful." I cupped the mouthpiece of the phone in vain.

On the other end the woman said, "Your doc sounds like an interesting character."

"Oh, he is."

"I'm calling up that report now."

"Anyway, you can check with the family if you need to. Let me just give you that number. It's Rainie Dixon, Ms. Hopkins's granddaughter." I rattled off the number. Gave her my own fax number. Hoped Rainie would remember and stick to our agreement from Saturday.

"Right. We have to be careful; I'm sure you understand."

Roosevelt said, "Gimme five, dude!"

"Of course." I hung up as quickly as possible. Roosie was chuckling and bobbing his head as if enjoying a private joke.

I saw a couple of appointments. While talking to a woman about the pros and cons of feline leukemia vaccinations for her new Abyssinian kitten I heard the fax machine go off. We'd already covered most of the other items on my check-off sheet so I told the woman to think about it, and get back to me if her cat was ever going outside. If it did, the risk of infection outweighed the chance of serious vaccine reaction, and the kitten should be protected. Ushering her out as quickly as I could manage, I headed for the lab to grab the report before someone else did.

It was Trinka's day in surgery. The OR was next to the lab, and I stood in the doorway perusing the form while she spayed a soft-coated wheaten terrier. Jimmy Buffett's "Fruitcakes" played on the stereo, and periodically Trinka stopped what she was doing to sing a line at the top of her lungs. She caught sight of me and I could tell she was grinning despite the paper mask she wore.

"Good weekend?" I asked.

"Hey! Went to see my mom."

"Well, you're in a better mood than usual."

"Yeah. She knew me."

Small wonders. "Heard from Cam lately?" Trinka had dated a TV actor the previous spring, garnering a couple of tabloid photos. But lately the relationship had tapered off.

She shook her head, her mood undiluted. "Nope. Being on TV doesn't make him any different from other men. Just makes the competition tougher. *But* . . . on the big-screen television of my life he'll always be the wavy lines that wiggle down the middle of the picture."

"Are you sure? I could never get rid of those."

"You're right, you're right. Wait, he's . . . *Fantasy Island*!"

"Out at sea with a midget upstairs?"

She laughed. "Okay, he's the special bulletin that interrupts my favorite show to tell us the Cowboys lost a football game I didn't know they were playing."

"He's the OJ trial?"

"Yes! That's it! He's the OJ trial in the regularly scheduled program of my life!"

Diane, assigned to help Trinka as needed, was not laughing. She twitched her lips when I glanced at her, as if she thought she should be.

To Trinka I said, "Did you really care about him? I mean, did it really hurt when he dropped out of sight?" Thinking of Clay. Getting ready for him not to be there.

She shrugged. "We have similar tastes in outdoor sports. I admit, it was fun having my picture snapped coming out of restaurants. But I wouldn't want to live that way. Why?"

"Just curious. You've handled it well." Meaning the breakup.

"Yup. Whatcha got there?"

I glanced at the page in my hand. "It's a . . . lab report."

She frowned but didn't argue and I went back to the office. The report format was not unlike those I looked at daily, but the numbers meant nothing. Twenty-eight micrograms per deciliter. Was that high? I needed to talk to someone who knew how to interpret this.

Chapter Twenty-five

It was nearly ten-thirty. I tried Alan Frank's office again. Used my efficient, aloof, professional voice to say, "This is Dr. Pauling, calling to speak to Dr. Frank."

"Just a moment." And I was listening to Sinatra. The song segued into a big-band piece, reminiscent of an era when Gilda's dilemma was unheard of.

His voice, when he came on the line, was guarded. "This is Alan Frank."

"This is Andi Pauling. We spoke last week?"

"The vet. What do you want?"

"You've seen the news accounts?"

"Yes." Not giving anything away.

"I'm trying to find out all I can about how Gilda Hopkins died. I'm sure I don't have to explain why."

After a while he said, "I don't see how I can help you."

"Can you interpret some lab values for me?"

Another pause. "Give me the values and I'll decide."

I did.

"That sounds high enough to contribute to her death." He sighed heavily. "The test should never have been run. When will society realize that death is a natural end to things? That poor woman . . . I really can't say any more."

"Thanks for your time. You've been helpful."

"I doubt it, Doctor. Good luck to you. You're going to need it, I'm afraid."

I thought so, too. I'd spoken to everyone I could think of who might help me. Everyone, that was, except Alexandra. Inevitably, I would have to talk to her and I did not look forward to it.

Sheila was paging me before I hung up. "Lara on two."

I picked up, a shiver of anxiety trickling down my spine. "Run out of stupid pet owners to impersonate?"

"Listen up. That morphine the cops took from your clinic? It was mostly water. What the hell's going on?"

"What?" I thought furiously. I wasn't as shocked as I should have been. I had my suspicions, but had been too wrapped up in my own problems to do anything about it.

Speaking slowly, irritably, Lara said, "Someone took the morphine out of the bottle and put distilled water in its place. Now what can you tell me about that?"

"Nothing. I—" *Damn it, Andi, cut it out! This is your lawyer you're talking to!* "Okay. I think Diane, the technician who works here, has been using it on herself." I told her about the injury to her thumb, her refusal to have it seen by a doctor when the X rays didn't show anything broken. "She hasn't missed a day of work, and I don't think she can afford to."

"But workers' comp—"

"Doesn't kick in with benefits unless you've been off work a few days. She decided to tough it out. It, um, didn't affect her performance." Not much. Just her personality. And my trust in her. She'd stolen drugs from my office; I wasn't sure I could prove it, and now I had to do something about it.

"Damn it, Andi, this is serious!"

"I know it is. I just hate having to face it. I'll talk to her."

"What the hell good will that do?" She only meant in reference to my defense.

"I might be able to persuade her to confess. She'll only get a warning for her first offense, right? And drug rehab? Will you represent her?"

"Too little, way too late! Andi, you are not taking this seriously!"

"Yes, I a—"

"Even if she comes forward now, it will look like you've twisted her arm. I don't care if she's guilty as Cain, you bought the drug and it's missing and the same drug was found in excessive quantity in the blood of a dead woman. The lab can't tell where it came from, Andi. The police are looking at you as a possible murder suspect. This is big news, and it will make TV tonight, and the paper tomorrow. That reporter has some kind of vendetta going, Andi, and he is not going to go away!"

"I know that, Lara. But what else can I do? Murder Thorpe?" Hah. I laughed without humor.

"You need to find out how so much morphine got into that woman's bloodstream, and prove it didn't come from your clinic and that you didn't put it there."

"Oh, is that all?"

I could almost hear her screech to a stop. "I don't know, Andi. Maybe not. I doubt this will go to trial. The cops don't even want to investigate. If it does, there's way too much reasonable doubt, not to mention public sympathy—you'll never be convicted. And I'll cut you a deal on the legal fees." My pal. "The main damage will be in the media, and you're a better judge than I am just how bad that might be."

I'd gotten that far all by myself, and told her so.

"Fine, so you know everything. You don't need my help, right?"

"Damn it, Lara, I don't want to fight with you. This is all pretty new for me, and yes, I do need your help."

"I think you should file a lawsuit against Alexandra, for harassment and defamation of character. It wouldn't be a bad idea to include that reporter, too."

I groaned, ran a hand through my hair. "We'd be playing right into poor Alexandra's misunderstood little hands. She has the money and the time to devote herself to a lawsuit. I don't."

"Think about it."

"She would also love it, and would get a lot more mileage out of it than I would. She craves attention, any kind. She has a very weird approach to life."

"You don't have to decide right now, Andi. Let me know."

I rested my forehead in one hand. "Right. I'll let you know in a second. Okay, I've decided. No lawsuit."

"Fine. It's your life. Just don't complain to me later on."

"That would never occur to me. I have a client. Talk to you soon."

In fact, Arlene was standing in the door to the office, holding up one finger: client in Room One. I didn't want to go. I had begun to fear my own clients and what they might request. I got up and headed for the exam room.

Two tearful faces and a very sick dog waited. I knew this dog. Porky the Yorkie couldn't have been more than eight years old, but he had a long medical history. Coupled with the owners' ability to ignore even the most blatant symptoms for upwards of two weeks, this made for several brushes with death. Each time I felt we should hang garlic over his cage to ward off the evil spirits, because we never reached a definitive diagnosis and he always seemed to rally after a few days of supportive care.

"We think it's time, Doctor," Mr. Medina said.

I wasn't surprised. Virtually every one of their visits began with these words. I examined Porky.

He lay listlessly on the table, a pile of bones under greasy matted hair, so dehydrated that his skin stayed in place when I tented it. His temperature was 97, far below normal. He had the same heart murmur he'd had for two years, which I'd never been allowed to work up. His ears stank and the hair clogging the canals was caked with wax and debris. He had most of the same rotten teeth I'd been after the Medinas to take care of for years, but a few had apparently fallen out on their own since I'd last seen him.

"Vomiting?" I asked.

They nodded.

"Diarrhea?"

Again, yes. These were his usual presenting complaints. When Porky felt better, he had a cheerful, feisty personality that drew people to him. Despite his unkempt, oily haircoat and room-clearing breath, he was hard not to like. With different owners he could have slept on a satin pillow with bows in his hair. And gummed the chicken and rice on which he did so well.

"How long?" I bit my lip to keep from saying ". . . this time."

"We're not sure. I think it started on the fifth."

This was the eighteenth. They were a day early.

"Anything else?" I asked.

"We think he's been drinking a lot of water."

"More than usual? Since when?"

They exchanged glances and shrugs. "A few months. Maybe. I first noticed it when he started making puddles on the floor instead of going outside."

I sighed. I wanted to growl. I wanted to scream. Instead I sighed again, more deeply this time.

"Is it the same thing?" she asked.

"His inflammatory bowel disease? Most likely." *Since you never refilled his medication. And, let me guess, you've been feeding him your leftovers again instead of the special diet we spent an hour discussing.* "Though it sounds like he might have another problem this time, too." The list of conditions that caused an increase in water consumption was long and tortuous, but all required long-term treatment of some kind.

"We don't have much money, Doctor. He just keeps getting sick. We've decided it's time to put him to sleep."

I could have argued. I could have pointed out that had they brought him in sooner—say, twelve days sooner—I might have treated him simply and inexpensively. I could have asked what they had expected when they purchased a Yorkie, one of the most troublesome breeds—from a pet store no less, where genetic quality is, shall we say, a secondary consideration. I probably could have persuaded them to treat him, and I might have once again pulled Porky back from the edge of the abyss. But looking at Porky, and ahead to the next episode and the one after that, I couldn't help thinking he'd had enough.

I said, "I can't disagree."

They looked a little surprised. For a moment I thought Mr. Medina was actually going to change his mind. Then his shoulders slumped and he said, "We feel awful for not realizing something was wrong."

That was not my problem. I was too angry to try to ease their guilt. I don't know why some people do awful things then think they shouldn't have to feel bad over it. I got out the brief euthanasia-authorization form and waited while he signed it. I carried Porky out of the room, handed Arlene the chart, and took the little dog into Treatment. Didi helped me place an IV and give him the injection, though I could have done it alone. Porky never even knew.

The Medinas would probably have a new dog before the weekend.

It was lunchtime and I had to get out. Porky's euthanasia had probably affected me more than it had his owners. I had saved that dog's life three times, each time sending him home with his owners who promised to make that appointment to have his teeth taken care of, to have him groomed more often, to look after his ears. Each time they had taken home a few cans of the special diet I recommended, and never returned for another can. I knew he liked it, because he ate it well in the hospital, but I knew that, once home, he returned to eating leftovers off the Medinas' own plates. I'd seen him obese and I'd seen him skin and bones, as today. I'd talked till my jaw muscles hurt, trying to educate them on his proper care. They'd nodded like puppets, and promptly forgotten every word. If I wrote it down, they lost the papers before they got home from my office.

Why did I keep at it?

Gilda Hopkins, one of the best clients I'd ever had, had asked me for a favor that horrified me. And now I felt convicted without trial. I'd done my best for Maui and extended her life for six months. Six months was still my record for hemangiosarcoma.

As I drove away from the clinic I felt I would never return. I'd struggled so hard to get into and through veterinary school, only to get to this point. I hated it. I wasn't up to the fight. Clients asked me to kill their pets because my fees for treating them were "too high." Yet every day it was a struggle to pay our bills, and we were falling further and further behind the times as equipment costs skyrocketed.

Trinka was right. Burnout had snuck up on me. At that

moment, I no longer wanted to be a vet. I didn't want the responsibility or the guilt, not to mention the poverty.

I didn't want to deal with employees who stole drugs from me. I dreaded the next client who said, "She's all I have in the world, but I can't afford to treat her."

Let someone else do it. Right now I could not.

I drove aimlessly as the car cooled. Eventually I turned the air conditioner to a saner level, and found myself in the middle of the desert on Indian, headed north.

The route to Clay Tanner's house.

And, with another half hour, Brad and Wayne's compound at the edge of Joshua Tree National Park.

I never even saw the car that followed me there.

Chapter Twenty-six

I passed the turnoff to Clay's house, barely slowing down. Later I thought about that, wondered what might have happened differently if I'd turned. Maybe nothing. Maybe everything.

I would be late getting back, no matter how fast I drove. But I wanted a dose of Brad's eccentric enthusiasm. I wanted a Sally hug. I needed to see little Andi in her crib, and be reminded that sometimes what I did had value.

I drove, fast. Up the long winding hill of Twentynine-Palms Highway, through Morongo Valley and Yucca Valley, past the signs announcing Joshua Tree National Park. African drums on the CD player filled the small space with urgency. I turned down the side road that would have been so easy to miss. Noticed the cream-colored Mercedes make the turn after me but gave it no thought except that it was the wrong car for the area, with all the dirt roads up here. No worse than my Miata.

Wayne's car wasn't in, but I'd expected that. Might not have come, in fact, if I'd thought he would be home. But Brad's van was gone as well.

I got out and knocked anyway. The only sounds that greeted me were the shrieks of chimpanzees, possibly enraged at my trespass or just greeting me in their own language.

The door was not locked.

If both men were out, the chimps would be caged. I could settle for an Andi fix. To gaze into those curious, clear brown eyes, to feel those incredibly strong, tiny fingers close around my own. Surely Brad wouldn't mind if I spent a minute with her.

I opened the door, leaned inside, shouting, "Brad? Are you home?" In case the van was in the shop and he was in the bathroom. But no one answered except the chimps, much louder now. Brad must have run out to the store. Surely he wouldn't leave little Andi for long.

I closed the door behind me and made my way toward the nursery. Realized I was tiptoeing and made myself stop. Shouted once more for Brad, who once more failed to answer.

Andi was there in her crib, and awake. She seemed glad for company. I cooed and gurgled over her for the better part of fifteen minutes, then glanced at my watch. I knew I had a two-thirty appointment, and now I doubted I could get back in time. I tried, but failed to feel badly about that. Trinka could handle everything on the books that afternoon.

I could call, though. Sheila answered. Trinka was at lunch, which was just as well. I told Sheila where I was and that I would not be back that day. She said, "Snowball—remember that poodle with the skin problem? She's coming in for her recheck. She asked for you."

"Trinka can see her. Or you can reschedule her." I fought a small bloom of shame that I would not be there. Not today. I simply wasn't up to addressing complaints about myself, about my profession, about this poodle's persistent scratching.

When Sheila started to ask if Andi was okay, I cut her off. I'd talk to her tomorrow.

I would talk to Diane tomorrow, too, and Trinka, and

we would begin the search for a new technician. Few things I dreaded more. Trinka didn't even know yet.

Andi's attention span was short. She soon fell asleep. I wandered back to where the older chimps lived, my presence causing an escalation of protests on the part of Jimbo. Sally leaned forlornly against the door of her cage, poking fingers out, or pushing her fingers, up to the knuckles, under the door of her cage. I stroked the backs of her fingers while she playfully tried to pinch mine against the grate. I'd learned from experience such grabs could hurt.

Both wishing that Brad would return and knowing how embarrassed I'd feel if he did, I finally left. I borrowed a liter bottle of cold water from the refrigerator first, and left Brad a note: LOCK YOUR DOOR. YOU NEVER KNOW WHO MIGHT WANDER IN HERE. I was going into the desert.

I got in the car and drove back to Twentynine-Palms Highway, up to the entrance to Joshua Tree Park, and went in past the deserted guard post. There aren't a lot of roads in the park, so after a few miles I stopped in a turnout. Though I hadn't seen a trace of anyone since entering the park, I locked my purse in the trunk and carried the bottle of water. I put the convertible top down, because it doesn't get as hot inside that way. My car keys went into the pocket of my scrub shirt.

I wasn't up for a strenuous hike, but I strolled through a patch of desert to a pile of boulders twenty or so feet high, and scrambled to the top. The view spread out for miles, not a street or car or human being in sight. Straining, I imagined I could see light reflected off the chimps' outdoor playground far in the distance, but that was all.

It was a cleansing view, Darwinian in its stark abundance. A reminder that life is hard sometimes, but possible—with a little ingenuity. Out there in the sun-baked harshness, small creatures lived and hunted and died and were eaten, many without ever taking a drink of water in their lives. Prehistoric Joshua trees, their limbs twisted, armored, spiked, thrived still and were host to rodents, birds, insects—all more recently evolved.

All this wilderness, so close to the glitter of Palm Springs. And yet so far.

I sipped water and reflected on all that had happened the past week. I tried to lead an ordinary life. What was it about me that attracted the dark side of humanity?

Poor Gilda, dying her mundane and miserable death; whose doctors might have made it easier but for the threats and protestations of her own daughter.

Rainie, growing up so normal in such a disturbed household. She loved her "gramma" and watched helplessly as one person after another refused to help her die. Did she possess the knowledge to do so herself?

Eddie, whose sense of injustice threatened to jeopardize his career in medicine before it ever started. If his premed science classes had not taught him how to induce euthanasia, he certainly had access to the information and knew how to find it. At his age, with his ideals, I doubted he could keep such a secret for long.

Eva Short, the wild card. She witnessed such petty tragedies every day. She needed the money provided by Gilda's lingering, by Alexandra's imagined emergencies. Surely she wouldn't risk everything to give Gilda what she craved. So why had she been so jumpy when I'd asked her about the morphine? I tried and failed to see her as an addict. Narcotics induced a mellow stupor, constricted pupils, needle tracks. None of these were consistent with the woman I'd met. But I'd failed to notice these symptoms in my own technician.

Alexandra, who watched her mother die by inches, and stood between her and those who would help. Who insisted Gilda was an abusive mother, yet continued to live with her into her own daughter's adulthood. Who welcomed me as a savior—scapegoat?—then accused me of murder. Whatever had really happened to Gilda, she was not currently my problem. Everything swirled around Alexandra.

There was no avoiding it. I had to talk to her. As soon as possible.

Still I lingered, gazing out at the subtle lushness of the High Desert wilderness. The sun, just past its peak, beat down on my back. My arms, the back of my neck, would be burned. Right now it felt good, purifying somehow. Even as sweat ran between my shoulder blades, down my neck and chest, and dust clung to the moisture, I felt refreshed.

Distantly a car door slammed, an engine turned over. It jolted me out of my reverie. How long had I been here? Only twenty minutes? It felt longer. But the skin on my forearms could not deny the sun's effects.

With a sigh I sipped my now-tepid water and climbed carefully off the rock. My light-cotton scrub pants afforded little protection and I felt them snag a couple of times as I slid from one level until my feet, in ordinary walking shoes, contacted the surface below. It took me another ten minutes to reach my car.

It wouldn't start. I tried again.

Nothing happened. Nor again, nor a fourth time. A faint click. No *chug, chug* of a dying battery, no whine, no growl . . . nothing at all.

Damn, damn, damn. I'd had this car since it was new, and it had never stranded me. I pulled the hood release and realized the hood was not latched. The hairs on my neck prickled. I knew then that I was being watched, that someone had disabled my car, leaving the hood unlatched so as not to bring me running at the sound.

Cursing myself for still not owning a cellular phone, I scanned the road. Not a car in sight. Yet someone had deliberately crippled my car. Left me here in the desert.

I lifted the hood and stared morosely at the motor. I hadn't examined it often, but it looked to me the same as it had looked any other time. Or was there a wire missing back there?

Not expecting to find it, I searched the immediate area. I didn't find it. I wasn't even sure what I was looking for, or what to do with it if it turned up.

I scanned the horizon, and suddenly the sun felt threatening. There was nothing to do but walk out.

My choices were the road (miles to the main highway, even more to town if no one picked me up; and, under the circumstances, would I want to accept a ride?) or, I could head cross-country to Brad and Wayne's. I thought the compound might actually be closer, if I stayed on course. That being the drawback—no trail, no markers. But there, at least, I knew I'd find a telephone, more water, and if Brad had gotten home, a sympathetic ear. Help. In town, if I got there, I would have to call AAA and wait for strangers to tow my car to more strangers.

Still, the road was a clearly marked path guaranteed to take me to civilization eventually.

It felt much hotter than it had even a few minutes earlier. The sun glared angrily and the sand cooked my soles through the thin surface of my shoes.

I brought the water bottle to my lips. Less than a quarter full. Not good, but I'd had no reason to conserve it till now. Sweat oiled my face and ran in streams and rivers down my neck, back, belly. I resented every dehydrating drop, but knew I'd be in worse trouble when it stopped.

It will be a long walk. But what are your options? Put one foot in front of the other and repeat, until you get there. Might as well get started.

But then I heard a car. The engine, smooth-running, hardly audible above the crunch of tires on sand. Most of the road was hidden by rocky hillside, the reason this spot had appealed in the first place. I caught my breath, waited for the car to appear.

Damn, I was thirsty. First I would drink a gallon of water. Then a cold, cold beer. I moved my tongue inside my dry mouth. Saliva flowed weakly and I pictured a silver can of Coors Light, imagined licking the moisture off its dripping surface, the incredible sound of the tab popping.

And a cool shower before the sunburn matured enough to make that thought unbearable. Water, water, cascading over my back in a never ending stream.

All these thoughts before I even drained the bottle in my hand. Thank God I wouldn't have to hike out.

A cream-colored Mercedes nosed around the bend.

I'd seen that car before. Had subconsciously noticed it make the turn behind me when I went to the chimp compound.

Not planning, I ducked behind a boulder, hot sand grinding painfully into my arm as I fell and rolled. I made myself lie still and listen. The car came to an idling stop. Had the driver seen me? I tried not to breathe. Tried not to notice the telltale marks in the sand where I'd rolled. Forced myself not to pick the grit out of my skin while I waited.

The car stopped, angled away from me, tinted glass preventing me from seeing the driver.

It was a comfort car, climate controlled, full of safe extras for people who did not take chances in their lives. Not the sort of car normally driven into the park in August. Certainly not a rock climber's car.

Was it a saboteur's car instead? Had the driver disabled mine, driven away, then turned around to effect a "rescue"?

I shifted my weight, crouching behind a rock, hunkered down where the driver couldn't see me. Unfortunately, I could no longer see the car, either.

Did I hear a door open? A foot crunch road sand? I waited, fought a need to look, a need to stand up and say, "Hello, there! I wonder if you could give me a ride. . . ."

"Andi?" A tentative shout. "Andi Pauling?" Feigned astonishment. A voice I knew. Alexandra.

I almost stepped into the open. But I waited. It could not be coincidence that she was here.

Did she sound sorry? I couldn't tell. If so, she could leave whatever she had removed from my car, and drive away.

"I need to talk to you, Andi. I, uh, recognized your car. Amazing that I would find you here."

Uh-huh. Miss Innocent. I remained silent.

An unconvincing laugh. "Okay, you caught me. I followed you up here. You'll never get that car to start, and it's a long way to town. I've got this thingy I took out of it, and I'll give it back after we've talked."

I had wanted to talk to her, too, but not here and not now. Moving very slowly, checking every spot before placing a hand on the ground, I moved to hands and knees and crept around the boulder until I could peek around it. I had the advantage of its shadow and the fact that my pale hair was similar in color to the desert. Still, sudden movement would draw her attention.

I risked a glance. Alexandra stood gazing past me, toward town. Her left hand shaded her eyes, but her right was hidden behind her thigh.

I sat back. "Andi, this is silly!" she said. "You could die of thirst out here. Don't play games, let me give you a ride!" Worried that her game had gone too far? Or just frustrated and eager to return to the cozy, air-conditioned car?

I picked up a fist-sized rock and threw it hard to my

right. It hit the rock I'd sat on earlier, and I leaned forward to see how she reacted.

As expected, she turned sharply toward the sound. In doing so, she brought her right hand up. It held a small handgun, aimed loosely in the direction of the noise. Almost immediately she seemed to realize it had been a ruse and the weapon vanished again beside her. She took a tentative step in my direction and I tensed. But she wore silk pants and ridiculous sandals, and she wasn't about to come looking for me. We'd hate to mess up that pedicure.

"Fine!" she snapped. "I hope you dry to a crisp!" I sat back and listened as her car door slammed, then she turned and took off the way she'd come.

There was nothing to do but start walking. My feet had gained weight. I put one in front of the other, and repeated.

What was Alexandra up to? Why had she followed me? She couldn't have known I'd drive into the desert and park—it had been a spur-of-the-moment idea. Had she followed me before today? Left crude threats on my door? Called my house and hung up on the machine? I'd given Rainie my number. Alexandra could have gotten it from her or found it in her room.

So she'd disabled my car, perhaps simply pulling randomly at wires under the hood until something came loose. Or maybe that weird brain actually knew something about cars.

But why? Because she thought I'd killed her mother? Destroying my career was too slow or not satisfying? Had I underestimated her fury so severely? I'd always known that certain people's minds worked so differently from my own that I simply could neither predict nor make sense of their actions. Witness Alexandra.

It was just possible that she herself had killed Gilda. I

recalled her interest in Gilda's "medicine," which I'd assumed meant pills. But Rainie and Eva had made it clear that leftovers from her drip were readily obtainable, and my own inspection of the cassette assured me it would not take a mechanic to break into one. But if Alexandra had done so, her actions made even less sense. Gilda's death would have gone unremarked had Alexandra not gone to extremes to draw attention to it.

So why had she done this to me? Had she seen me as a convenient scapegoat on which to blame her mother's death? But there would have been no blame, no investigation, without her determined insistence.

I sipped water. The bottle was very light. I scanned the distance. Miles of sameness. Brad's compound was invisible, but I was sighting on a boulder pile in the same general direction. Distance in the desert was impossible to gauge, but it couldn't be more than a couple of miles. I kicked a battered Coke can, evidence that someone had come before me. People hiked farther in this park than I was going, every day. Except, apparently, today. Today nothing moved but an occasional hawk, floating lazily high above. Maybe it was cooler up there.

Did Alexandra really think she could cause my death by stranding me in Joshua Tree? If so, did that prove a naive unfamiliarity with the terrain, or a conviction that I would be willing to die easily? Or was she merely trying to inconvenience me, not kill me? Get me out of the way?

I needed to think like her, but could not make my brain work that way. What motivated such a person? Why did she do anything she did?

Alexandra, Alexandra . . . her name echoed in silent cadence to my footsteps.

The first time I met her, I'd come to visit her mother. Gilda lay dying in that upstairs bedroom, begging for a gentle death. She'd sent for me, and I came.

Alexandra answered the door. Overdressed and made up, with high tea prepared. Ready for a social event, prepared to force her cookies on me if necessary. Behavior that was, as a college psych teacher would have said, inappropriate to the situation.

But, damn it, I was no psych major. How was I supposed to know what motivated someone like her?

I tipped up the water bottle. Nothing ran out. Then, a tiny drop moistened my tongue. That was it, though I stood for a long minute with the bottle up-ended over my mouth. I kept the bottle after that, a sort of talisman against dehydration.

That morning I'd gotten up and gone to work like any other day. I'd seen cases, joked with my partner, made some phone calls. What I wouldn't give for a phone at that moment. For the daily concerns that led me to drive away, to momentarily hate my life and my job. How petty those grievances sounded now! I wished I was rechecking Snowball's skin at that very moment.

My right calf began to cramp.

I put one foot in front of the other, and repeated.

Chapter Twenty-seven

Alex . . . andra. Alex . . . andra.

The name like a drill sergeant, pulling my feet forward. Alexandra was the key to everything.

She professed to love her mother. She'd rather keep her alive as a shell than let her die peacefully. Was it control? Money? Had her identity simply been so wrapped up in caring for her mother that she could not imagine life beyond Gilda's death?

Gilda specifically and unequivocally asked me to end her life. Yet the first time I went there Alexandra wanted to sit and have tea, as if nothing about my visit was unusual.

What had she said? *"After everything she did to me."* What had Gilda done?

No, what did Alexandra *think* Gilda had done? The letter, unmailed according to Rainie. A young husband, suicide.

Drawing attention to herself, her own stale tragedies, while her mother lay dying miserably. I understood how introverted people could get when their own troubles threatened the daily ins and outs we've grown to expect. I'd done exactly the same thing that morning—ignored my clients' grief, my patient's suffering, and felt sorry for myself for having to euthanize little Porky.

And look where that had gotten me. I might have laughed if my mouth weren't so dry.

And yet, *and yet, and yet* . . . The new refrain took over in silent cadence to the muted *whunch, whunch* of my endless walking. And yet, there was a difference between normal concern for one's own interests and the constant attempts Alexandra made to draw attention back to herself. Other people's attention. *Poor me, look what I've been through. My mother is dying, a productive, professional person's life may be ruined*—that was me, I couldn't help it—*but look how hard all this has been for poor Alexandra.*

Yet she was consistently ignored by those around her. Rainie, that first day, had walked past her without a word. Eddie hadn't spoken to her. They had, no doubt, learned that every exchange led to confrontation, and chose to avoid it.

Her mother died. Poor Alexandra. She'd called the police, who failed to take her allegations seriously. Poor, misunderstood Alexandra. She'd obtained a blood test that showed Gilda's morphine level was high—which proved nothing. Finally she contacted the media, eventually finding Bud Thorpe, who already bore me a grudge from a year ago. Had some mental pathology been held in check by her mother's presence, only to decompensate upon her death? Or was she simply getting mileage from the first genuine tragedy to touch her life in years?

Had she imagined herself the focus of media attention, national television interviews, public sympathy? Tabloid headlines?

But it backfired. They came to me instead. And I ducked them.

I stopped abruptly.

I had what she wanted, what she craved—constant attention. Yet I had done my best to get rid of it.

Not only had I gotten what she felt she deserved, but *I didn't even want it*. From her point of view, I'd thrown it away. Shown that what she wanted most in life wasn't worth having.

So she'd stalked me. The police had assumed it was right-to-life advocates, but that was wrong. I wasn't important enough for them to waste time on.

What was Alexandra's plan today? It had not been thought out, obviously. Did she expect me to die in the desert? Really? Is that what she would do in my position, just lie down and give up? I didn't think so.

Eddie had pegged her as having borderline personality disorder. Unlike mental illnesses, I knew that personality disorders went to the soul of who a person was. They featured total self-absorption, and were not treatable.

I had entered a wide valley, deceptively deep in its center. I could not see the tumble of boulders that had been my visible goal. I raised the water bottle to my lips, wishful thinking. It was dust dry. Moving my tongue still produced enough saliva to make the movement possible, but my lips felt swollen to twice their size. I ran a hand across my forehead, and felt the ominous dryness there. Pictured my purse in the trunk of my car, the lipstick no doubt melting to a greasy puddle. Should have applied some before I left. Should have brought it with me. Didn't football players use something on their cheeks to ward off glare and sunburn?

Next time, I thought. *Next time I'll know.*

I felt furious with myself for having driven so conveniently into the desert, alone—like some airhead movie heroine who enters the dark building where the audience *knows* a killer is hiding. But I often sought wilderness when I needed to think. Had my life gotten so weird that I always had to look over my shoulder?

Maybe not always, Andi. But this one time it would have been a good idea.

Behind me, the ground was too hard for footprints to show. I could only keep walking and hope I was moving straight. Both my calves threatened to seize up, and my knees ached. My feet hurt, too, from the unstable going. Next time I'd wear better shoes. Hah. I sighted on a cactus near the top of the rise ahead.

It was a barrel cactus. I'd seen them before, not given them much thought.

As a kid in the lush agricultural greenness of southern Illinois, I'd known that, if ever lost and thirsty in the desert, I should crack open a barrel cactus. It would be filled with water, which I could drink, and save myself. I think this came up as a result of watching either an old western movie or a nature show. At the time, I didn't know what thirsty was. But it stuck in my brain like thousands of other heretofore useless bits of information.

At any rate, the squat round plant, maybe a foot in diameter, looked capable of holding the promised liquid. Then I'd seen one, an ornamental sphere on a median near the clinic, which a drunk driver ran into with his car. The car, as well as its driver, had fared much better than the cactus. I clucked along with everyone else, grateful that he had only killed a plant. But added a new piece of trivia: The barrel cactus was not, in fact, full of water. Instead it held a bright pink watermelonlike pulp. I did not taste it. But now I stood and gazed longingly up the hill, remembering that colorful mush and salivating a tiny bit.

Watermelon. *Water . . . melon.* Walking again, a new refrain.

My eyes were drying, too. Blinking was becoming painful. I hadn't considered that.

Years earlier a soldier from the marine base in Twentynine Palms had become separated from his unit during an exercise in the desert. His body was found three days later, miles from where it should have been and in a direction away from base. Mummification had already begun. It was speculated that he'd hallucinated at the end, pursued a mirage perhaps. It was flatter out there. Maybe they didn't have barrel cactus. Or maybe no one had taught him how to survive in the desert. Or maybe the rumor of salvation was a lie. The pulp inedible.

Water . . . melon.

Or maybe, like me, he had no tool with which to cut one open. They protected their precious moisture with an armor of interlaced spines two inches long. Beneath that, the skin was leathery and thick.

My purse contained a pocketknife. Why hadn't I lugged it along?

Maybe I could bash it open with a rock. God knows, there was no shortage of rocks.

At any rate, it was on my way. I had to climb that hill anyway. Had already begun. Hot air seared my throat as the deceptively gentle incline stretched onward, revealing itself in increments as I climbed. It hurt my eyes to look, so I kept my head down, put one foot ahead of the last, and repeated.

Water . . . melon.

Why had I seen this trek as preferable to riding with Alexandra? Couldn't I have simply snuck up behind her, hit her with a rock, taken the gun? Left *her* to walk home. Driven over her on my way out.

I shook my head. Such fantasies were not productive. I was here, surely past the halfway point, and a little moisture was all I needed. I looked up.

The cactus was gone! My throbbing feet stopped and I blinked frantically, glancing around. There! Ten feet behind me, twenty feet to the right. How had I gotten so far off course? I went back. Found a rock. It took several tries, but at last a fissure appeared in the tough hide. I used the mouth of my water bottle to pry it apart, nearly sobbing as a rivulet of moisture trickled into the sand. My reaching fingers met cactus spines and I jerked them back. Pried some more. Kicked at it. Finally the plant lay riven and bleeding.

My greedy hands plucked at the warm pulp. My mouth expected watermelon, found bitter mush instead but hesitated only a second. The wetness coursed down my throat. My stomach, after brief consideration, decided to accept the unfamiliar gift. Fluid flowed once more.

The thought of getting up, resuming my journey, leaving this life-giving plant, was impossible to contemplate. But I couldn't eat it all now. Using a key from the ring in my pocket, I carefully creased the plastic water bottle where the neck widened out and succeeded in removing the narrow part. With sticky, filthy hands I scooped pulp into the bottle to take with me. Gooey as it was, I wiped some over my face and neck in an effort to cool myself. I could not tell if the sticky result was a good thing or not.

Moments later I crested the rise and spotted the outcrop that had been my previous goal. It was much closer, and off to my right. Adjusting my course, I set out with renewed optimism.

Brad's van was in the driveway.

Exhausted, I stumbled to the front door and pounded. By now my legs were a mass of cramps and tremors, threatening to quit any moment. After a long time, Brad opened the door. His expression would later seem comical, but now it made me realize how I must look from his perspective. In torn and filthy scrubs, my face streaked with dust and the sticky residue of cactus juice, clutching an empty plastic bottle like a lifeline.

"Andi?"

"Brad!" My voice a croak. I swallowed, licked my lips, tried again. Not much better. "Hi. Bathroom?"

"Um, sure. Of course." He stepped back. Sally was not with him, but I recognized the simulated explosions and whistles that represented her videogame in the back room.

I walked, with as much dignity as I could muster, into the bathroom, which was past the living room and near the chimp quarters. I drank from the tap, splashed my face, drank, ducked my head under and let the water run over my neck, drank some more, vomited what I'd drunk, drank less the next time, splashed my face again.

Grimacing at my image in the mirror, I finger-combed my hair, wiped my face and the countertop with a hand towel, and went out to face Brad.

Alexandra stood there, with her gun.

I hadn't seen her car. Damn it, should have known she'd realize a desert hike would not be fatal. She'd followed me up here, seen me stop, would easily figure out where I was going.

Brad gaped at her, his face ashen. "You said you—"

"Shut up! Shut up!" Her eyes were beyond rationality. Something behind them had altered, lost whatever had once tethered her mind to logical thought. "I should have killed you when I first saw you!"

Oh, damn. How did I get into this? "Alexandra, there's no need to involve Brad in this. This is between you and me. Brad is going to give us some privacy now. Brad?"

Alexandra knew she should object. I saw protest in those eyes. But my words weren't what she expected, and before she came up with a reason, Brad had stepped into the chimp quarters and out of sight.

I hoped he had a phone in there.

To keep her focused I said, "Now, it's just the two of us." Should I mention my trek through the desert? She couldn't know for sure I'd seen her out there. "My car broke down in Joshua Tree. I had to walk a long way. I'm beat, Alexandra. How 'bout if we have a seat?" Slowly I moved toward the living room. It was a pleasant open space, if a bit jarring with all the bright colors.

"Stop it! You're trying to confuse me!"

Well, yes, I was. "I'm just tired. I want to sit down."

I knew she was trying to remember why she shouldn't let me do that, but I just kept walking, reached the deep cushions after about an hour. With silent apology to Brad for my filthy condition I sank into it. My brain had been occupied too long with putting one foot ahead of the last. Sitting disoriented me. And there stood furious Alexandra, who had not walked through the desert. Who had not cared a hoot about her mother's suffering. Who trained a handgun on my face and wanted the world to pity her for her trauma.

Ironic that only now I would understand what went on behind those wild eyes. In my own mind, something slipped.

The previous spring, a very evil person had tried to shoot me. The bloodbath that followed still haunted my dreams sometimes. I still had scars on my right arm, and twinges when the weather changed. I knew it would bother me for years.

I looked at Alexandra's gun and recalled that scene.

In this civilized, colorful living room I saw that other room, a brutalized child and the bighearted dog that was her lifeline. In this serene house full of love, I felt the need to kill.

Maybe she saw it, maybe not. The gun wavered. I didn't move. Where fear should have been, I felt numbness.

Still, part of me stood aside, watching. And whispered of folly and future and healing.

I took a deep breath, stopped the words that wanted out.

"So now what? You're going to shoot me in a stranger's house? Then what?"

"Then you'll be gone. Then everything will be better."

"What will be better? What could be so bad you can only fix it by killing me?"

"Everything! My whole life is ruined because of you!"

Damn, I was doing this all wrong. This was a woman desperate for attention. She craved an audience. "Tell me about it, Alexandra. It's obvious you wanted to help your mother. Even after all she did."

"You don't know what she did!"

"Tell me. Tell me what she did."

"Always needing, always using me. She couldn't let me go."

"You mean when you were married?"

"She killed my Jeffrey! She did it to keep me tied to her. I could have been . . . whole. I wasted my life, and it was all her fault."

I gasped. Gilda? A murderer?

"As sure as she pushed him off that roof. You think I didn't know? I saw that letter. Years ago. She didn't think I saw it, but I did. And when I went to look, it was gone." Her eyes narrowed. "You took it. You must have."

"I never even saw it, Alexandra."

"My Jeffrey . . . He was going to be a doctor. She couldn't stand it, wouldn't let me go. Everything would have been so different."

A doctor. Like the man her own daughter had chosen. The young man Alexandra had nothing good to say about. Did any of them see the irony? "How terrible! Please, tell me everything that happened."

"Mother called him a gold digger. We had to elope, when I wanted a big white wedding. He said we could have all that later, the important thing was that we'd always be together."

"How sad. What happened?" Listening for sirens. Jimbo shrieked in the next room and Alexandra's hand tensed on the gun.

"She said she'd get it annulled! She would have, too, but I fooled her! I got pregnant, that showed her. She tried to say it was never consummated, but she couldn't say that anymore, could she? Jeffrey didn't want a child, but I did. I showed them. I got mine."

I wondered if young, idealistic Jeffrey hadn't simply awakened one morning and realized what he'd married, who was then pregnant with his child. Keeping my face rigidly neutral, I said, "You love your daughter very much."

"Hah! What do you know? She drove my Jeffrey to suicide, and look at her! She should be grateful, after all I've sacrificed to raise her right."

A pounding in the other room, something heavy against the door. The gun went off and Alexandra screamed, short and clipped. Silence then. A wild bullet, I hoped.

Alexandra's eyes were wide. Terrified. "I'm not crazy!" she said. "Not crazy."

"Of course not," I managed, thinking that, unfortunately, it was probably true. "You just need someone to listen."

"Jeffrey wasn't crazy either. Medical school was all he needed. Just needed some focus. Some . . . direction. That's all. Not crazy."

I had no idea what to say to that. My silence ended my usefulness, and Alexandra sighted the gun in my general direction. "I'll kill you and they'll all say you deserved it. They'll understand. They'll ask me questions and take my picture and they'll want to write a book about me. You'll see. You'll see!" She held the gun in both hands, shaking wildly, the gun wavering.

Jimbo furiously threw toys in his cage.

The door to the chimp room flew open and Sally ran out. Teeth bared, she charged Alexandra.

"Sally, chill!" I shouted. Would she listen? "Friend! She's a friend!" I didn't want to see her ripped apart.

Sally barreled into her, arms outflung. They hit the floor, the chimp's arms wrapped tightly around Alexandra.

The gun discharged as it hit the floor ten feet away, the bullet taking a chink out of the quarry tile before zinging in the other direction.

Brad ran past us, intent on the nursery.

Stray bullets . . . but surely not—

A simultaneous pounding at the door, and a shout: "Police! Open up!" It would later seem like dialogue from a bad movie, but I felt only relief when the door flew open and a very scared young deputy entered, weapon first.

I don't know what he thought when he saw Sally get up. I said, "Sally! Come here! Brad?"

He had Andi in his arms. Sally, confused and terrified, went for the deputy. Brad's hand touched the remote at his waist and Sally hit the floor as another shot rang out. If he'd been a tenth of a second slower she'd have been dead. The bullet hit the wall three feet from where I sat.

My hands went up. Brad said, "Oh, my God!" and hugged Andi to his chest. A second cop had him covered. "I can't drop the baby!" he screamed. "Don't shoot! Don't shoot!"

Alexandra, dazed, started to rise from the floor.

"Freeze! Police!" I heard terror in the deputy's voice.

Alexandra hesitated, and the fight left her. Slowly her hands went up. She threw a venomous glance at me, and a calculating one toward her gun on the floor. The first deputy reached it, stepped on it, said, "Don't move!"

More uniformed officers entered. They cuffed Alexandra on the floor and patted her down before moving to me.

Meanwhile Brad held little Andi while telling Sally,

"It's okay, 'Tato-bo, Sally-tater, don't move, it's okay!" He wanted to go to her, but didn't dare move. He was on the verge of breaking down himself. My greatest fear was for Sally, dazed and terrified. And for what could happen if, now that she could move, she went after the deputies again.

But she didn't, and after a few minutes of sorting things out, Brad was allowed to lead her back to her cage. He handed me the baby first, and I cradled her while her mother looked on. The sadness in Sally's eyes was so human I could have cried.

Chapter Twenty-eight

Two hours later I was headed home. Alexandra had surrendered the wire from my motor, and a deputy drove me back to the car and replaced it. Despite swallowing two ibuprofen from my purse upon retrieving it, my whole body ached, and my knees rebelled against the pedals. But the muscles obeyed my orders if I went slowly. Sunburn made me feverish, and my shoulders scraped painfully against the back of the seat with every movement.

Alexandra had been held overnight, but was sure to be out on bail the next morning. Would she come after me? They would take her gun, but they could not stop the weird workings of her mind.

It was nearly dark in Palm Springs when I got there. The dogs greeted me with their usual curiosity. The cats, with indifference.

The long-awaited shower failed to wash away the horror of the day. But it was a start. I threw away the torn scrub pants.

It was early yet, and my day was not over.

I dug out a well-worn business card and dialed.

"Thorpe here."

I pitched my voice low and whispered, "Alexandra Dixon is in jail in Joshua Tree." Then I hung up. He would have no doubt who called him, but could not prove it.

It occurred to me that Rainie might not know what had happened to her mother, and would worry when she failed to come home. It wasn't my job to tell the girl her mother was in jail for trying to kill me, but I liked her and hated the thought of her being frantic so soon after losing the one other constant in her life. So I called.

Eddie answered. When I identified myself, he became guarded, even hostile. I guessed Alexandra had called, and the version she'd given might differ from my own.

I sighed. "How's Rainie?"

"Fine. Considering."

"Look, Eddie, I don't know what Alexandra told you. But she's pretty unstable right now and it might be best if Rainie was away from her awhile."

"It would be best if she never saw her mother again," he said bitterly.

"She tried to kill me today, Eddie. She stranded me in the desert, then waited around to shoot me when I came out. I don't think she really has it in her to murder someone in cold blood, but things could have escalated. I'm not exaggerating. Can you take Rainie and stay somewhere else until things get sorted out?"

"Rainie owns this house. It's in trust right now, but it's hers. She won't be driven out. Alexandra will have to go stay somewhere else. Jail, for example."

Stubborn damn kid. "I'm not saying it's right, Eddie. Just prudent."

I heard Rainie's voice in the background, then silence as Eddie covered the mouthpiece. Almost a minute later Rainie was on the line.

"Hello? Andi, is that you?" Weak, exhausted. Very, very young.

"Hi, Rainie. Yes, it's me."

"Thanks for calling. I feel so bad about what happened today."

"I think you should get out of the house until your mother gets help. Can you do that?"

"Yeah, I'll think about it. How long will she be in jail?"

"Probably not more than a night or two."

"That's what her lawyer said, too. We'll work on it tomorrow."

I pictured Eddie sulking beside her. She was defying him, where she had usually deferred to him. Good. I thought he could handle it, and their relationship would be better.

"I'll stop in tomorrow to see how you're doing," I promised.

Then I called Trinka. Her voice sounded torn between worry and anger. "Where the hell were you?"

I told her about my afternoon. Her response was predictable: "Christ, Andi. The situations you get into—"

". . . situations I get into," I'd said simultaneously. "Yeah, I know. And the day's not over."

"Well, I got news, too. The kid dropped the charges."

"What kid?"

"Against Wayne. There never was any molestation."

The degree of my relief surprised me. "Thanks for letting me know. Wayne's whole reputation could have been ruined by the father's homophobia."

"So true."

I said, "There's something else." And I told her about Diane and the missing morphine.

"Oh, shit. Let me think about this."

"Okay, now I have a favor. Could your sources go as far as getting me a nurse's home address?"

"What are you up to?"

"I'm still trying to piece things together the night Gilda died. I want to talk to Eva Short again, but I don't want her to know I'm on my way over."

"I can't get that kind of information. Besides, she works for the hospice home-care outfit, not for the hospital itself."

"Okay, it never hurts to ask. I'll try a different approach."

"We need to get this thing with Diane sorted out. Want to deal with that tonight?" Trinka asked.

No. I emphatically did not. "Only if you're driving."

"Deal. See ya in a few."

I thought about calling Lara but didn't. I thought about calling Clay. But didn't.

Eva's listing in the telephone book did not provide a street address, but the other Short did. The man who had answered that phone clearly knew Eva. I got my Thomas Guide from the car and found his street in Cathedral City. When Trinka pulled up in her aging Jeep, I carried the guide out with me.

"Today was her day off. She can't come back in." Trinka's voice was grim, determined.

"No, you're right. I feel bad, though."

Trinka glanced at me. "You ever have to fire anyone before?"

"Not really."

"Me, neither."

That kind of surprised me.

"I hired her. Want me to do the talking?"

She considered. "No, it's got to come from both of us."

I felt gratitude. "She's got two kids. She's been a tech for years. Losing her job is going to be tough."

"She stole drugs from our lockup. She can't be trusted

around narcotics ever again." Meaning she'd have to find a whole new line of work.

"We have to decide now what to do to help. We can't just cut her off."

"Christ, Andi—"

"I just want to give her a month's severance pay on the condition she starts rehab immediately. And we'll keep up her insurance for the duration."

Trinka nodded. "Great minds think alike. Her check is in this envelope. I like the insurance idea."

We drove in silence for a minute. Then Trinka said, "I'll call in a new ad tomorrow."

"Fun times. I hate looking for new staff."

"Yep. We had a pretty good team there for a while."

I'd have to sort out my different feelings later—resentment at Diane for screwing up our team, sympathy versus anger at what she had done. I knew I'd been very lucky up to now, but this incident would foster suspicion of future employees. Perhaps I was too trusting by nature, but the thought of living with that sort of distrust made me feel old, tired . . . burned out.

Better watch that, Andi. There may be other stressors at work here. Ya think?

Diane lived in a kid-heavy apartment complex in Cathedral City. Neither of us had been there before, but Trinka had brought her address and with the help of Mr. Thomas we found it easily. We entered a courtyard with a pool, the pavement strewn with various toys, and latched the gate behind us.

As soon as Diane answered the door and saw our faces, she knew why we'd come.

"Ohmigod, how'd you find out?"

Trinka handed her the envelope containing her check.

I said, "I'm sorry it happened this way, Diane. And it's not just the missing drug. It's the fact that you were willing to risk an animal either experiencing pain it shouldn't have, or not being sedated and injuring one of us."

Trinka said, "It's the fact that we can no longer trust you with an essential part of your job."

"That check will keep you going for a few weeks while you get help."

She started crying. Her daughter, whose ninth birthday party we'd all seen pictures of in July, peered into the room with big, frightened eyes. I felt horrible.

"I don't have a drug problem. If I'd went to the doctor, he would of gave me Vicodin. It really hurt. I only took it when I was at work, so I could still use my thumb. Please, I won't ever do it again."

Trinka said, "It was a hard decision for us to make, Diane. The fact that the police know means we'll have to report the missing drug to the DEA. They'll want to talk to you, but if you're already getting help on your own, you probably won't be arrested."

At this word Diane grew nearly hysterical. "Arrested? I didn't do anything! It's not my fault! I have kids, I can't afford to take time off from work. You should appreciate my dedication!"

"It's out of our hands," I said. "But we will see that your insurance remains in force as long as you seek treatment. The Betty Ford Center is close to home."

"There's nothing we can do." Trinka. I was grateful she'd come along. "We'll need your key to the clinic."

She could have refused, but she went inside and returned with the key. In the morning we would change the security code for the alarm, just in case she'd had a new key made. But I thought this would be the end of things.

Diane said, "I think my mom could come stay with the kids a few days if I go to rehab."

It was a good sign.

* * *

Back in the car I said, "You know that nurse I told you about? Eva? I got a relative's address from the phone book. It's here in Cat City. Would you mind swinging by?"

Trinka laughed. We were both a little giddy from having gotten Diane's firing out of the way. "Where do I turn?"

I directed her.

"You're the one she told us about."

The man who had opened the door was somewhere between sixty and eighty. He wore a yellow polo shirt and shorts. I saw Eva's eyes in his, both the gentle and the suspicious parts. Behind him the TV chattered—an interview with, ironically, Cam Delaney, the TV actor Trinka had dated briefly.

Trinka scowled deeply.

"I'm sorry to bother you," I told the man for the third time. "I just wanted to talk to Eva a minute."

"I'm her dad."

"I guessed you were."

"You want to know about the drugs."

My eyes widened in surprise.

He nodded. "I told her you wouldn't make trouble. It's not like she's selling them on the street."

I waited.

"Come on in. You want a beer?"

"Well . . . sure. Thanks."

Trinka asked for water.

He got it for her, and a beer each for himself and me, and settled into a chair that fit like an old friend. He picked up the remote that waited on one chair arm and turned off the TV. Cam and his new girlfriend blinked into darkness. I perched uncomfortably on the edge of a pleasant orange sofa and waited.

"Ever heard of a group called 'Hospice for Humanity'?"

I had not. Neither had Trinka.

"How 'bout 'Doctors Without Borders'?"

"Of course. They travel to other countries to work on poor children."

"Surgeons," Trinka said.

He heard something in our answers that satisfied him.

"Right. Kids that wouldn't get their cleft palates and other problems fixed otherwise. Well, these docs, they pay their own way, take their own drugs and anesthetics and stuff. They can do that, cause they're docs. They got prescription rights, an' all."

"Okay." I thought I knew where this was headed now.

"Eva's always liked helping people. Only, the American medical system's so screwed up, being a nurse wasn't what she expected when she went into it. She really wanted to help people, instead she's wound up fighting with doctors and fighting with patients, and getting in the middle when they fight with each other. So, the past few years she got involved in this group, see, Hospice for Humanity. Got a nice ring, hadn't it."

"Very nice, yes."

"Anyhow, once a month or so, these nurses, they travel down to Mexico. Not Tijuana or Mexicali. They drive, cause it's cheaper, and no customs. Not that they'd have a problem going in, it's coming out you get checked. Anyhow, they go into these poor areas and they help the Mexican docs. They teach 'em how to take care of the old folks. And others, might not be so old, but they're dying anyway, and with no money for fancy treatments. These nurses go down and show their families and the docs how to take care of 'em, make 'em more comfortable. You follow?"

"And the drugs?"

"Let me show you something." He got up and headed out of the room. I followed. In a small den he opened a closet and pointed. A stack of three boxes sat on the closet floor. The top one was open, and I peeked inside. It was about half-full of pill vials, morphine cassettes, syringes, and IV tubing. In a back corner sat an IV pump and a small oxygen tank.

"It would all go to waste," he explained. "It's not like stealing. It's trash. Stuff that got opened then they changed their mind, or pills left over when someone died. IV bags underneath, sometimes a whole box of them blue pads they put under people that can't get out of bed to pee. You wouldn't believe."

I didn't point out that the equipment would have belonged to the survivors. Heck, maybe they'd have donated the machines and tanks just to escape the reminder. But I could almost hear the wheels turning in Trinka's brain at the sight of that pump.

Quickly I spoke. "And they take these things into Mexico and give them to people who otherwise couldn't afford them."

"And glad to have it, too. Won't save any kids' lives, but it gives some folk a little dignity they might not get otherwise."

I felt both humbled and shamed, while my heart beat with a quiet gladness that people existed who were willing to take risks to help others.

"Don't you tell her I showed you this, hear?"

"I won't. Thank you."

I felt obligated to finish my beer before I went, lest it be wasted in this house. Trinka didn't argue. Mr. Short turned the TV back on, and together we watched a rock singer I'd never heard of breathlessly describe her ongoing concert tour. Trinka and I left after a few minutes.

Chapter Twenty-nine

The following morning there was another letter from a woman who wanted help committing suicide. This one lived in Kansas, and included a phone number. When I called, a very old man answered, his voice reedy and weak.

"Hello, this is Dr. Andi Pauling. I'm calling for Emma Anderson?"

"She won't be needing any more doctors," he said.

"She wrote me a letter. I'm calling from California to speak to her."

"You're not listening. She's dead. My wife died last night. Heart failure. It'd been coming on awhile."

From Trinka's desk, Roosevelt said, "Cool!"

I hoped the old man hadn't heard. "I'm sorry for your loss," I said.

"All right."

Silence. Had he helped her? I didn't want to know. "Good-bye, then."

"All right." And he hung up.

Trinka said, "What's so funny?"

"That bird of yours is going to get me in trouble."

"If he doesn't electrocute himself first." She extracted a computer cable from his beak and gave him an almond instead. He never declined an almond.

I handed Trinka the letter. "She died last night."

"Oh. Hm."

I laughed.

"Well, it's not exactly funny."

"I know." I giggled. "I'm sorry, I don't know why I'm laughing."

Sheila called to tell Trinka she had an appointment waiting. I had a couple of surgical procedures, including a bilateral mandibular fracture in a cocker named Mandy. I'd vaccinated her and spayed her the previous year, and knew her as an irrepressibly cheerful pup. Her owners were a couple in their eighties, who took excellent care of her but weren't always able to control her. She had slipped her collar and been hit by a car the night before, stabilized at the emergency clinic, and sent over for surgery. She was in remarkably good spirits despite her disorienting appearance—the front half of her jaw hung at a right angle to the back half. Her tongue, dried and crusty, lolled helplessly with nothing to hold it in her mouth. I would use wire and acrylic to piece it back together, and if I did it right she would heal without a scar. It was the kind of case I liked best—a chance to make a visible, tangible difference for a pet whose owners valued her presence in their lives.

The procedure went well, and I was able to call the Muirs afterward to tell them I expected full recovery. I felt so damned normal. The good feeling carried through the rest of the day.

Then, around four o'clock, Detective Majors arrived, alone. I met him at the front desk and he followed me into the office. I could not tell from his expression why he had come. But he accepted my offer of a place to sit, which I took as a good sign.

"The coroner's office has decided not to investigate further," he said without preamble.

I waited while the news reached my brain. *Not to investigate* . . . "Then that's it?"

"That's it."

"You're kidding."

"No, ma'am."

I couldn't believe it. Just like that, no more media, no more threat of a murder charge. Gilda's death would be ruled natural causes. The letters would stop, maybe even Alexandra would leave me alone.

"Well, thank you for coming to tell me. I was sure, when you showed up, it would be more bad news."

"No problem. We like to deliver the good stuff in person once in a while, too." He was definitely smiling now.

As soon as he left I called Lara. "They should have called me!" she said. "They shouldn't have gone there. I'm your lawyer."

"Oh, give it a rest! It's over, get it?"

"We'll have to make a statement. I'll call a press conference."

"Do what you want, Lara. Just don't expect me to show up."

Then I dialed Clay's house. " 'Lo?"

"Hi."

"Hey! How are you?" He sounded pleased to hear from me.

"There's no investigation!" I blurted.

"You mean . . . Great! That's great news! Hey, I'll take you for sushi to celebrate."

I laughed, a healthy laugh this time. "It's a deal. What time?"

We arranged to meet at Otani at eight, and hung up.

I felt damn good. When I told Trinka and the staff, they wanted to have a party. We settled for lunch—pizza ordered in. Diane's absence lightened the atmosphere, or it could have been my imagination. The ad would start the next day, and we were optimistic.

* * *

I had promised to stop in to see Rainie. But first I called the sheriff's office in Joshua Tree and determined that Alexandra was still being held, and her arraignment would not take place until the following morning.

Rainie answered the door herself. Her eyes were swollen and bloodshot. She seemed to have shrunk into herself, the grace and poise that had so impressed me when I first met her replaced by a desperate sadness.

Without a word she turned and walked inside. She'd left the door open, which I took as invitation and followed her. She sat in the living room, arms crossed and bent forward, rocking slightly.

I wasn't sure what to say. She'd lived an intense series of tragedies the past week, if not throughout her life. She would have to grieve, learn to accept, live with who she was and how she'd gotten there. I knew a couple of good counselors, as clients, and could give her names. But she'd have to take the initiative herself and I thought that would take a while.

I sat next to her, awkward and uncertain. Mine was not the comfort she needed.

"I'm sorry, Rainie," I said.

"It's all my fault."

"No, of course not."

"It is. I ruined everything. I was only trying to help."

And it finally clicked. Gilda's deterioration those last few days. Rainie's anxiety, Eddie's presence in the house that night. Eva's guarded defensiveness, which had nothing to do with Hospice for Humanity. "You turned up the morphine rate." Such a simple thing, so easily done.

"You knew?"

No. But Eddie had. Eva had—she couldn't have missed the altered setting on the cassette. Maybe even Alexandra had known. She'd insisted that someone be charged in her mother's death. Only now did I realize that could have been a preemptive strike to protect her daughter.

"It's okay, Rainie. Detective Majors came by today and told me they stopped the investigation."

A sob escaped her. Damn it, covering things up further wouldn't assuage this girl's guilt.

"I miss her so bad."

"I know. Rainie, it's okay. Really. Think about it." As if she'd thought about anything else. "Rainie, the morphine didn't kill your grandmother. The cancer did. The morphine just made it a little easier for her." And if her mother hadn't been threatening lawsuits, Gilda's doctor would have had the rate turned up weeks ago. Months, even.

"But Mom said . . . and you wouldn't have . . . She almost killed you, Andi! She ruined your life."

"Not at all. In fact, I'm glad I got to know you. I learned a lot from this whole thing. That there are plenty of awful things in this world that I can't change, but a few I can. And it made me think about the value of life. It helped solidify my conviction that people should have choices over their own fate."

"It ruined Mother's life."

Hm. "Your mother made her own choices. Nothing she did was in any way your fault. Do you understand that?" It was very important that she do so.

After a hesitation she nodded. "I kind of do. But I feel so guilty."

"That's okay. As long as you recognize the difference between feeling guilty and being guilty."

Her eyes widened. "Yeah! Wow."

I smiled.

She said, "I've been doing a lot of thinking. I've decided to become a doctor, too."

"That's great! Good luck to you!"

"Eddie doesn't know yet. I don't think he's gonna like it."

"The two of you have a lot to figure out."

"Yeah, I guess. I don't want to go to South America. I want to stay right here and fight for patient rights."

"I think that's terrific. If I can help in any way, let me know." In fact, I dug the crumpled card given to me by Marin Connor from my purse and handed it to her. Humanity for Humans. "I don't know anything about them, but they have a Web page you could check out."

"Thanks." She studied the card. Her shoulders moved higher, her eyes filled with possibilities.

When I got back, Trinka was just leaving. We stood at the back door in the cooling twilight and chatted for a minute. "I've been on the VIN," she explained. I understood. The hours could fly.

I was due to meet Clay for sushi. First I had to get home, shower, and change. I wasn't even sure why I'd come back.

Her expression was unreadable. "I saw you throw the syringe in the Dumpster."

I didn't answer, but my mouth went dry and my heart raced.

"The night she died, when you came back to the clinic. I just thought you should know."

Still I didn't answer. Trinka put her helmet on, inserted the key in her Harley's ignition, and mounted.

"It's okay, Andi. I'm glad you did it."

She revved the engine and took off. I wondered if I'd ever tell her the truth.

Don't miss
the first two Andi Pauling mysteries
by

LILLIAN M. ROBERTS

RIDING FOR A FALL

The return of Ross McRoberts—an old flame from vet school—spells trouble for Andi Pauling's fledgling new business. First Ross's horses become the targets of malicious sabotage, and then a popular Argentine polo player turns up dead. . . .

THE HAND THAT FEEDS YOU

Palm Springs vet Andi Pauling fears the worst when a client brings a severely battered pit bull to her for treatment. Even more disturbing is the mute, withdrawn little girl accompanying him. When the dog's owner is murdered and the child vanishes, Andi infiltrates the nightmare world of the illegal dogfight circuit to find the girl—and becomes fair game for a vicious pack of very human predators.